Adva
BLOOD MOUNTAIN

"Make room on your shelf of favorites: Peter Brandvold will be staking out a claim there. Fast, gritty and wonderfully well written."

—Frank Roderus,
Spur Award–winning author of *Leaving Kansas*

"*Blood Mountain* takes off like a shot, never giving the reader a chance to set the book down."
—Douglas Hirt, author of *Deadwood*

"Peter Brandvold weaves a fast-paced, exciting yarn. He is welcome around the campfire anytime."
—Andrew J. Fenady,
author of *The Rebel*

Berkley Books by Peter Brandvold

ONCE A MARSHAL
BLOOD MOUNTAIN

BLOOD
MOUNTAIN

Peter Brandvold

W
BRANDVO
1999
PBK

BERKLEY BOOKS, NEW YORK

BLOOD MOUNTAIN

A Berkley Book / published by arrangement with
the author

PRINTING HISTORY
Berkley edition / July 1999

In memory of my mother, Yvonne,
and all the fun we had together.

". . . and round me too the night
In ever-nearing circle weaves her shade."

—Matthew Arnold

Surely there is nothing more wretched than a man, of all the things which breathe and move upon the earth.

—Homer

Always in the end, the hunter becomes the prey.

—Old Indian saying

BLOOD
MOUNTAIN

1

On the sage-pocked, sun-scorched tables east of the northern Rockies, five covered wagons clattered single file across a shallow creek, then climbed the bank lined with chokecherry bushes and storm-twisted willows. The sky was ablaze, and the air was heavy with the musk of burning sage and buffalo grass. Two teal slapped the muddy shallows and took flight, quacking. A killdeer shrieked.

The driver of the last Conestoga, a blond young man in a wool cap and sweat-stained, pinstripe shirt and suspenders, was studying a pile of wolf dung in a patch of burning nettles when the wagon drifted off the trail and slammed into something hard.

Jolted from his reverie, the boy leaned back on the reins. "Aw, shit—*hooah!*" he yelled.

When the mules had stopped, he stood and looked down at the right front wheel with a worried expression on his blunt face. It wasn't the first time he'd let the mules wander and gotten in trouble with his father. Hoping against hope he hadn't busted an axle or cracked a wheel, he set the brake and climbed down for a look.

A young woman poked her head out of the canvas, squinting her blue eyes against the afternoon sun. She was a Nordic beauty with high cheekbones, wide, full mouth, and a surprisingly matronly figure for a girl of eighteen. Wisps of tawny hair blew around her sunbonnet and suntanned forehead. She slipped onto the driver's seat and arched her creamy, slender neck to regard the boy below.

"What was that, Nils?" she said with a heavy Scandinavian accent.

Too worried to reply, the young man ran his hand over the wheel and suppressed a gasp. The girl winced and set her worried gaze to the wagon ahead of them, its steel-rimmed wheels crunching prickly pear and sage and sending up twin dust streams.

The young man sighed and stood, cursing under his breath. Turning his crestfallen face to the other wagon, he tipped his cap back from his broad, sunburned forehead and said weakly, "Pa?"

The second wagon continued on, and the boy wanted to let it go. In spite of himself, he cupped his hands around his mouth, yelled, and watched the wagon squeak to a halt, the mules blowing in their traces. The boy felt his heart pounding in his temples and bile churning his gut.

When his father jumped down from the other wagon and walked around the box with his jaw set in a hard line and his small blue eyes squinting severely from their deep-set sockets, the boy's knees nearly buckled.

"What?" Imbert Kohl said in his harsh old-world accent.

"I hit a rock."

"You what?"

"I hit a rock. Think I cracked the wheel."

The elder Kohl gave a sigh and approached his son on short, stubby legs, swinging his meaty arms. He pinched his faded trousers up at the thighs and kneeled down with a grunt. When he craned his head to peer behind the wheel, his battered black hat rolled off, revealing the sparsely haired crown of his head.

He cursed, ran a hand over the spokes and down the wheel's steel rim, cursed again, and pushed himself to his feet. "Yah, that's what you did, all right. You cracked the goddamn wheel!"

"Sorry, Pa. I—"

"You what? Weren't paying attention? What have I told you about paying attention? Now we'll have to stop for the night and replace the goddamn wheel and there's only one spare—one spare to get us through!" Kohl's voice rose until it cracked. Spittle strung from his lips. "I tell you, I don't know what to do with you sometimes, Nils. You make me so goddamn mad. . . ."

Her face pale with anxiety, the girl lifted her skirt and crawled gingerly down from the wagon. She stood several feet from Kohl and his son, who bit his lip and nodded while his father berated him.

The girl took a step forward, pushing the sleeves of her dress up her slim arms and wincing as though in pain. "Oh, Uncle Imbert—it was just an . . . accident," she said, searching for the right word.

Kohl regarded the girl but spoke to his son. "What you got your mind on, huh? She's your cousin, for the love of God!"

"Oh, Uncle Imbert!" the girl protested.

Kohl ignored her. With a quick jab, he cuffed the boy's head, knocking his cap off. Then he walked ahead and told the other travelers to go on; he and the boy would change the wheel, get an early start in the morning, and catch up with them the next day. Then, grumbling and cursing under his breath, he returned to his own wagon and rummaged around in the jockey box for his tools.

Flushed and humiliated, the boy picked up his cap, slapped it against his thigh, and snugged it on his head. The girl smiled sympathetically and wrung her hands together. "Nils, I am sorry."

Unable to meet her gaze, the young man walked away to unharness the mules. She watched him, feeling sadness wash over her—not only for Nils but for all of them, so far from home in this harsh, empty land, headed for the wilds of the Northern Plains, as foreign as the moon.

"Help me get the pots out, Corinne."

At the sound of Mrs. Kohl's stern voice, the girl turned to see the round-faced woman, in a faded print dress and soiled sunbonnet, standing beside the other wagon. At her side, the glum, twelve-year-old Ida Mary twisted her back to peer at the dirty sole of her bare foot.

"We'll unload the gear and boil up some coffee for Pa. You best stay out of his and the boy's business."

"Yes, Wilomene. It is just—"

The woman's gray eyes blazed. "Just you get to work!"

Corinne jumped at the harsh retort, then dropped her eyes. "Yes . . . ma'am."

Unloading the camping gear and firewood, Corinne couldn't help feeling sorry for herself. Last year at this time, she'd been home in Norway with her parents and brothers and sisters. Then her father had taken ill and died, and her mother, too poor to feed and clothe four children, had sent Corinne, the oldest, to live with her brother's family on a farm in Illinois.

Only her brother's farm turned out to be a cold and lonely place. Aunt Wilomene seemed to resent Corinne's presence, and saddled her with enough daily chores to keep the girl up from five-thirty in the morning until midnight. Little Ida Mary, inexplicably jealous of Corinne, tattled on the foreign girl's every underdone loaf of bread and crooked linen crease.

As for Uncle Imbert, when he wasn't ignoring her, he was gazing at her lewdly from behind his newspaper; more than once she'd turned from a household chore to find his gaze retreating from her backside, his brows furling and his face flushing, blue smoke lifting around his pipe.

She wasn't sure, but once while bathing she thought she heard the floor squeak beyond the locked kitchen door, saw an eye blink through a knot in the log wall, and smelled the honey-rich aroma of Uncle Imbert's tobacco.

Nils was the only one in the family who treated Corinne with respect, who spoke to her as though she were a person and not a slave. The boy fairly doted on her, in fact, which Corinne attributed to his big heart—a family anomaly to be sure—and his sympathizing with her loneliness and long distance from home. The problem was he tended to dote on her a little too much, which peeved the others, who then lashed out at them both.

"The fire's going, girl—stop staring at it!" cried Wilomene Kohl, who sat fanning herself in the shade of the wagon, Ida Mary playing in the dust at her feet. "Get the cloth on the table. You know how Pa likes a proper table for his afternoon coffee."

"Yes, ma'am, I know," Corinne said, leaving an armload of kindling next to the fire ring.

"Don't forget the sugar. . . . And there might be a little of that hard candy we got at Fort Reno."

"Yes, Aunt Wilomene," Corinne said, hiking her backside onto the wagon's open tailgate and turning to rummage through barrels and shipping crates in the musty twilight under the canvas.

After a supper of hot porridge, sidepork, and coffee, Wilomene Kohl and Ida Mary did their toilet, spread their blankets under their wagon, and lay down for the night. It was only seven o'clock, and the sun was high, but both were exhausted from the long ride from Fort Reno, where they'd left the railroad and joined the others for the long overland journey north.

When Mr. Kohl and Nils had gone back to work on the damaged wagon, Corinne washed the dishes in the creek, put them away, and laid out blankets for the men. She stoked the fire, gathered wood for breakfast, then stole off alone, as was her habit when she found the time.

The sun burnished the sentinel peaks of the Big Blue Mountains rising in the west, the pine-dotted benches purpled, and the bottomland grayed. Mosquitoes and the miserable green-headed flies, thick all day, were finally thinning with the approach of dusk.

When Corinne had wandered for a half hour along the stream, which rolled over its white-sand bottom alive with waterbirds and mayflies, she came to a wide, black pool, a backwater bay lined with water lillies and saw grass. She knelt down, tested the water with her hand, then stood and gave her lip a wistful nip.

She remembered the summers in Norway when she and several other village girls would steal away to the ocean, where they swam and giggled and talked about boys. The bay was a bearable temperature three weeks in July, and the mountains rose behind them and on the fjord across the inlet, casting toothy, snowy reflections on the water.

Now, longing for a home she would never see again, Corinne looked around, then reached behind her, unbuttoned her dress, slid it down to her waist, and let it fall to her ankles. She looked around once more, gave a girlish giggle, and slipped her crochet-edged chamise over her head, then bent over and slid her white cotton drawers down her long, slender legs.

She spread the undergarments on the grass, removed the pin that held her hair, and shook the honey blond mass across her shoulders, enjoying the caress of it against her naked back. Sucking her lower lip, she cupped her full breasts in her small hands, stepped up to the pool, took a deep breath, and plunged in.

She swam back and forth across the bay, marveling out loud at how good the icy water felt against her sweaty, sunburned skin. She slapped the delicious snow-melt with her hands and feet, drank until her head ached, then stumbled up the rocks above the pool, held her nose, jumped in, and came up screaming with unabashed joy.

As she swam to the grassy bank and lay in the last of the sun's rays, she felt wonderfully at home in the world.

She did not realize that, perched atop a shaley escarpment a hundred yards up the creek, five men watched her through a spyglass. They were a long-haired, hawkish, unshaven group in greasy buckskins.

"You ever seen such a thing?" said Pete Hill, handing the spyglass to J.L. Wood.

J.L. brought the glass to his eye and adjusted the focus. He stood frozen for a long time, casting his gaze at the naked girl lifting her chin to the sun. Her hair hung straight down behind her. The white globes of her breasts tilted upward.

"I'm first," muttered J.L. Wood. He swallowed, his Adam's apple bobbing like a plum in a rain barrel.

Sonny Laagerman, a tall, thin man with a salt-and-pepper beard and buck teeth, reached for the glass. "Let me see, J.L."

"You're always first, J.L.," complained J.L.'s brother, Dew.

"I knew when I first seen her on that wagon she was mine."

"Not this time," Jim McCluskey said with a high-pitched laugh.

He sat on his butt and slid down the escarpment, knocking rocks and sand into the water. Pete Hill and the Wood brothers took after him, whooping and hollering. Sonny hesitated. J.L. pushed past him, cursing.

Hearing them, Corinne grabbed her dress and drew it across her bosom. She stared for several seconds, unable to work her mind around four men hopscotching the rocks along the creek. Then she recognized them. The other day, when they had stopped the emigrant caravan to ask for water, they had ogled her and the other women, and made lewd comments. She realized now, with goose bumps rising along her shoulders and arms, that they were running toward her.

Fear engulfing her, she scrambled to her feet, clutching her dress in her hands.

"No!" she screamed.

She slipped, caught herself, and ran back along the creek, ignoring the brush stabbing her feet, the thorns poking her face and hair. She cast a fearful look behind her and saw the men closing in a loose, wolfish pack. They whooped and yelled.

"No, no, *no!*" she cried.

A rough hand closed around her neck and pushed her to the ground. She screamed again, turned, and saw the thin, hawk-faced man bending over to catch his breath. "Lookee here, boys, what I found!" he whooped.

Corinne got to her feet holding the dress over her breasts and sidled away, flushed and shaking. She'd never felt more exposed or more alone. "Leaf me . . . leaf me alone."

"Now, honey, what'd we want to do that for?" Jim McCluskey said, breathing hard. "A pretty little thing like you needs some lovin'."

J.L.'s brother, Dew, a wiry lad with a thin blond mustache and nervous eyes, came up last, pushing through the others. He stopped. His eyes grew bright. "Well . . . hello there." He licked his lips and swallowed.

The others laughed. J.L. grabbed him behind the neck and pushed him out of the way. "Easy there, little brother. You'll get your chance, but not before I get mine."

"Bullshit, J.L.," McCluskey objected. He was a big shaggy man with a pockmarked face and huge arms straining the sleeves of his fringed buckskin jacket. "I got first dibs on this one."

"Don't even think about it, Jim," J.L. said tightly. "Don't you think about it!"

J.L. turned to him, sliding his belt scabbard into view. It bore a wide-bladed hunting knife. He laid a big hand on the carved elkhorn handle and regarded McCluskey with a savage grimace. "Remember this, Jim? Remember this and that Shoshone bitch?"

Sonny Laagerman grinned his buck teeth and shook

his head at the high jinx. Corinne dropped her dress, wheeled sideways, grabbed a piece of driftwood, and swung it before her.

Remembering previous hostilities with the savage J.L., McCluskey welcomed the diversion. He laughed with the others.

Pete Hill said with a whoop, "Lookit that, J.L. The Norsky girl likes it rough!"

J.L. looked at Corinne and smiled, lifting his thin lip above a row of small, square teeth. "Now, honey," he said, deadpan, "why didn't ya just say so?" He bolted forward, ducked under the swinging stick, and grabbed her around the waist.

Corinne screamed. "No! Leaf me . . . *alone*!"

She fought with everything she had, kicking and lashing out with her fists. She clawed at his face, tried to gouge his eyes, but his arms enfolded her like iron. Cackling and making a mockery of her efforts to evade him, J.L. sunk his teeth into her neck until she saw red. Then he picked her up like a doll and slammed her down.

"Go, J.L.!" Pete Hill cheered.

· Corinne bounded to her hands and knees and tried to scramble away. J.L. grabbed her left leg and pulled her back. He turned her around and straddled her.

"Bitch!" he yelled, lips pursed with fury. He slapped her, hard, with the back of his hand.

Her mind fogged. Her ears rang. The fight left her. "Please . . . no," she begged. "Please. . . ."

Grunting with an animal anger, J.L. slid back and spread her legs, long and lovely despite the scrapes and bruises. He unbuckled his belt and pushed his trousers down to his ankles.

"Save some for me now, J.L.," McCluskey said. He turned, walked away, and sat in the grass.

"Yeah—me, too," Sonny said.

The laughter had left J.L. His eyes were black as coals. "Bitch," he muttered.

Corinne squeezed her eyes closed against the grunting animal on top of her and heard her own voice, thin with anguish.

"No. . . . No. . . ."

2

A violet sky brushed with salmon mares' tails shone between the gaps in the western ridge when Nils and his father finished replacing the cracked wheel. While the elder Kohl threw logs on the guttering fire to heat some coffee, Nils replaced the tools in the jockey box and supply wagon, then headed for the stream to wash the grease from his hands and arms.

On the way, he glanced under the main wagon and did a double-take. Only his mother and Ida Mary lay mounded in wool blankets between the wheels. Corinne wasn't there.

He couldn't help feeling protective and proprietary of the girl. She was his cousin, and he knew it was an unnatural attraction, but he'd fallen in love with her the first moment he'd laid eyes on her in the dingy stage station at Grogan Creek.

He took a quick look around the camp, then approached his father, who sat before the fire, where coffee gurgled in a chipped enamel pot. His crock jug of coffee enhancer lay at his feet, pipe and tobacco in his lap. "Pa, you seen Corinne?"

Imbert glanced around and shook his head. "She's asleep, no doubt. Don't pester her."

"She ain't under the wagon."

Imbert's voice grew shrill. The boy's affection for the

girl irritated him, though he wasn't sure why. "Then she's off tendin' to nature. Leave her be, I said."

Ignoring his father's demands, Nils made a wide circle of the wagons, calling softly for Corinne so as not to awaken his mother and Ida Mary. When he turned up no sign of the girl, he headed to the creek, his heart starting to beat faster and his chest growing tight with concern.

When he'd walked up and down the creek for fifteen minutes, he finally stopped, cupped his hands around his mouth, and yelled, "Corinne!"

He listened. An owl hooted. The short grass rustled. To his right, about thirty yards away, the creek gurgled over rocks. He looked west where the light was fading and east where the first stars flickered. "Corinne!"

Footfalls grew behind him. He turned and watched his father come out of the dark and approach him, puffing and wheezing, a Springfield rifle in his hand. "God-damnit, this is all I need! Where did that crazy girl go, anyway?"

"She musta got lost."

Imbert sighed. "You walk along the water; I'll head for the woods. We'll meet at that bend up ahead."

They searched for a half hour, calling Corinne's name, answered by only the ethereal howls of distant wolves and owls. Finally, drawing up beside Nils along the river, Imbert said, "We have to go back. It's getting too dark to see."

"Pa, we can't leave Corinne!"

"We don't have a choice, boy," Kohl said with an angry wheeze. "In a few minutes we won't be able to see a hand before our faces."

"There's a little light left."

"Not enough," Kohl said. "Come on." He snugged his hat lower, turned, and started back toward the camp. When he did not hear the boy following, he stopped and turned around. "Don't make me tell you twice."

Nils's eyes jumped from tree to rock to chokecherry tangle. A few yards away, a game trail creased a natural levee. He wanted to follow it. Torn between Corinne and his father, his heart pounded. "There's a little light left," he said desperately. "I have to keep looking."

He bolted up the trail.

"Nils!" Kohl barked, but the boy disappeared in the dark.

Nils followed the trail to the river, calling above the evensong of prairie larks and doves. Maybe she *was* his cousin, but cousins married cousins; it happened all the time. Besides, she was the only girl his age he'd ever been able to talk to without getting all thick-tongued and hot-faced and stupid. If he ever saw her again—*when* he ever saw her again—he would tell her how he felt.

He climbed a rise and peered downstream where the water back-eddied in deep pools. A thought knifed him suddenly, nearly bringing him to his knees.

What if she'd fallen in and drowned? Or . . . what if Indians . . . ?

Skirting a beaver dam, his ankle caught on a stick. Reaching out to break the fall, his hand landed on cloth. He brought the white garment to his face and smelled her. He filled his lungs, lifted his head, and yelled, "Corinne!"

"I am here, Nils."

Startled, he swung around. She sat in the brush a few feet away, the skirt of her dress draped over her knees, one bare foot planted girlishly atop the other.

"Corinne." He smiled, curious but relieved. "What are you doing here?"

She shook her head and bit her lip, fighting tears. Her hair fell in wet curls to her shoulders. She took a short breath and said thinly, "I cannot go back to the camp." When she looked up, he saw the bruises.

He dropped to his knees. "Corinne . . . your face." He studied her, frowning. "What . . . ?"

"Leaf me alone, please . . . "

"What happened?"

The girl's chest heaved, and she convulsed with a deep-throated sob. "Leaf me alone!"

Nils stood and backed away. He opened his mouth to speak, and she screamed again, louder. "*Leaf me alone!*"

Nils screwed his face against the terror in her voice, held his hands over his ears, and took three steps back. Stumbling, he turned and ran back along the creek, realizing that whatever trouble had befallen his sweet Corinne was beyond his resolving.

It took him a half hour to find the camp in the dark. His father was sitting by the fire, a cup of coffee in his hands. "Nils!"

Breathless, Nils yelled, "Pa, I found her! Somethin's wrong!"

Before Kohl could say anything, Nils was rousting his mother under the wagon. "Ma, it's Corinne. Come quick!"

Later that night, Nils and Imbert sat around the dying campfire. The night was black as pitch, and the glowing embers sparked.

Several yards away, the wagon creaked as Nils's mother tended Corinne. Nils and his parents had found her sitting on the beaver dam, staring downriver. When she saw Wilomene Kohl, she broke down in tears. The woman wrapped the girl in a blanket and led her back to the camp, where now occasional moans pierced the silence. Nils winced.

A half hour later, Wilomene Kohl stepped down from the wagon and pulled a quilt around her shoulders. She stared at her husband until he rose stiffly and walked to her. Nils watched them, brows knit. They spoke in hushed tones for several minutes. Kohl shook his head. "Oh, for the love o' Christ!"

When Mrs. Kohl had returned to the wagon, Kohl retrieved his rifle and returned to the fire.

"What happened, Pa?" Nils asked him desperately.

Kohl did not reply. He sat heavily down in his folding

camp chair and laid the gun across his thighs.

"Pa—"

"You stay out of it!"

Kohl propped the gun against a log, stood, walked a few feet away, and opened his pants to relieve himself. "She went out and got herself befouled by five men," he said with stern derision.

Nils's back stiffened. He felt as though he'd been hit with a sledgehammer. "Wha . . . who . . . ?"

"Those men we met yesterday. At least, that's what she told your mother. They musta followed us. One of us will have to keep watch tonight with a rifle."

Sick to his stomach, Nils bent over with his head in his hands. The image of his beloved Corinne ravaged by five men in the woods was unbearable. The elder Kohl regarded him with disdain. "Thought she was so almighty pure, did ya?"

Nils shot him a hurt look. "How can you talk about her that way?"

"Her mother was just like her. Pretty to look at, but . . ." Kohl spat into the fire.

Nils bounded to his feet and clenched his fists, eyes smoldering. Kohl returned the stare, and Nils wheeled into the darkness, groaning and holding his head. "How could they do that to her!"

"Don't make a fool o' yourself, boy."

Nils stumbled back to the fire, regarded his father across the salmon glow. "What are we gonna do about this?"

Kohl squinted his eyes, said at length, "We've women and children here, boy. We don't make trouble for ourselves. Hopefully, those men will go on about their business, now they got what they wanted, and we'll keep movin' . . . get up to the Basin before the fall time."

Nils shook his head slowly and stared, disbelieving. "Nothin'?"

Kohl stood and walked to his son until his face was a few inches from the boy's. "Don't be a fool for her.

A girl like that—she'd have nothin' to do with you."
He thrust his rifle into Nils's arms. "You keep watch.
Anything comes near, you shoot. No noddin' off, do ya
hear?"

He walked toward the wagon, stopped, and turned
around. "She didn't have to go wanderin' off by herself." He raised his eyebrows and nodded knowingly.
"My guess is she went off lookin' for trouble and found
it."

Kohl retired to his bedroll under the wagon, and
sighed. He'd known that taking in his sister's daughter
was a mistake. Uncle or not, he knew from experience
a man couldn't look at a girl like that without feeling
. . . well, like a man.

Nils fingered the rifle and sat down by the fire. He
stood the rifle between his knees and stared into the
flames. If his father didn't have the sand to do what
needed to be done, then he'd have to do it.

When Kohl's snores sounded in the dark beneath
the wagon, Nils gripped the Springfield in both hands
and walked to the mules picketed by the creek. As
quietly as he could, he slipped a bridle over Ned's
ears and swung astride, walked the mule across the
creek, stopped, and looked back at the encampment.

His heart drummed beneath his breastbone and he
heard a rushing in his ears. He touched his heels to the
mule's flanks and rode up a dark rise, squinting his
eyes to see the ground. The moon had risen over the
peaks, gilding the meadows. Wolves howled like ban-
shees.

A mile from the camp, a low fire burnished a dry
creekbed in a hollow about thirty yards away. Nils dismounted behind a hogback, tied the mule to a lone cottonwood, hefted his rifle, and crept around the hill,
stumbling over sage clumps and stones.

A horse nickered. Nils stopped, held his breath. Trying to quell his pounding heart, he looked right. Four
black figures milled in a grassy flat about twenty yards

away. He stepped toward them. Skittish, the animals sidestepped and shook their heads.

"Sh-sh, easy," Nils cooed. He unhobbled them quickly, slapped a rump, and watched them scatter.

When he came within ten paces of the camp, the silhouettes of five prone sleepers, heads propped on saddles, appeared in the flickering shadows cast by the fire. Snores rose. Someone groaned. Nils kicked a bottle, froze, and watched.

When none of the sleepers stirred, he drew a deep breath and gripped the rifle in both hands. He shuddered, his resolve weakening. Then he remembered the look of anguish on Corinne's lovely face, licked his lips, and thrust his arm through the rifle's sling.

Reaching behind him, he unsheathed the Green River knife given him by Jack Thompson, the grizzled old guide he'd met on the train. He raked a thumb across the blade he oiled and sharpened regularly, as the guide had instructed, and moved forward, hunched like a coup-hunting Sioux.

Approaching the first man, Nils knelt down, studying the man's unshaven face—eyes closed, chin drawn—sound asleep. Nils frowned. The man had wrapped something white around his neck, partially hidden by his blanket. Smelling the raw alcohol on the man's breath, Nils pulled the blanket down to his chest, revealing the thin, white garment knotted loosely around the man's neck.

It was a woman's washworn undergarment. A chamise, Nils thought it was called. It was Corinne's chamise! Nils gritted his teeth.

"You bastard," he whispered, pushing the man's collar down, lowering the blade, and drawing it across the prickly neck in one quick motion.

He froze. The man's chin came up. The eyes opened. He opened his mouth to speak but only gurgled. Then he grunted loudly, wide-eyed, as the death spasms began.

Across the fire, another man lifted his head. "Huh?"

Nils slipped the rifle from his shoulder, brought it to
bear, and fired. The rifle butt smashed his shoulder,
jerked him back. The boom felt like an open hand slapping his ears. Fleet with fear, he turned and stumbled
down the hollow as fast as his jellied knees would carry
him, stumbling in the loose rocks of the creekbed. Pistols barked behind him. Men yelled and quarreled. His
heart felt as though it would explode.

"Oh . . . oh, god . . ." he groaned. The hair on the
back of his neck bristled.

He stopped and looked around. He'd run too far. He
had to find his way around the hill, where Ned was tied.
Guns popped. Bullets spanged rocks and thumped in the
grass.

A clear voice behind him climbed to a high pitch and
echoed. "Come back here, you sorry fucking bastard!"

Nils climbed the hill, panting, his lungs as raw as
sandpaper, brush tearing his clothes and skin. When he
finally came to the mule, he untied the frightened animal
and jumped awkwardly onto its back, nearly sliding
down the opposite side.

Three quick rifle shots exploded nearby. An unintelligible cry followed. "You killed my brother, you son
of a bitch! I'm comin' fer you!"

Nils held the mule's reins taut, listening and shaking.
Brush popped under running feet. The voice rose again—
an animal wail.

"*I'm . . . comin' . . . fer you!*"

The echo died long after Nils had raked the mule with
his heels. "Oh, my god—what have I done?" he
gasped, leaning forward over the mule's ears, slapping
its rump.

When he found his way back to the creek, he picketed
the mule with the others and made his way toward the
camp.

A figure appeared out of nowhere, dark and round,
and cuffed him to the ground. Nils's ears rang. He
fought for air against the knee on his chest. The cold

steel of a knife blade pressed against his cheek. His father's deep voice resounded in his ear, the sour breath
hot against his face.

"Now you've done it, boy. Now you've done it!"

3

It took J.L. and the boys most of the next morning, in the blazing heat, to gather their scattered horses. Sunburned and foot-sore, they returned to their dugout built into the side of a low ridge peppered with ponderosa pines. The dugout was nearly covered with animal hides of every shape and size, tacked to the walls for drying. Bones lay scattered as though dropped from the sky.

J.L. buried his brother on the knoll behind the smokehouse. His jaw was set and his eyes were dark. Pete Hill approached him with a crock jug and a tin cup. He filled the cup and offered it to J.L.

"Here ya are, J.L. Have you a shot o' that; make ya feel better."

J.L. leaned on the shovel and gave Pete a look that would have cowed a grizzly. Pete smiled timidly. J.L. slapped the whiskey in his face, said through gritted teeth, "Don't you know it ain't proper to offer a man drink when he's buryin' his brother, you fuckin' heathen?"

Hill blinked his eyes against the burning whiskey, working his mouth. "Sorry, J.L. Thought it'd make ya feel better."

"The only thing's gonna make me feel better is to hang that kid's head above that door," J.L. said, jabbing a finger at the dugout. "And that girl's right beside it."

Jim McCluskey was sitting on a stump in front of the dugout door, blistered feet submerged in a pail of salt water. He pursed his lips. "Wasn't the girl's fault."

"It's always the girl's fault," J.L. countered, rubbing the long, bloody groove below his ear.

"I say we bring her back to cook, clean, and keep us company," Jim said. "What do you say, Sonny?"

Clad in only long johns, boots, and a floppy-brimmed hat, Sonny Laagerman ceased his work carving an elkhorn into a knife handle, and grinned.

"Who're either o' you to say anything?" J.L. barked.

Ignoring the comment, McCluskey squeezed a quirly between thumb and middle finger and held it to his lips, took a deep drag, and shook his head. "I seen that kid the other day. He didn't have spine 'nough to look me in the eye, much less cut my throat."

"Well, it wasn't your throat he cut, was it?"

"That doesn't make sense, J.L. How's your neck?"

"It hurts."

J.L. tossed more dirt on the grave, then erected the cross he'd made from rawhide and two green willow sticks. He got Pete to help him mound stones around the cross.

McCluskey poured himself a drink from the crock jug beside the stump. "You keep messin' there, that kid an' his old man are gonna be across the Deadman before we even get started."

Pete Hill squealed, "You just want more o' that Norsky girl, Jim!"

J.L. looked at them with a fire in his eyes. "If you two don't mind, I'm burying my brother here when it shoulda been one o' you."

He lifted a rock, carried it to the grave, and set it down. He sat on top of it and aimed his hawk face at McCluskey. "Besides, I ain't in no hurry. I aim to take my time an' enjoy myself." His lips spread in a mirthless grin.

McCluskey studied him, nodded, and turned away. He

knew from experience that J.L. could get right nasty,
and it wasn't a very pleasant thing to see.

The Kohl family found the other three wagons of their
caravan around noon that same day, stopped for lunch
in a horseshoe of a creek lined with cottonwoods. Blue
smoke curled up from the fires where coffee simmered
and buffalo boiled. Lazy voices rose, trimmed with
laughter.

Imbert halted his wagon behind the others, set the
brake, and stepped down. He walked into the ring where
the Townsends and the Langs reposed with filled plates.

"Well, look who's here. Kohl, pull up a seat and roll
up your sleeves," Major Lawrence Townsend cried
when he spied Kohl between the wagons. "We're fixin'
to eat the last of Lang's buffalo." Townsend was a trim,
tall Southerner, impeccably mannered and dressed,
who'd lost his plantation and his right arm in the War
Between the States. His silk cravat and the ends of his
bushy gray mustache lifted in the breeze filtering
through the cottonwoods.

Kohl sighed and tipped back his hat. "Like to talk to
you men, if you don't mind."

Townsend frowned and glanced at John Lang. "Trouble, Kohl?"

Kohl gestured for the men to follow him behind the
wagons, and they gathered at the head of Kohl's mules—
Townsend, Townsend's son, Douglas, and John Lang,
the mild-mannered schoolteacher from Indiana.

"What is it, Mr. Kohl?" Lang asked. He was a sandy-
haired, blue-eyed man, with a big, clean face and an
affable smile. Standing about five-nine, lean but broad
shouldered, he had muscular hands and the look of a
farmboy who, tired of the plow and the hay wagon, had
turned to books.

Kohl scrubbed his brow with the back of his wrist and
told them about the rape and about Nils killing one of
the girl's attackers. When Kohl finished the story, Lang

looked around for Nils, suddenly conspicuous by his absence.

Reading the teacher's mind, Kohl said, "He's back with the supply wagon. I've confined him there to keep him out of trouble."

"That boy actually *killed* a man?" Townsend said, unable to contain his surprise.

"Wouldn't know it to look at him, would ya?" Kohl grunted.

"That's an awful thing," Lang said, shaking his head. "How's the girl?"

Kohl shrugged. "She'll live. Lucky they didn't kill her, if you ask me. Lucky they weren't Injuns. Injuns woulda done worse than that, most likely."

"Well, we all saw them the other day," Lang said. "They're dangerous men. We were warned about their kind back in Fort Reno. They ride the trail looking for easy targets."

"I wouldn't say we're all that easy a target," Townsend objected, his old soldier's pride surfacing. "If you're worried about them coming after us, don't be. There were five of them, if I remember right, so now they're four. Well, there's four of us, and if you include Kohl's boy—and I guess you have to since he already cut one of their throats—we're five." Townsend punctuated the sentence with a resolute dip of his knobby chin.

Lang looked around at the group, silently sizing them up. Imbert Kohl was a poor dirt farmer, handier with a scythe than a rifle. Townsend was a one-armed Southern gentlemen, in his mid-sixties, whose skill at fighting, whatever it may have been in the past, was obviously reduced. His son, Douglas, stood quietly beside his father, taking every cue from the old man.

He had his father's height and build, not to mention his taste for expensive clothes and adornment, but he had the pompous, weak-eyed look of a pampered heir. Lang judged him even less handy with his fists or a firearm than he, John Lang, a country schoolteacher trav-

eling west with a well-thumbed volume of Shakespeare's sonnets in his vest.

Townsend stretched his arm across his son's shoulders
and continued in his slow South Carolina drawl, "No,
if we hang together, men, we'll be fine. There's strength
in numbers. Those men might be renegades, but they
can count. Now, I think it's best Cynthia and Mrs. Lang
don't hear about what happened to Kohl's niece." He
slid his cool, humorous eyes to the Illinois farmer.
"Kohl, can your wife and son keep a secret?"

"If I tell 'em to, they can," Kohl said.

"Fine, then," the major said. "Now, the women are
goin' to be gettin' right nervous if we don't stop skulk-
ing around back here with the mules."

Giving a self-satisfied chuckle, Townsend turned back
to the fire and the smell of meat boiling in wild herbs.
His son gave Kohl and Lang a nervous smile, then followed his father.

Lang turned to Kohl. "What do you think?"

Kohl ran a big hand down his two-day growth of salt-
and-pepper beard. "I think we better keep extra close
watch at night—that's what I think."

The company traveled until late in the afternoon, then
halted for the night by a creek surrounded by good grass.
They turned the wagons in a protective circle and sealed
the gaps with rope, then turned the mules and horses
into the circle to graze. The men examined the stock for
loose shoes, scrapes, and bruises, then gathered buffalo
chips and carried water from the creek.

Normally, the women would have started setting up
folding chairs and tables in preparation for supper, but
word had gotten out that the poor foreign girl traveling
with the Kohls had gotten hurt falling down a ravine.

As soon as the wagons had stopped, Grace Lang and
the major's lovely daughter-in-law, Cynthia, walked to
the back of the supply wagon Nils had been driving, to
offer sympathy and assistance to the poor thing. Wilomene Kohl stood between them and a little behind, fists

on her hips, making a show of patronage by shaking her head, but her jaw was set and her eyes were cold.

When camp was finally set up and the women had begun making stew from Lang's buffalo, Major Townsend decided to go hunting. With Lang's buffalo about gone, the party would need meat tomorrow. Besides, the major's rheumatism had been acting up, which made him feel old and the need to prove himself.

He unpacked his riding tack and saddled his gold, white-maned stallion, Windjammer, who'd made the trip tethered to the major's wagon. He wrapped a brace of Confederate revolvers around his waist and slid his Maynard rifle in his saddleboot, then rode over to his son and daughter-in-law's wagon.

Douglas was sitting sideways at the back of the wagon box, only his head and shoulders visible above the endgate, the delicate bones and sallow skin of his long, feminine face bunched as though with pain. His full red lips drew back from his perfect teeth. The major was about to ask what was wrong when Cynthia lifted her head from between Douglas's knees, a look of bemused concentration on her face.

Horrified that he'd interrupted his son and daughter-in-law in carnal pleasure, the major gasped, "Lord o'mercy!" and was about to rein away when Cynthia regarded him casually, holding up a small green bottle and a cottonball.

"Bee bite," she said.

"Oh, thank heavens," the major chuckled.

"No," Cynthia said, shaking her head and rolling her lustrous brown eyes, apparently reading the major's mind. She had the dark-haired, heart-stopping beauty and offhand air of good Southern breeding. To the major, the girl conjured images of misty hills and oak-shaded lanes. "The only thing that's been swollen on Douglas for the past two months is the inside of his thigh where the bee stung him. The poor dear doesn't travel well."

She doused the cotton from the bottle and applied it

to her husband, who stiffened and tipped his head back in pain. "Ouch—Cynthia, it *hurts!*"

"How'd you get stung there?" the major inquired.

Wincing, Douglas said, "I was just riding along when the beast landed right between my legs."

"And the fool boy got so frightened he jumped around until he sat on it!" Cynthia laughed.

"It's not funny, Cynthia. I've always been highly allergic to bee stings."

The major leaned on his saddlehorn and shook his head. "Well, I take it you won't want to go huntin' with me, then, eh, boy?"

Douglas regarded his father with exasperation, his girlish locks of auburn hair bouncing on his shoulders, "My thigh's swollen up like a dinner plate, father!"

"No, I didn't think so," the major said, reining away and raking Windjammer with his spurs. It bothered him that Douglas was the only man who hadn't contributed meat to the supper table. They were Southern aristocrats with names to uphold—a job no easier since Bobby Lee's debacle at Appomatox.

Townsend cantered his horse out to a hogback about a mile from the camp, and looked around. To the north, the creek coursed under buttes. Dun-colored prairie rose and fell in the south and east.

Through a swale punctuated with willows to the west, the major spotted a pond trimmed with saw grass and flanked with a white blotch—probably a salt lick. He nodded to himself, clucked to his horse, and rode toward the lick, hoping to scare up a deer or two, maybe a pronghorn.

About a hundred yards away, the major dismounted and tethered his horse to a tree, careful to remain upwind of the pond so his scent wouldn't give him away. He shucked his old, scarred rifle, crouched, and moved through the high grass. Red-winged blackbirds screeched. A skunk poked up its black-and-white face, then turned and scuttled away.

The major circled the pond. A right-handed man before he'd lost the arm in the war, he felt awkward with the rifle in his left hand, but he'd convinced himself that, considering the injuries he'd witnessed at Chickamauga, it was a minor inconvenience. He just needed to take his time and think about what he was doing.

Stopping twenty yards before the lick, he peered through the grass and spied a medium-sized buck and a heavy-shouldered doe feeding in a raspberry patch just beyond the lick. Using the stub of his right arm, he hefted the rifle to his left shoulder and steadied the barrel until the bead lay on the neck of the heavy doe whose meat would be more tender than the old buck's.

"Steady . . . steady. . . ." He held his breath and increased the pressure on the trigger until the rifle popped and the barrel bounced, smoking.

Letting the rifle sink to his chest, he squinted his eyes at the lick and saw the buck leap away through the grass. The doe remained standing as though frozen. She took a step and keeled over on her side, legs quivering.

"Now, that wasn't so godblame hard a'tall," the major congratulated himself, dropping the rifle to his side and moving toward the dying deer. "Not a'tall."

When the major was sure the doe was dead, he retrieved his horse, then regarded the fallen game with skepticism. He rubbed his left shoulder. "The only problem with shooting a lassie your size is my rheumatism," he said through bared teeth, kneeling down and shoving his arm under the doe's neck to test the weight. "Nope. You're a heavy gal, that's for sure," he said, shaking his head.

Suddenly a chill ran up his spine and lifted the hair on the back of his neck. He felt an evil presence, and heard the rustle and clomp of hooves on the grassy ground. Windjammer whinnied. The major raised his eyes slowly.

Four mounted buckskin-clad men closed around him in a tight circle, grinning.

4

"Hello there, old-timer," said the man who'd pulled up nearest the major.

He was thin and long-muscled, with a coyote face and eyes, and long cords in his neck. His flat-crowned hat sat at a rakish angle over his whiskered face. Two pistols, butts forward, snugged up against his ribs, and a long cartridge belt did a figure eight over his deer-hide tunic.

The major stood slowly, feeling his blood warm. He gave a slow nod, eyes glancing off each rider's prominently displayed pistols, rifles, and knives. He was hoping they were only hunters from another pack train, but their bold demeanors and impertinent eyes told him they were the men he'd seen the other day who'd raped the foreign girl.

"Good afternoon," the major said, trying to dredge up his Southern charm. "Just shot a deer here and was trying to figure out how I was going to get the damn thing on my horse. The good Lord must have heard my silent plea and sent you men to give me a hand." The major let the sentence trail off into a chuckle that sounded wooden even to him.

The lead rider gazed at him with his sharp coyote eyes and spat. "You from that group camped yonder?"

The major's smile weakened. "That's right."

"You a reb?"

"I'm from South Carolina." The major squeezed the stock of his rifle and prepared to raise it. He thought he could get one of them if he had to. He was outnumbered and had no chance of surviving a firefight, but he'd give them something to remember him by.

"You look rich. You rich?"

"Poor as a hind-tit calf, sir."

"Yeah, well what's that around your neck? Looks like silk to me. And that hat must've cost you plenty. Where'd you get it?"

"My daughter-in-law bought it for me in Fort Reno."

A gaunt man with grinning eyes said, "That's a nice hat, J.L."

"Real Western hat, ain't it?" the lead rider said, turning to the others. "Only you never see 'em on any Westerner. Only in Eastern magazines or on the heads of rich yellow-bellies. . . . You like that hat, Pete?"

"Sure do. That's a nice hat."

"Mister, give my friend your hat."

The major frowned and tightened his jaw.

The man called J.L. said, "That's a Western hat. You're not a Westerner. My friend here is a Westerner, born and raised, and look at that silly old hat he has to wear!" He gestured to the limp, sweat-stained hat covering the head of the grinning rider one horse down from him.

Involuntarily, the major took one step back. The lead rider's eye narrowed. "Give it to him. He'll give you his—a real Western hat."

The major said, voice swollen with pride, "I'll not give up my hat."

"If I have to come down there and take it from you, you ain't gonna have a head to put *any* hat on . . . Reb!"

The major's heart throbbed in his throat, and he felt dizzy and sick to his stomach. His hand greased his rifle with sweat. He hated fear in any man, but especially in himself. He tried to lift the rifle and lower the barrel, but his hand wouldn't budge.

"You don't really want to die for your hat, do you, old man?" the coyote-faced man said, leaning forward on his saddle horn, looking wistful.

"You'll kill me anyway," the major muttered, hating the weakness in his voice.

"I'm an honest man. I give you my word. Your hat for his, and we'll move along."

"You the ones attacked the girl?"

The man fabricated a wide-eyed look of innocent surprise. "Attack? We didn't attack no girl. There was a girl out swimmin' naked and lookin' fer some fun. And we gave it to her. But we never *attacked* her." He looked at the others and laughed as though at a preposterous injustice.

The major gritted his teeth, seeing red bleed up from the corners of his eyes. "You're a lot o' scum," he growled.

The man sighed and studied the major with eyes cold as a Yankee winter. "Give my friend your hat. Then we'll let you go back to your camp and tell that boy I'm gonna cut his throat just like he cut my brother's."

Silence hung for what seemed minutes. Finally, the rider with the battered hat spurred his horse forward and stopped beside the major, doffed the hat, and offered it to Townsend with a mock flourish, thin lips spreading a grin to match the one in his eyes.

The major looked at him. He felt a sharp pain behind his left eye as he lowered his rifle under the stub of his right arm. With his left hand, he removed the flat-brimmed plainsman and handed it to the rider, then accepted its wretched replacement with a look of eminent disdain and reluctance.

He looked at the smelly, sweat-sogged thing, as though it were from a different world. He wondered how something so insignificant could make him feel so small.

"Jim, why don't you and Sonny tie that deer to our friend's horse?" the lead rider said.

"Sure thing," the big, bushy-headed rider said jovially, dismounting.

The major just stood there, looking around and blinking, as the two men draped the doe over his horse. So this was how it felt to be a coward. He'd survived umpteen skirmishes on the fields of his beloved South, had slept in sloughs of his own blood and that of his friends, and he'd always resisted the urge to run . . . until now.

Giving his hat to these men without a fight, despite his knowing he didn't have a chance against them, was the same thing as running, sure as he was standing here.

When the deer was tied behind the major's saddle, the men mounted up, and the lead rider turned to Townsend. "Now, Mister Reb . . . don't forget to tell that boy I'm comin' fer him, hear?" He raised his eyebrows and nodded his head. "He won't know when or where, but I'm gonna get him and get him good." He gave his coyote eyes a hard blink, then reined his horse around, raked his spurs against the gelding's flanks, and led the others westward across the salt lick, hooves clomping through the tall grass.

Crestfallen, Townsend watched the men ride away. When he realized he was still holding the hat, he dropped it, brushed his hand on his pants, picked up his rifle, and returned it to the boot snugged against his stallion's ribs. He grabbed Windjammer's reins and swung into the leather with an involuntary groan of bereavement for his lost pride, and started back to the camp at a slow walk.

He was in no hurry to see the other members of his wagon train. How could he ever hold his head up to them again? Not even Douglas would have given those renegades his hat. He turned his head to spit, but there was no ridding his tongue of the bitter taste of cowardice.

Back at the camp, everyone had eaten, and having washed the dishes in the creek, the women were sitting around the fire patching clothes, and Kohl and Lang were puttering around their wagons, greasing the wheel hubs and checking for cracked axles and canvas

tears. It was nearly dusk, and long shadows swelled
from the cottonwoods, and cotton drifted in a gentling
breeze.

Townsend dismounted and tethered his horse to his
wagon. Having heard him approach, his son poked his
head out of the wagon next to the major's, apparently
still laid up from the bee sting. "Father, you shot a
deer!"

"Yes," the major grunted, unsheathing his belt knife
and cutting the ropes that held the deer to his horse. The
doe fell in a heap. Ignoring it for now, the major unsaddled Windjammer and packed the tack in his wagon box.

"What happened to your hat?" Douglas asked him,
looking up from the magazine he was reading.

"The wind got it," the major mumbled.

"Oh, that's a shame! Cynthia will be disappointed."

Silently, the major went to work on the deer, dressing
it out and skinning it, making a horrible mess of the
thing. All he could think about was his hat. Finally, deciding to quarter the carcass in the morning, he hung the
doe from a tree and drifted silently to bed. He knew he
should tell the other men about his encounter, warn them
of the danger.

But how could he ever explain giving up his hat?

The next morning the party headed out just after dawn
and the breakfast fires were doused. Nils rode alone on
the driver's seat of his family's supply wagon, bringing
up the caravan's rear. Corinne was behind him in the
box, where there was enough room for one person to
ride comfortably amid the barrels of foodstuffs and trail
gear.

He'd tried to talk to her since the attack, but the girl
had only looked at him distantly, as though she hadn't
heard him or couldn't bear the sound of his voice.

That's why he was so flabbergasted when, that afternoon, she appeared through the opening in the canvas
behind him.

"Corinne?" he said.

Clutching a shawl around her shoulders with one hand, she crawled over the seat, smoothed the dress beneath her, and sat down beside Nils, who appraised her cautiously.

She wore a black felt hat with a wide, floppy brim and a round crown. Its cord drooped beneath her chin. One eye was still brown, her right cheek still bore the rip from a man's knuckle, but she looked much more familiar to him than the girl he'd seen only last night returning from her toilet near the creek, eyes glazed with fear.

"I thought I would get some air," she said quietly.

"How do you feel?"

"OK."

"Really?"

"No," she said with a thin, ironic smile, staring straight ahead, shoulders swaying with the wagon.

They rode in silence, Nils handling the reins and Corinne peering through the dust of the forward wagons. Nils was thinking about the men who'd raped her, and he kept imagining it over and over—his lovely Corinne!—until he'd worked himself into a lather. His eyes narrowed and the muscles bunched in his face. He had to tell her.

"I got one of 'em," he said.

He looked at her. She kept her eyes straight ahead. Then she turned to him, slowly, blinking. "What?"

"I got one of 'em." A smile tugged at his mouth.

She watched him for several seconds, a shadow passing over her face. "No, Nils," she said, pleadingly.

He nodded, and the grin grew larger. "Yeah. I sneaked into their camp that night and cut one of their throats."

"Oh, Nils!"

"At least one of 'em paid for what they did to you. Goddamn dirty snakes!"

"Nils, tell me you did not do this," she pleaded.

He looked at her, replacing his grin with a frown. One

man who'd raped her was dead. He'd thought she'd be pleased.

"Well, sure I did," he said.

Corinne swept the horizon with her gaze, looked to the buttes and mesas tapering around them. The haunted cast returned to her eyes. "It is not over, then," she said, her thin voice catching in her throat.

Nils did not hear her. The other wagons were halting and he was wondering why. It was too early to stop for the day. He hauled back on the reins and considered walking forward but decided against it. He was giving his father a wide berth these days, since the elder Kohl, having heard the gunfire and surmised what Nils had done that night, had nearly slit the boy's throat. Nils would wait here, and if he needed to know what the stop was all about, Mr. Lang would no doubt tell him.

Ahead, Nils's father set his wagon brake, got down from his seat, and walked up to Major Townsend's van. John Lang, who'd been scouting the trail on horseback, had returned, dusty and sunburned, and was talking to the major, perched atop his wagon hatless, silk cravat lifting in the wind.

"What's goin' on?" Kohl inquired.

Lang turned to him. "I spotted what looked like a ranch or a roadhouse up ahead a ways and north."

"Might be a good place to spend the night," the major said. "Might even be some other women around."

"Wilomene would like that," Kohl allowed.

Lang wiped the sweat from above his lip. "Might be . . . safer, too."

Repelled by Lang's candor, the major sighed loudly. "Well, you know me—I could go all day. But I know our stock could use the rest. What do you say, Kohl?"

Like the others, Kohl was tired of looking over his shoulder for the renegades who could appear at any moment to shoot him and the other men, rape the women, and loot the wagons. If only that damn boy of his would have left well enough alone. . . . A ranch or a roadhouse would be a safe haven for the night.

The farmer worked his jaw and sucked a tooth, nodding. "Why not?"

5

Glenn Nordstrom stepped out from his cabin and set a steaming coffee cup on the rail of the rough pine veranda. Blinking away the sleep from his afternoon siesta, he fished around in his shirt pocket for his tobacco and built a quirley.

He yawned and rolled the kinks out of his neck as his fingers smoothed the paper around the Durham and curled the ends. Firing a lucifer on the porch rail, he lighted up, blowing smoke and lifting his gaze across the dusty, hard-packed ranch yard to mesas shelving to distant blue mountains.

Nordstrom was a good-sized man, an inch or two over medium height. He had a lean, angular face, with a strong jaw and pale blue eyes contrasting the red-brown of his deeply tanned cheeks and sun-bleached eyebrows. His straw yellow hair had grown over his ears since his last trim, and his beard of the same color, while not bushy, had gotten a little shabbier than he liked. He wore a faded blue bib-front shirt and smoke-tanned buckskin pants tucked into high brown boots. Shirtsleeves rolled halfway to his elbows revealed the hard cords in his forearms.

Nordstrom had built his ranch here in the Big Open after twenty years of cowboying, game hunting, prospecting, and scouting. In the last three years, he'd made peace with the Indians and had held the land against rustlers, drought, and blizzards while waiting for the railroad rumored to be heading this way.

He had cut timber in the river bottoms and hauled it out by wagon. He had built a cabin, a small, three-room affair with a lean-to pantry and a big fieldstone hearth. When the railroad arrived, he planned to expand his holdings, buy some Texas cattle, and hire seasoned cowboys to string fence.

Though it was still wide open country, Nordstrom knew it would be the next big cattle range. The scattered parks, long draws stirrup-high in forage, and wide valleys shaggy with berry thickets provided ideal graze and shelter, and the deep running streams were a boundless supply of water. The mountains offered game.

It had taken him a long time to save enough cash and muster enough courage to settle down, but he'd finally done it. He congratulated himself now, dropping his gaze from the distant peaks to his stock pens and barns and the rough pole corrals just beyond the main gate, where fifty wild mustangs milled. Yes, he'd finally settled down. After three years here, he just kept feeling more and more at home.

Nordstrom heard a floorboard squeak behind him and turned to see his wrangler, Charlie Decker, stroll through the cabin door, looping his suspenders over his shoulders and blinking his eyes against the afternoon glare.

"What time is it?" he asked.

"Must be pret' near three. Hell of a habit—sleepin' in the middle of the day," Nordstrom said.

Charlie raised his eyebrows and blinked his eyes, smacking his lips. "Feels right sweet, if you ask me."

Twenty-three years old and one-quarter Cheyenne, Charlie was a short, powerfully built young man with coarse dark brown hair curling over his ears, and olive skin that turned a rich dark red in the sun.

His round, hard-boned face was distinctly Indian, and his full mouth appeared to be smiling most of the time. He wore a faded blue collarless shirt, red bandanna, and denim jeans rubbed white where his thighs and seat snugged the saddle.

Nordstrom puffed on his cigarette, then took it between his thumb and index finger and leaned against the rail.

"Your old man got me in the siesta habit when he lured me down to Mexico to dig our El Doradoes. I swear we did as much sleepin' as diggin'. Your pa never had much use for the pick and shovel, I discovered only *after* we got to Mexico."

"I bet you had fun, though," Charlie said, grinning.

Nordstrom and Charlie's father, Clem Decker, once scouted for wagon trains on the Oregon and Overland Trails. They were hunting a marauding grizzly near the Patched Skin Buttes in Dakota six years ago when, on a whim, Clem decided to cut a two-year-old pinto from a wild band he'd stumbled upon.

Somehow he'd roped the tail, and the mustang outran Clem's stallion and pulled the mount down on top of Clem. Nordstrom found him, cursing and grunting with a stove-in chest and broken back a half hour before he died.

After he'd built the ranch, Nordstrom gave Charlie a job wrangling and breaking horses. Nordstrom had never known anyone who could handle a horse like this kid. In his twenty-three years, he'd learned twice what most men learned in a lifetime, and he had all the right instincts to back it up.

Nordstrom clamped a hand on his shoulder. "Your old man was the worst miner I ever knew, the best tracker I ever saw, and the most fun a man should ever have!" He laughed and flicked his cigarette into the dirt. "Well, I suppose we better get those broncs in the yard before they jump the poles and head back to the mountains."

"I s'pose," Charlie agreed, snatching his wide-brimmed plainsman off the cabin wall.

It took them over two hours to separate the stallions, mares, and foals, line them out and haze them past the brush wings of the corral gates, and to repair the inevitable damage to all three pens. By the time they had all the horses secure, the sun was sinking in the west, casting shadows, and a green haze cloaked the near foothills.

The older horses moved to the far side of the pens and milled in circles, kicking up dust and shaking their heads. The mares whinnied loudly for their foals, who pricked their ears over the closed gate before them and bleated like sheep. Rippling their big muscles, the stallions screamed and threatened the gate.

"Fine-lookin' bunch," Charlie said.

Nordstrom nodded. "I hope the army hostlers think so."

"Pshaw—what do they know about ridin' stock?"

"That's the problem. I could bring them the finest stock in the mountains, and they'd still try to dicker me down to pennies and pisswater."

"You'll still make enough to lay in good for the winter, Glenn."

Nordstrom looked at the stocky young horseman, frowning. "I take it you ain't gonna winter out here?"

Charlie shook his head. "Got business in Denver."

Nordstrom scowled. "Who is it this time?"

"Millie White."

Nordstrom's eyes widened. "Mrs. Reginald Dawson White?"

"One and the same," Charlie said, giving a self-satisfied grin.

"Son, you keep messin' with important men's women, you're gonna get yourself tarred, feathered, and greased for the pan!"

Charlie laughed. "There's just somethin' about us bronc busters that gets those society ladies hotter'n a spring bitch. Why don't you come with me and find out for yourself?"

Nordstrom shook his head. "I promised myself a long time ago that when I could, I'd spend no more time in a city than I needed to get a haircut and fill my flour sack."

He lifted a coiled rope over a corral post and opened the gate. He stepped through the gate, shook out a big horse loop, and stepped slowly forward, trying to keep the broncs from boogering. A big gray and a blue roan stood facing him, heads low. The others trotted up and down the far side of the corral shaking their heads, long manes dancing.

Behind him, Charlie said, "Heather wouldn't want you to stay out here all by yourself. She'd understand if you went to town, got yourself some company."

Nordstrom nodded, remembering his lovely wife, the daughter of a Lutheran missionary he'd met at the Red Cloud Agency in Dakota. She'd died two-and-a-half years ago of influenza without having enjoyed one full season with Nordstrom on the ranch. He could hear her mentioned now, could remember the way she looked, without dropping to his knees in tears.

"I know she would, Charlie. My staying here has nothing to do with Heather. She's gone, and I've let her go." He gave the young man a sincere look and added, "Really."

Charlie pursed his lips and nodded.

Two-and-a-half years, Norstrom thought, turning back to the horses. Has it really been that long? Had he really let her go?

He shook his head and moved into the corral, holding the wide loop about an inch above the ground. He swung it back and forth in front of him, then brought it up and over his head, spun it outward in a long arc, and settled it over the gray.

The brown eyes widened, white-ringed and wild. Squealing, the horse lifted its head and reared as Nordstrom jerked the slack from the rope and tightened it.

"Ho now, ho now," he said as the horse reared and plunged.

He worked his way up the rope to the bronc as Charlie made his way around the corral and poked a hackamore through the poles. Nordstrom grabbed it. Charlie ducked into the corral and held the rope taut while Nordstrom wrestled the hackamore over the bronc's ears.

The rattle of trace chains and the complaints of squeaky wheel hubs rose in the west. A mule brayed. Nordstrom secured the hackamore and removed the rope from the bronc's neck.

"Looks like we got company," Charlie said, coiling the rope and poking his chin westward.

"You don't say," Nordstrom said.

The ranch stood about a mile off the Lone Wolf River, in the rough, sagey expanses south of the Deadman. Although a prominent cattle trail cut the nearby buttes, visitors to the ranch were few and far between.

Nordstrom knew from newspapers that the West was filling up, but the Big Open—at least, this part of it— was still too remote and rough around the edges for most folks. That's why it was a surprise to see an outsider lifting dust at his door.

Nordstrom held the bronc by the hackamore rope and glanced under the horse's chin. Five mule-drawn wagons bounced across the shallow creek shaded by cotton-woods and willows, approached the log cabin, and clattered to a halt, the thunder of their industry dying as the crimson dust rose.

Nordstrom studied the five dusty vans, the lathered, blowing mules twitching their ears at flies, the men and women perched on the wagon seats sweat-soaked and sunburned. Their eyes were dull with what Nordstrom had once called trail shock: the tired, wary, eager look of civilized people traveling in an uncivilized land and not quite remembering why.

"Good afternoon," he called with a nod.

"Good afternoon," the man on the lead wagon echoed in a deep-rolling Southern accent. A South Carolina accent, Nordstrom thought, his years on the trail guiding thousands having taught him such things as accents. "Hot one today."

"Sure is."

The man set his brake, threw his reins over his seat, and stepped awkwardly down from the wagon. The awkwardness came from his having only one arm, Nordstrom saw—an all-too-common trait in Southern men these days.

He was tall, lean, and white-haired, with a broad straw hat shading his forehead. He walked toward Nordstrom and Charlie, setting his lips in a friendly smile.

To Charlie, Nordstrom said, "Let's turn the horse loose. It's getting too late to start working 'em today, anyway."

"I got him," Charlie said, taking the hackamore rope from Nordstrom, who crawled through the corral to meet the visitors.

"We didn't mean to interrupt your work," the man said. "We were just passin' through on the trail south of here, saw your place in the distance, and thought it might be nice to rub elbows."

"Glad you did, friend." Nordstrom smiled. Two other men had gotten down from their wagons and were walking up to flank the first man.

"I'm Major Lawrence Townsend," the tall Southerner said, thrusting out his hand.

"Glenn Nordstrom."

Turning to the other two men, Townsend said, "This is Imbert Kohl and John Lang. Kohl, Lang—meet Mr. Nordstrom." Nordstrom shook hands with the other men, feeling awkward. He hadn't shaken a man's hand in over a year, but he warmed to the prospect of company. It was nice to hear an unfamiliar voice, see a face from elsewhere.

"Where you folks headed?"

"Cottonwood Valley," Townsend said proudly. "I've homesteaded me a ranch in the Cottonwood Basin, and persuaded these two gentlemen I met on the train to join me. The makin's of a town up thataway, and when the railroad comes through, we'll all be shittin' in high cotton—if you'll pardon my French." The man smiled broadly, revealing big, horsey, tobacco-stained teeth.

Nordstrom smiled back. "Larkspur and witchgrass, more like. Where's your cattle?"

"All in good time, Mr. Nordstrom. All in good time."

Lang cleared his throat. "Would you mind if we camped by your creek for the night?" he asked politely. "We promise to stay out of your hair and be on our way first thing in the morning."

"Not a chance," Nordstrom said, shaking his head. "You'll stay right here in the yard, and let me and Charlie serve you at our fire."

"We can't let you do that," Lang said.

"Nonsense. It's our pleasure. We don't get many visitors out here."

The pilgrims looked at one another and shrugged.

"Unharness your mules," Nordstrom urged. "There's good grass along the creek."

"We don't want to be any trouble," the major said, spreading his hands.

"No trouble at all." Nordstrom had led four caravans over the Rockies in as many years, survived cholera, cyclones, floods, and Indian raids. How much trouble could a few trail-weary pilgrims be?

"I'll start the vittles," he said, and headed for the cabin.

6

When the travelers had unharnessed their mules and hobbled them in the grass by the creek, they accepted Nordstrom's invitation to wash in the big tub behind the cabin fed by a pipe running from a hillside spring.

While Charlie gathered wood and built a fire out in the yard, Nordstrom chopped up the venison, smothered it with salt, pepper, and home-grown garlic, and tossed it into a big cast-iron stewpot, which he lugged outside and hung from the wrought-iron stand over the fire.

While the meat browned, he and Charlie dug three hills of new potatoes and several pounds of onions from Nordstrom's irrigated garden, and dumped the washed and peeled vegetables into the sizzling pot from which the smell of charred venison issued. Then Nordstrom produced a five-gallon crock of chokecherry wine he'd been aging in his springhouse since last fall, and poured the scarlet liquid into the smoking pot. The fruity, liquory steam mushroomed skyward to the delight of the onlooking visitors.

"Have you ever smelled anything so heavenly?" asked John Lang's wife, Grace. At over six feet tall and stout as a rain barrel, she dwarfed her husband, who stood next to her basking in the sweet-smelling steam.

"Lordy, Mr. Nordstrom," Cynthia Townsend said,

looking smitten, "where on earth did you learn to cook like that?"

Nordstrom tossed several sprigs of fresh sage into the pot and brushed his hands on his breeches. "On the Oregon Trail, ma'am," he said with a grin.

"I can cook, Cynthia," Douglas Townsend snapped, obviously irritated by his wife's fascination with the rancher.

"On what planet!" Cynthia replied with a wail, rolling her lovely, impetuous eyes.

Later, when they were eating quietly around the fire, stirring only for another of Nordstrom's sourdough biscuits with which to soak up every ounce of the rich, dark-brown gravy congealing around the thick chunks of meat and potatoes, Major Townsend pulled his chair up beside the rancher's.

He was dressed for dinner in a linen shirt, long cutaway coat, and black wool trousers. His gray mustache was brushed to sharp points above his mouth.

"Mr. Nordstrom, did I overhear you tell my daughter-in-law that you spent some time on the Oregon Trail?"

"That's right. I led a few expeditions when the trail was still a main thoroughfare."

"You know your way around the frontier, I take it?" the major said thoughtfully.

Nordstrom forked a gravy-drenched potato into his mouth and nodded. "I guess you could say that."

"Any advice?"

"Just follow the rivers and the cattle trails," Nordstrom said with a shrug. "It's Indian country, of course, so you have to watch yourselves, but it's really the white people you have to look out for these days. For every decent citizen who moved west in the past twenty years, ten cutthroats had the same idea."

"You don't say," the major said absently, forking his stew.

"Anything wrong, Major?"

The major gave his head a quick shake, scowling. "No . . . no . . . nothing. Tasty stew, Mr. Nordstrom."

"Help yourself to more, Major." Nordstrom regarded the rest of the group. "Help yourselves to more stew, folks. Nobody gets Charlie's juneberry pie till the pot's been cleaned!"

When everyone had finished with the main meal, Charlie rolled out the dough for his pie while Nordstrom gathered the dishes, fending off the women who insisted on handling that chore themselves. He knew how hard the women worked on the trail—he'd always thought they had it tougher than the men did—and it made him feel good to give them the night off.

He was walking around behind the Kohl wagons when someone suddenly jumped off the tailgate and landed in front of him. He stopped abruptly, nearly running into the girl and losing his stack of dishes. Seeing the tall man before her, the girl gasped, stiffening and bringing a frightened hand to her throat.

"Woah—excuse me, miss!" Nordstrom said. "Didn't mean to run you over."

She was a pretty young blonde, maybe eighteen or nineteen years old, with high, wide cheekbones and clear Nordic eyes below the floppy brim of her black felt hat. Her thick, wavy hair framed her face and curled on her shoulders. She wore a plain, linsey-woolsey dress that did nothing to hide the blossoming figure beneath it.

The hat brim went up and the girl's eyes met Nordstrom's and held his gaze for several seconds. That's when he saw the bruise shading her right eye and spreading a yellowish cast over her cheekbone. The blue eyes were afraid. There were several, faded knuckle-shaped marks in the hollow of her cheek and above her lip, swollen as though from a bee sting.

Nordstrom frowned. The marks weren't much now, but they had been. And she hadn't gotten them falling down, either.

Nordstrom opened his mouth to speak, but before he could get the words out, the girl brought a hand to her face and self-consciously turned away, moving around him and walking off down the line of open tailgates.

He watched her go, scowling and wondering. He'd thought he'd met all the travelers in the caravan, but he hadn't seen her until now. He wouldn't have forgotten a face like that. He remembered spying the queer-acting Kohl boy taking a bowl of stew around behind the wagons. It must have been for her.

While Nordstrom washed the dishes in the tub behind the cabin, Charlie made a display of baking his pie over the fire, and served coffee to their guests, who'd gathered to watch. Nordstrom heard the lad entertaining the pilgrims with his jokes and stories gleaned from the young man's frequent forays to Denver and Julesburg. Having been privy to Charlie's repertoire, Nordstrom hoped he'd save his more risqué material for after the ladies turned in for the night.

But that didn't happen until nearly midnight, for the women seemed to be having as much fun as the men were—talking, laughing, telling life stories, and shooting the bull.

It wasn't long after the women had retreated to their wagons, thanking the two ranchers over and over for their hospitality, that the men turned in, as well. They had another long day ahead of them, and they needed every minute of sleep they could squeeze out of the night.

Nordstrom thought it was just as well Charlie didn't have time to get into his late-night material. The young man liked to kick up his heels as much as any bronco-buster Nordstrom had ever met, but you never knew who you might offend among strangers—especially when Charlie started tipping back the chokecherry wine.

Nordstrom had been thinking about the girl with the bruised face since he'd first seen her behind the Kohl wagons. He hadn't wanted to ask the other travelers about her; she was none of his business. But keeping a girl hidden away in a wagon was odd. Those bruises made it odder, and the whole thing smelled of a rat.

He mentioned the girl to Charlie when the two men sat on the veranda drinking the rum Charlie had brought back from his last trip to Milestown, keeping their voices low so they wouldn't wake the pilgrims.

"Damn strange," Charlie agreed, regarding the dim shapes of the wagons crouched beyond the light from the cabin's two front windows. He turned to Nordstrom. "But you know, girls get slapped around by their pas."

"And hidden away in wagons?"

Charlie shrugged. "Maybe she didn't want to be seen like that."

"Damn funny," Nordstrom said. "None of those men look like the type that would hit a girl. Maybe Kohl, but even he doesn't seem that rough around the edges."

Charlie tossed back his drink, stood, and stretched. "Well, you figure on it. I'm goin' to bed."

"I'm right behind you," Nordstrom said.

But he sat there thinking about the girl for another fifteen minutes, finally deciding what bothered him most was the incongruity of bruises on such a face. How could anyone lift a hand against such beauty?

He was asleep in the cabin when something woke him. He lifted his head, wondering what he'd heard. The front door latch? A hinge squeaked above Charlie's soft snores on the other side of the log wall.

Sure enough, someone was entering the cabin.

Nordstrom reached for the Colt hanging from the bedpost. "Who's there?" he called.

He heard the curtain over the bedroom door rustle, watched a shadow move. A whisper: "It's me—Cynthia."

Instantly the room filled with the smell of perfumed hair and body powder. It nearly took Nordstrom's breath away. A high half-moon slanted a shaft of white light through the sashed window over Nordstrom's head, limning a silhouette above him.

"What's going on?"

"Shh. You'll wake your friend."

"What do you want?"

"To thank you for supper."

She giggled and lifted her chamise over her head. A

shaft of light fell on her long hair fanned around her shoulders and on her round, hard-nippled breasts. Nordstrom swallowed, feeling his heart throb in his temples.

Before he could even begin to work his mind around what was happening, she'd grabbed his revolver away, thrown back the single wool blanket, and scooted in beside him on the cot. She threw her arms around his neck, flattening her breasts against his chest. Her breath was hot on his face. Groaning with desire, she pushed her lips against his, probing his mouth with her tongue.

So forceful was her passion that he couldn't have stopped her even if he'd wanted to.

It had been a long time since he'd been with a woman, smelled a woman, touched a woman. . . .

7

The women were screaming, the mules were braying, and the smoke was so thick the major could barely breathe.

Four howling renegades were raping Cynthia while the wagons burned. Kohl, Lang, Douglas, and Nils lay sprawled on the ground with bullets in their backs.

The major was crawling away from his burning, over-turned wagon, his pants afire, the flames leaping at his thighs. He beat the flames with his arms while moving to help Cynthia, who lay naked in the circle of hollering men.

"Stop! Stop!" the major rasped, wincing against the pain of his burning legs. No matter how far he crawled, he couldn't get away from the burning wagon, nor get any closer to Cynthia.

One of the renegades turned to him, face flushed and twisted. His eyes were devil eyes, small, round, and red.

"Lookee here—a one-armed reb!" the man squealed.

"Please stop!" the major begged. "I am Major Lawrence Townsend. I fought at Chattanooga! I knew Longstreet and Jackson . . . !"

The man parted his lips in a snaggletoothed grin and stepped casually toward the major. "Mister, out here you're just another sorry pilgrim," he said, lifting his gun.

The major watched the big round hole of the barrel yawn as the gun rose to his forehead. He stared down the black bore and struggled against the gun with both hands, grunting and panting and pleading for his life. But the weapon remained firm against his skull, as though the hand of god were gripping the butt.

"No!" he cried when he heard the hammer click back, squeezing his eyes shut.

The gun boomed like a cannon.

The major lifted his head from his pallet, pressed both hands against the wagon floor, and clipped a yell. Panting, he looked around the wagon box, slowly realizing he'd been having a nightmare, then, remembering the yell, wondering self-consciously if anyone had heard him cry out like a frightened child.

He listened for movement in the other wagons, but there were only the usual sounds of bugs slapping the canvas, the screeches of distant nightbirds, and Imbert Kohl's muffled snoring. Satisfied everyone else was asleep and hadn't heard him, the major lay his head back on the pallet. Trying to relax, he thought about home and his favorite horses—all lost in the war.

Then the faint sound of a door latching set his heart to beating again. He knew it was probably only one of the ranchers stepping out to the latrine, but the nightmare had stirred him too much to let the sound go at that.

He grabbed one of the old Griswold and Gunnison Confederate revolvers he kept on either side of his pallet, crawled to the back of the wagon, peered over the tailgate, and looked toward the cabin the sound had come from.

The moon was angling over the western mountains, illuminating clouds and spreading silhouettes across the barnyard. The cabin hunched darkly beneath it, moonlight nickeling its pitched roof. A slender shadow within the cabin's shadow moved, stole out from under the awning, took the form of a human figure as it passed into the moonlight, then vanished amid the black hulks

of the wagons. At least, it looked like a human figure;
the major was too far away to be sure.

He scowled. Now, who could that be?

He crawled clumsily over the tailgate and hopped
down, bringing the revolver to bear on the nightmare
images still flashing in his mind. He looked around cautiously, moved left toward his son's wagon, stepped over
the tongue, and stopped. The driver's seat bounced
lightly. A muffled thump issued from the box.

Someone had just crawled inside, the major thought.
Or so it seemed. Probably Douglas or Cynthia returning
from answering nature's call. But what about the person
who'd left the cabin and headed this way?

The major stood quietly looking around, listening, and
thinking, warm fingers of agitation pricking his spine.
Could it have been Cynthia stealing across the yard? But
what business would she have had in the rancher's
cabin?

The major winced at the only possible answer for the
time of the night, and turned away from his son's wagon
as though from the thought itself. Cynthia was the wife
of a Townsend. Douglas may not have been the prodigal
son, but no Townsend had ever let his wife stray.

No, the major thought, the figure had to have been
one of the men from the cabin using the outhouse or
checking their horses.

Or one of the renegades sizing up the camp for a
raid . . .

With that thought in mind, the major crept around the
wagons with his revolver held before him. He stopped
occasionally to listen, to peer between the wheels, and
to sweep the ranch yard with his gaze. From the wagons,
he moved to the pole barns and corrals, stepping quietly
over the hard-packed yard.

When he found the mules lounging in the silvery grass
by the creek unmolested, the major decided his imagination had gotten away from him. His confrontation with
the renegades who'd raped the girl had turned his nerves

to jelly. He'd probably even imagined the figure leaving the cabin.

"You old fool," he told himself, dropping the gun to his side and heading back to his pallet.

He dozed until dawn, then rose, poured water from the oak barrel strapped to the wagon, and washed at the basin beneath it. He heard a door shut followed by the clomp of boots and jangle of spurs on wood, and turned to see Glenn Nordstrom walk off his porch and head across the ranch yard toward the corrals.

The major greeted the rancher with a wave. "Good morning, Mr. Nordstrom."

"Mornin'," the rancher returned with a wave of his own.

Toweling his face dry, Townsend watched the slender-hipped, broad-shouldered rancher fork hay into the three corrals where wild broncs trotted back and forth, shaking their manes and snorting. Nordstrom was talking to the horses in a conversational tone, though the major couldn't make out the words.

The rancher wore a denim tunic with the sleeves rolled up his muscular arms. A flat-brimmed Stetson kept the rising sun from his face that had tanned the color of a well-used saddle. His jaw was straight. His eyes bore the look of a self-possessed man, a man who'd made his own way in the world at a considerable cost, attained pretty much everything he figured attainable for himself, and bore not a trace of arrogance for his accomplishments. Only confidence.

Yes, he was every bit the capable Westerner, Townsend reflected, looping a silk cravat around his neck and going to work on the knot. Big and self-assured and quiet. Dependable. The kind of man you'd want on your side.

With that thought in mind, Townsend stuffed the tie down his worn linen shirt, snugged a big straw hat on his head, and made his way over to John Lang's wagon. Lang's wife, Grace, a big, fleshy blonde with a high chortle of a voice, was giving poor Lang down-the-road for not filling the water barrel at the creek the night before.

"If I told you once, John, I told you a thousand times—always fill the barrel before you settle in for the night. That way we'll never wake up to no water. But what do you do? You open your book and read until you fall asleep, and we get up and there's *no water*!"

Lang opened the supply box strapped to the outside wagon and pulled out two tin water buckets with a grimace. "Sorry, Grace. I know—you told me a thousand times...." Turning toward the creek, he nearly ran into Townsend, who'd just stepped up to the wagon.

"Good morning, Lang," he said, smiling as though he hadn't heard anything not meant for his ears. "Good morning, Grace."

Lang mumbled good morning through a tight smile. Grace trilled her usual cheery greeting, pink fleshy cheeks balled with a grin, beady eyes flashing, tightly curled blond hair bouncing around her neck. You'd never have thought she'd just been hacking her poor browbeat husband into bite-sized chunks.

"How are you this morning, Colonel? Wasn't it just a beautiful dawn?"

"Major," Lang corrected his wife for the hundredth time. "He was a major during the war, Grace. Not a colonel."

"Oh, Major, I mean. Do you think I'll ever get that straight?" Grace drew her small blue eyes wide and laughed her grating laugh, setting the major's teeth on edge.

He knew a devil lurked behind the woman's gregarious facade. He also knew that devil did not like him, because he'd worn butternut gray in the War Between the States. Lang had informed the major that Grace's brother, Harvey, had ridden for the Union, been taken prisoner at Pea Ridge, and died in the Confederate camp at Copper Mountain, Georgia. The major figured that calling him colonel was the woman's way of showing her disdain. He supposed he should feel grateful, though.

He'd been privy to her disapproval of her husband, and it wasn't pretty.

"No problem at all, Grace, no problem at all," the major sang, trying to hide his contempt for the woman at least as well as she hid hers for him. "Colonel, major—what's the difference to a simple Yankee girl from Indiana, eh, Mrs. Lang?"

The major gave a false guffaw and turned from Grace to her husband, letting his laughter settle to a slow chuckle. He wanted to see the woman's reaction to his barb but didn't dare linger. Instead, he clamped his hand on the back of Lang's neck. "Heading for the creek, John? I'll join you."

When they'd left Grace behind and had exchanged their morning pleasantries, the major got down to business in as subtle a way as possible. "Sure was a good meal we had last night, wouldn't you say, Lang?"

"Best damn meal I've had in years—no offense to the women, of course."

"Of course not. Yes, that Nordstrom seems a capable sort. You know, he was a scout on the Oregon Trail."

"I heard you and him talking about that," Lang said with a nod.

"Sort of reminds me of myself at that age—full of vim and vinegar, and not afraid of one pea-pickin' thing!"

As if on cue, squinting up at the morning sun as they walked toward the cottonwoods along the creek, Lang said, "Yeah, it would be nice if he'd offer to guide our party to the Basin. Probably save us a lot of time and trouble, none of us knowing the trail very well and all. He'd probably know how to get those renegades off our trail, too."

The major smiled to himself. He couldn't have been more pleased. "You know, I never thought of that," he lied. He feigned deep thought, lifting his chin to take the dewy breeze full in the face. At length, he said, "It probably would save us some time—money, too, in the long run."

Lang shot the major an expectant look. "Think he would?"

Casually, with an air of distraction and raised eyebrows, the major said, "What? Guide us north? I don't know. Guess we could ask him. . . ."

Thus, to even Townsend himself, it seemed to have been John Lang's idea to ask Nordstrom to head up the caravan. The major couldn't have articulated why that made a difference to him, but it did.

When Lang had finished filling his water barrels with enough for Grace's morning toilet, he and the major talked Lang's idea over with Imbert Kohl, whose only reservation was cost.

"It cost me a round bundle to take the train to Fort Reno," the farmer said as he harnessed his mules. "I don't think I can afford a guide."

The major nodded, prompting Lang with his eyebrows.

"Well, you know—like me and the major were thinking—hiring a guide would probably save us money in the long run. You know, shorten the trip and the amount of supplies we'd use, and we'd get settled in sooner in the Basin. And . . . uh"—here it comes, Townsend thought with an inward grimace—"he'd probably know how to handle those renegades, too."

From Kohl's expression, the major could tell that the farmer had already considered that aspect of the equation. Kohl nodded, turned his head to regard Nordstrom pumping water from a stock well, and fingered the beard spikes on his pointed chin. The younger man, Charlie, was chopping wood out behind the cabin, the ax blows sharply rising in the cool morning air.

"We gonna tell him about the hardcases?" Kohl asked dully.

"I don't see any reason to," the major said with a shrug. "Hell, they're probably not even after us anymore."

"We should tell him, I guess," Lang said guiltily.

"Prob'ly up his price," Kohl warned.

"And they're probably not even behind us anymore," the major added, though he knew that wasn't true.

The way he saw it, the less the ex-scout knew about the renegades, the more likely he'd be to accept their invitation to guide them. And the less cowardly the major and the other men would look for needing his help. When the renegades showed up again, Townsend and the other men could feign ingnorance of the threat. That shouldn't be too hard for Kohl and Lang, for only Townsend—and the foreign girl, of course—knew just how much of a threat they really were.

Lang didn't like the sound of this, Townsend could tell. But after further discussion, the schoolteacher shrugged his shoulders and nodded his head, turning with the major and Townsend toward the well where Nordstrom was working.

When the rancher saw the three pilgrims heading his way, he wondered for a moment if they were coming to defend Cynthia Townsend's honor, or to seek revenge for Nordstrom's cuckolding of the major's son-in-law.

Nordstrom had never slept with a married woman before; he'd always considered himself above such tawdry weaknesses of the flesh. But Cynthia Townsend had caught him in a weak moment, though he supposed any man would have a weak moment when a woman like Mrs. Townsend flung herself into his bed and mawled him like a she-griz with the springtime craze.

What was he supposed to have done—hogtied her and dragged her back to her husband for safekeeping? The way he saw it, if young Townsend couldn't keep his wife at home, whatever happened was his own damn fault.

Nordstrom was just glad the pilgrims were leaving. Though his two hours in Cynthia Townsend's clutches had been pure, unmitigated bliss, their aftermath made him feel edgy, guilty, and aloof, not to mention tired.

That's why he watched the three pilgrims approach with a tentative cast to his gaze, irrationally worried his and Cynthia's tryst had been discovered. What could the travelers do, anyway—hang him?

"Mornin' there, pilgrims," he said heartily—maybe a little too heartily, he thought—lifting his arm from the stock tank and throwing into the yard the clump of wet hay and algae that had clogged the pipe. "How did you sleep?"

"Just fine, thanks," John Lang said with a nod and his affable smile.

"Not bad a'tall, not bad a'tall," the major said when he and the others had gathered at the tank. "A fine meal, a fine night's sleep. We'd like to thank you again, Mr. Nordstrom, and offer you breakfast at our fire. Nothing near as grand as the vittles you laid out last night, but our women have a right artful way with johnnycake and bacon."

"Well, I appreciate the invitation, but Charlie and I already had some coffee and biscuits. That should tide us until lunch. You don't want to break wild horses on a full load, if you get my drift."

"I understand," the major said, smiling and furtively sliding his eyes to John Lang.

Lang caught the look and licked his lips to speak. "We had a thought, Mr. Nordstrom. Seeing as how you once led travelers on the Oregon Trail, we were wondering if you'd like to show us the way to the Cottonwood country. We'd pay you, of course."

Nordstrom rested a hip on the edge of the stock tank and folded his arms. "Well, I tell you, a few years ago I wouldn't have hesitated, but I'm not in that line of work anymore. As you can see, I have a few horses to break and a ranch to run. You men don't need me, anyway. Hell, you only have a couple hundred miles left."

Lang shrugged his shoulders and stuffed his hands in his pockets. "We were a little worried about the route, not bein' Westerners and all." He looked off, squinting his clear Indiana eyes.

Kohl, who'd been hovering behind Townsend and Lang, stepped forward and tipped his hat brim back.

"We just thought you could take us through a little faster. A little easier. You know, fewer stops and turnarounds, you knowin' the way and all, and prob'ly the best places to camp and hunt."

Nordstrom shrugged. "True, it's always best with a guide, and I wish I could help, but I can't, that's all. I have too much work to get done here before the snow flies." He couldn't help considering the obvious problem of Cynthia Townsend, as well. He'd seen more than one wagon train driven to the brink of chaos by uncontrolled passions.

The major cocked his head to one side, and his eyebrows crawled up his forehead. "Are you sure we can't entice you? Might be fun."

Nordstrom shook his head and pursed his lips. "I couldn't leave Charlie here to break all these horses himself."

"Seems a right capable lad to me."

"Sorry, Major."

"All right, then, Mr. Nordstrom." Townsend's voice betrayed disappointment; his eyes studied the ground. Nordstrom felt he'd caught the man in an unguarded moment.

"You're really not apt to have any trouble," Nordstrom assured him. "The trail is pretty easy to follow, and most of the Indians are causing trouble farther south these days."

"No doubt," Lang agreed, nodding, though they all looked worried.

Why? Nordstrom wondered. What had happened to these people? Was it just trail shock, or had something spooked them out there? He didn't want to ask because he didn't want to offend them, but he couldn't help studying them with a frown.

"All right, then," Kohl grunted. "Just figured we'd ask." He was eyeing the other men and edging away.

The major had turned westward with his jaw set in a line, a scowl wrinkling his brows. "It was just a thought, Mr. Nordstrom. Just a thought," he said vacantly.

"I'm sorry . . . ," Nordstrom said again, meaning it.

"Nonsense," the major said, turning and lifting his left hand for Nordstrom to shake. "Thanks for your hospitality. Maybe we'll meet again someday."

"I'd like that."

Nordstrom shook hands with the other two men. Townsend had already started back to the wagons. "Come on, gentlemen," he called crisply over his shoulder. "We're burning daylight."

Within a half hour, the breakfast fires were doused, pots and pans put away, chairs and tables stowed. The pilgrims climbed aboard their wagons and headed out, waving as they whipped their mules into motion and turned their wagons in a wide circle around the yard, heading back the way they'd come.

Nordstrom was sitting on the top rail of the corral where the stallions were penned, watching Charlie try to drop a broad loop over a big-chested bay with a spotted rump. He turned to see one of the wagons break from the line and stop near the corral.

Oh, Christ, he nearly said out loud. It was the Mr. and Mrs. Douglas Townsend van, and Cynthia had a big grin on her face. What the hell was she up to?

"Just wanted to thank you personally for a wonderful evening, Mr. Nordstrom," she said, bright brown eyes flashing, smooth cheeks fairly glowing. Wearing a pale blue dress with a deliciously low neckline, a crisp white shawl, and blue ribbons in her thick black hair—not exactly trail gear—she turned to her husband, grinning. "Didn't we, Douglas?"

"Yes, of course," Douglas said tightly, concocting a smile.

Nordstrom wanted to slink down off the fence and hide among the horses. Hot with embarrassment, he fixed a smile on his face. "My pleasure, ma'am . . . Mr. Townsend."

Douglas whipped the reins, and as the wagon pulled out to join the others, Cynthia lifted her chin, laughing.

Nordstrom watched them go, his smile fading, cursing under his breath.

"Well, Mrs. Townsend sure looks spry this mornin'," Charlie said from inside the corral. He was holding the big loop above the ground, watching the wagons fade in the distance.

Nordstrom wondered if the bronc buster had heard the love play through the cabin wall. Turning to see Charlie's white-toothed grin, he got his answer.

"Boss," Charlie said, "your ears get any redder, you could boil lead in 'em."

"Don't you have some horses to break?" Nordstrom snarled.

Charlie laughed, teasing. While he continued toward the bay, Nordstrom lifted his gaze back to the dust rising in the wagon train's wake, still chafed from Cynthia's Townsend's hijinx, and wondering what in hell the men were so afraid of.

He guessed he'd probably never know.

8

Later in the day, big sooty thunderheads rumbled over the mountains, jabbing lightning at the dun-green prairie. The rain approached the ranch like a giant wedding veil, fronted by a cold wind and flanked with cloud shadows. The cool, moving air freshened with the smell of sulfur and greasewood.

The cowboys returned their tack to the barn and loped to the cabin with their heads tipped to the rain funneling off their hat brims, and set coffee to boil.

In a few minutes, they were tilted back in their porch chairs, boots crossed on the railing, steaming mugs perched on their thighs. They watched the rain glisten the backs of the wild broncs trotting around the corrals like spoiled monarchs. Finally, Nordstrom drained his coffee and went inside to fix some beans and tortillas.

"Boss," Charlie called a few minutes later.

"What is it?"

"Company."

"What the hell?" Nordstrom said, stepping outside. Company two days in a row was unheard of out here.

Charlie was standing against the rail, looking eastward. He pointed his arm, and Nordstrom gazed down it until four riders grew out of the short grass and sage, heads bobbing stiffly, hats tipped against the rain. Gouts of mud and wet grass blew up from the loping horses' hooves.

"Who could that be?" Charlie said.

"Your guess is as good as mine." Nordstrom disappeared inside the cabin and returned a moment later with his Winchester, and stood it against the cabin wall behind his chair. Four men on horseback could mean trouble.

It took the riders several minutes to pass through the cottonwoods along the creek, splash through the water, and trot their horses under the horizontal rail over the front gate. In the yard they slowed to a walk, their horses' shod hooves making sucking sounds on the wet ground. Saddles creaked and bridle chains jangled.

From the porch Nordstrom appraised the group. One man was lean and wiry, with eyes like a snake's. The one beside him was big and barrel-chested; his beard grew as thick as grizzly fur.

The other two men, bringing up the rear, were small and scruffy and owned the lightless eyes of the mean and simple. One stood out for the hat he wore—an expensive felt plainsman with a tooled leather band. All four riders carried Henry rifles in their saddleboots, wore bandoliers heavy with .44s, and had wide-bladed skinning knives sheathed in belt scabbards. Wet tobacco stained their lips, and from ten feet away Nordstrom could smell their odor of bear grease, rancid sweat, and raw alcohol.

His instinct for danger gnawed his gut. In the corral, the skittish mustangs lifted their tails and squealed.

"How do," the snake-eyed rider said with a tip of his broad-brimmed black hat.

The rancher nodded. "Afternoon."

"Wet one today."

"I'll say."

"Even the elk are stayin' low," Snake-Eyes said, hollow face friendly except for the eyes. "Just seen a whole herd of 'em hunkered in a ravine." He turned to the big, bearded rider beside him. "How many did you count, Jim?"

"Seventy-two," the bearded man replied under his waterlogged sugarloaf sombrero.

"Seventy-two elk," Snake-Eyes repeated. "They were so goddam purty I don't think I coulda shot one if I was starvin' to death."

"They're a fine sight, that's for sure," Nordstrom agreed.

He would have invited most travelers to light and sit a spell, but he didn't like the looks of this crew. He saw that Snake Eyes carried a 40–90 BN target rifle in a second saddle boot. The big-caliber gun told Nordstrom these men were probably game hunters for the markets in Milestown and Denver. What else they were, you never knew.

Snake Eyes tipped his hat and crossed his hands on his saddle horn. "We're lookin' fer some friends of our'n. Lost their tracks in the rain. They appeared headed toward your ranch, last we saw. 'Bout ten folks in five wagons."

A warning hammered at the base of the rancher's skull. He stared at the man, thinking. Snake Eyes pursed his lips and eyed Nordstrom intently.

He said, "We met up along the trail aways back and thought we'd throw in together, seein' as how we're all headed in the same direction. Me and the boys here broke off to hunt, day before yesterday. Been trying to catch up with the wagons now for most of the afternoon. The rain hasn't made it easy."

"Where's your meat?"

"What's that?"

"You said you broke off from the wagons to hunt," Nordstrom reminded the man.

Snake Eyes scowled and shifted uneasily in his saddle. "Well, sure—we cached it back along the trail. Wouldn't expect us to pack it, would ya, friend?"

Nordstrom didn't say anything.

"Pass this way, did they?"

Nordstrom thought he knew now what—or whom—the pilgrims had been so skittish about. These men were probably following the wagons, waiting for a chance to rob them, or worse. Or maybe they'd already tried and failed and were trying again. Nordstrom remembered the bruises on the pretty girl from the Kohl wagon, and his jaw tightened in anger.

"Yeah, they were here," he said grudgingly. Since the riders knew the pilgrims had been headed this way, denying they had been here would have been pointless. "Spent the night and left early this mornin'."

"Which way'd they head?"

"West along Conni Creek," Nordstrom lied.

"West along the Conni, eh?"

"Said they wanted to do some hunting, so I directed them to a dogleg that feeds into the Conni. Lots of deer in there."

Snake Eyes frowned, and said thoughtfully, "You don't say."

Nordstrom nodded and wondered how long it would take to get his Winchester in his hands and a shell levered into the breech.

The lead rider turned in his saddle to regard the others. "West along the Conni, the man says. . . ."

The bearded rider snapped, "That don't make sense, J.L. The Conni country's too rough for wagons."

"Not through the dogleg I told 'em about," Nordstrom countered.

Snake Eyes looked at Nordstrom for several seconds. Then he shrugged and nodded. "Well, boys, I guess we'll be ridin' west, then," he said, eyes still on the rancher. To Nordstrom he said, "Much obliged, friend."

He tipped his hat, reined his horse around, and led the others from the yard. Hipped around in his saddle, the bearded man watched Nordstrom as he rode away.

Watching them, Nordstrom felt the muscles in his back relax and the sweat dry on his palms. Behind him, Charlie heaved a long sigh of relief. "What you supposed those owlhoots want with those pilgrims?"

Nordstrom snorted and walked onto the porch. "Last spring I came upon a family walkin' along the Bozeman Trail—half-starved and the baby bawlin'. Thieves had looted their wagon and shot their oxen, left the family on foot. I outfitted 'em with horses and an old tool wagon."

"Suppose it was those men?" Charlie asked.

"Or others just like 'em." Nordstrom walked into the cabin. A moment later he appeared in the doorway hitching his cartridge belt, holster, and short-barreled Colt around his waist. "Help yourself to beans and tortillas," he told Charlie. "I'm gonna ride out and warn those pilgrims what's behind 'em, in the off chance they don't already know." He knew it wouldn't take long for the hardcases to realize they'd been duped and to loop back for their quarry.

"Why don't I go with you?" Charlie said. "If you run into those men alone . . ."

Nordstrom shook his head, reaching for the Winchester. "You stay here and keep an eye on the horses. I'll try to be back before nightfall."

"Watch yourself," Charlie called as Nordstrom headed for the barn and his saddlehorse.

"Same to you."

As Nordstrom rode the dry creekbed northwest on his grulla mustang, he tried to hold his anger at bay. It wasn't easy. The pilgrims should have let him know who was behind them. Those renegades could have stormed the ranch and taken him and Charlie completely by surprise.

He knew Cynthia Townsend hadn't been aware of the danger; no woman could have performed like she had in bed last night and been worried about renegades. But Nordstrom was sure Kohl, Townsend, and Lang had known about the owlhoots tracking them.

That's why the major had seemed so distracted last night, and why they'd asked Nordstrom to guide them up to the Cottonwood country. Only what they'd really wanted was a bodyguard; they were just too damn proud to admit it.

Damn funny way to treat a host, Nordstrom thought with a shake of his head, turning the grulla westward through a shallow draw. He leaned out from his saddle as he followed the wagon trail he'd cut about an hour out from the ranch.

It was best not to get too overheated, though, he knew. He wouldn't know the whole story until he caught up to the vans.

Which didn't happen until after another hour of hard riding. Ascending a knoll on the other side of a cotton-wood motte, he brought the big horse to a halt and peered west. Rounding another motte about a mile ahead were several wagons in haphazard formation, their white cotton covers glowing in the sun that had peeked through the rain clouds.

Though he was too far away to be certain, Nordstrom figured they were the Townsend, Kohl, and Lang parties. The country didn't see much traffic these days, especially this late in the year.

He spurred the horse ahead, galloping in a wide circle around the wagons, so the pilgrims could spot and identify him before he got within rifle range. Skittish as they were, the emigrants were liable to shoot him before they found out who he was.

"Hello, the train!" he yelled, waving his arm. "It's Glenn Nordstrom."

The lead wagon jerked to a slow halt, Townsend peering Nordstrom's way. The other wagons, spread out behind in a ragged line, kept coming through the dust.

"Well, Mr. Nordstrom . . . ," Townsend said as the rancher approached at an easy trot, "change your mind?"

Nordstrom said crisply, "There's four men on your trail. Hardcases, by the looks of 'em. They stopped at my ranch lookin' for you about three hours after you pulled out."

The major lowered his eyes and winced. ''You don't say.''

''Said they were friends of yours.''

''They did, did they?''

''But they aren't, are they? And this isn't really news to you, is it?''

Reacting to Nordstrom's sharp tone, the major met the rancher's gaze, narrowing his eyes.

''You've known those men were trailing you for some time, haven't you?'' Nordstrom continued. ''And you led them right to my door without telling me. Why?''

Before the major could answer, John Lang pulled his wagon up beside the major's. Lang's wife sat beside the schoolteacher, squinting her eyes against the dust catching up to them.

''Mr. Nordstrom,'' Lang said by way of greeting, nodding his head and hauling back on the reins. ''Thought we'd seen the last of you.''

''You almost did see the last of me, thanks to the hooligans on your trail.'' Nordstrom grunted and gave the schoolteacher his cold gaze.

Lang's face fell. His wife turned to him. ''What's he talking about, John?''

''It's OK, Grace.''

''What hooligans?''

The major said to Nordstrom, ''You're frightening Mrs. Lang, Mr. Nordstrom. Maybe we better chat in private.''

Nordstrom reined his horse around, poked its flanks with his spurs, and galloped fifty yards ahead of Townsend's van. He dismounted and tied his mount to the branch of a cottonwood, and stood with his arms crossed, watching Lang and Townsend walk toward him.

The schoolteacher had a guilty, tentative look on his face. The major looked sheepish. Wisps of gray hair blew out from his well-worn slouch hat.

''Why didn't you tell me you were being dogged?'' Nordstrom said as the two men approached. It still galled him that they'd led those renegades to his door without warning. People looked out for each other in the West; it was an unwritten code. But then, he thought with a pang of shame, the code didn't really allow for bedding other men's wives, either.

"Didn't know we were being dogged," the major said sharply but without heat.

Lang looked at him tiredly. "Come on, Major," he said. He turned his gaze to Nordstrom. "I don't know why we didn't, Mr. Nordstrom. I guess we just didn't want to admit it to ourselves, or talk about it. It's a pretty frightening thing, really—having savages like that stalking you out here in the middle of nowhere."

"They could have hit us last night when we weren't ready for 'em."

Lang nodded. "I know."

"That what you came all this way for, to give us hell?" the major snapped.

"No, I came all this way to make sure you knew they were back there, and to give you some advice. . . ."

"Let's have it so we can get a move on," Townsend said impatiently.

Nordstrom looked at him. The old bastard was feisty, he'd give him that. But too damn proud to survive out here.

"Head for low ground and water, and strike a cold camp," Nordstrom advised them. "No fires until you're sure they're not behind you anymore. Keep a sentry posted after dark. At Henry's Crossing on the Deadman you might find an out-of-work hide hunter to ride shotgun for you, but don't turn your back on him. There's more bad eggs out here than just the border ruffians eating your dust."

"That it?" the major asked.

"You know why they're doggin' you?"

Lang shrugged his shoulders, said dourly, "Our women, I guess."

Nordstrom nodded. "What happened to the girl riding in the Kohl wagon?"

"They raped her," Lang said. "Kohl's boy snuck into their camp and cut one of their throats."

Nordstrom winced and shook his head. "Not a smart move."

"No."

"So it's women and revenge . . . ," Nordstrom said thoughtfully. "Hell of a combination. You people are going to have a long road to the Cottonwood." He turned and untied his horse from the tree. "Just remember to stay low."

"We will," Lang said. "And . . . sorry, Nordstrom. . . ."

The rancher felt his anger dissipate. He suddenly felt sorry for the men, but he didn't know what to say. They were out here alone against four renegades, and he couldn't help them. He had a ranch to run. Anyway, it wasn't his fight.

He mounted up, then turned to the two men standing beneath him. The major didn't say anything, just watched him with an angry, defeated look on his face.

"Good luck," Nordstrom mumbled, and spurred away.

9

Charlie Decker was splitting wood behind the ranch cabin, working up a good sweat in the warming sun. The clouds had broken an hour ago, but the ground was still too wet for horse breaking.

Since Nordstrom sold most of his horses before winter, he didn't need much hay stacked in his pole barns, so wood splitting was about all there was to do on wet days. Charlie brought the sharp head of the woodsplitter down with a grunt, laying open a well-seasoned box elder log to a hollow of dead ants, froze last fall.

Charlie had split a good half cord when he sunk the splitter in the chopping block, scrubbed sweat from his forehead with the back of his hand, walked over to the pipe poking from the hillside spring, and stuck his head under the icy flow. He was drinking from his cupped hand when a horse's whinny penetrated the sound of splashing water. Hooves pounded and corral rails clattered.

Charlie lifted his head, water dripping from his chin, and looked toward the cabin. Something had spooked the horses.

Charlie's heart quickened. He glanced at his gunbelt coiled on the ground near the chopping block, a good thirty yards away. Suddenly anxious, he started that way, walking fast, hearing the horses snorting and thundering around the corrals.

Charlie was within fifteen feet of the Remington six-shooter when a rider suddenly appeared to his right on a big chestnut gelding.

"Whoa!" Charlie yelled, startled.

"Whoa yourself, cowboy!" The leader of the group that had visited the ranch earlier in the day came around the cabin on Charlie's left. Hearing the ring of shod hooves on stone behind him, Charlie turned to see the other three riders loop around the hill and ride toward him—slowly, like they had all day, thin smiles curling their lips, hands on the walnut grips of their sidearms.

Charlie's heart throbbed in his temples. He looked at his holstered gun, then at the bearded rider moving up on his right. "Go for it, slick," the man said. "You're so smart—go for it."

Charlie looked at the man, the bearded face flushed with anger. "Why would I wanna do that?"

" 'Cause you're so smart."

Charlie shook his head. "I ain't so smart."

"He thinks he's smart, don't he, Jim?" the lead rider asked the bearded man bearing down on Charlie. "Him and the other fella think they're real smart, sendin' us off on a wild goose chase."

"They sure do, J.L."

To Charlie, J.L. said, "Nothin' makes Big Jim madder than bein' took for a patsy."

Charlie played dumb. "We didn't take nobody for no patsy. You didn't find the wagons along the Conni?"

The bearded man's eyes glowered. The lead rider regarded Charlie with a look of bemusement, leaning on his saddle horn. Charlie licked his lips, looking between them, feeling his knees go soft. Nordstrom had left two hours ago, and Charlie knew he wouldn't be back for several more.

"Well, we directed them west along the Conni," he said, shrugging.

The bearded man spat. "Sure ya did." His horse

swished its tail at a deerfly and craned its neck around.

The lead rider changed the subject. "You got any money in there?" he asked, tipping his head at the cabin.

Charlie felt a flicker of relief. Maybe they'd take what was left of his last pay and go. He and Nordstrom would hunt them down later, deal some frontier justice. He shrugged. "A few dollars. It's in a coffee can under my cot."

"How 'bout the other fella; he got any money inside?"

"Doubt it. He doesn't like keepin' cash around."

"That right?"

One of the men behind Charlie laughed, but Charlie didn't turn to look at him. He regarded his gun, considered making a dive for it.

"Go for it, chump," Big Jim said, reading his mind. "I want ya to."

One of the men behind Charlie said, "No sign of the other fella, J.L."

"Where's the other fella at?" J.L. asked Charlie.

"Go fuck yourself," Charlie sneered, his fear giving way to anger. The sons of bitches thought they were real tough—four against one, and he wasn't even armed!

J.L. leaned on his saddle horn. "What makes ya think you can talk to us like that? You need to be taught some respect, half-breed." He slipped his lariat from the leather thong on his saddle and weighed it in his hands, tipping his head to one side and giving Charlie a cold, dark look.

The cowboy slid another glance to his gun. It was his only chance. In a minute, they'd have that rope around his neck.

"Go ahead," the rider called Jim urged, leaning forward and jutting his face out.

Charlie looked at him, a smile growing on his lips, his heart beating faster. He could do it; he was fast.

He lunged forward, sprang off his feet, and lofted into the air, seeming to hang there for a long time, the

woodchip-littered ground and his revolver growing
slowly before him.

Guns exploded.

Charlie hit the ground on his chest and raked his holster with his hands. The barrel of his Remington had just
cleared leather when he felt the hot dull pain of lead
hammering into him and slamming him forward, knocking the revolver from his hand. He twisted around,
arched his back, panting, as the pain skewered.

He glanced up until the four riders swam into view,
revolvers raised, powder smoke wafting about their
heads. "You . . . sons o' bitches," he said tightly, his
breath coming hard as he winced against the pain.

He pictured Millie White moving to a window, drawing the shade, reaching up to remove the pins from her
hair, allowing the thick red curls to spill across her
shoulders.

He tipped his head back, saw his revolver an arm's
length away. He lifted his arm, twisted around, and
reached for it.

A gun popped. The bullet went through his back and
came out his armpit. Charlie gave a grunt and fell forward, his face in the woodchips and dirt.

He heaved a long sigh. "You sons o' bitches!" he
rasped.

Nordstrom's horse was tiring, so the rancher walked the
grulla into a draw where a spring creek gurgled over
mossy stones. He dismounted, loosened his saddle cinch,
and let the horse drink. The ranch was another two hours
away. It was shading toward sunset, and long shadows
were bleeding out from the hills, but he figured there'd
be enough light to see him home.

While the horse stood in the water, drinking and swat-
ting mosquitoes with its tail, Nordstrom sat on the bank
of the creek and chewed a weed. Downstream, a beaver
slapped the water and a startled duck quacked.

The grulla lifted his head sharply, working his nose.
His eyes were intense. Nordstrom studied him, frowning.

"What's the matter, boy? It's just a duck."

But Nordstrom knew the mustang well enough to know he wouldn't start at a duck. The hair on the back of the rancher's neck lifted. Glancing around with cautious eyes, he walked over to the horse, shucked his Winchester, and headed up the rise behind the creek.

From the top of the knoll, he swept the prairie with his gaze. Shadows had angled enough that it took him several seconds to make out the four riders loping from his left to his right, about three hundred yards away.

"Shit!" he grunted, dropping to his belly.

He crawled backward down the rise, removed his hat, and peered over the ridge. From this distance he could make out only silhouettes, but he was certain the riders were the men who'd stopped at his cabin. They were following the trail he'd taken when he'd left the ranch, and the thought filled Nordstrom with foreboding.

He watched the riders until they'd disappeared around a grassy shelf, then jogged down the ridge, slid his rifle into the saddle boot, tightened the cinch, and mounted up.

"Come on, boy," he said to the horse, reining around. "You've had your rest. Let's lift some dust."

For the next hour and a half he pushed the horse hard, feeling the stone in the pit of his stomach grow heavier by the mile. By the time he started the last leg to the ranch, the sun had set and the prairie had purpled, but there was enough light in the sky to silhouette the ragged column of black smoke rising in the north.

He raked the horse with his spurs, crouching low in the saddle, his heart racing. Climbing to the top of a chalky bench, he saw the glow beneath the smoke. Though the barn didn't seem to be involved, the cabin was on fire.

"Son of a *bitch*!"

He pushed the horse on, crouching low and yelling in its ear. Charlie would need help, for the cabin stood only fifty or so yards from the main barn, and a blaze of any size could spread to the barns and stock shed.

Within a hundred yards of the gate, he saw there was no use trying to save the cabin—it had already been reduced to charred rubble—but they'd have to haul water from the spring to keep the other buildings safe from cinders.

Near the gate he reined the horse to a sliding halt. His stomach turned and his heart jumped, nearly taking his breath. He muttered a curse and set his jaw in a grim line.

Around him lay ten or twelve dead horses with their necks stretched out and their eyes rolled back in their heads. Gaping bullet holes glistened. Beyond them, the corral gate hung open. At that moment, with his pulse throbbing in his temples, he figured it out.

The renegades had raided the ranch, setting fire to the cabin and shooting as many horses as they could before the herd galloped out of range.

Nordstrom cupped his hands around his mouth. "Charlie!" he yelled above the pulse drumming in his ears and the crackle of pine resin.

Then he noticed something above and right of his field of vision, and lifted his gaze to the figure hanging from the rail over the front gate. Though it was silhouetted against the burning cabin, Nordstrom knew who it was.

"Charlie!"

He jumped down from his horse, latched and climbed the gate, then threw his hands up to the rail. When he'd steadied himself, he used his right hand to retrieve the bowie from his belt scabbard. Grabbing Charlie around the waist with his left arm, he reached up with his right and cut the rope. As the cowboy plunged, Nordstrom yanked the body over his shoulder and squatted with the burden before the sudden weight could topple him.

Awkwardly and quickly negotiating his way down the gate, his boot caught on the bottom rail. Twisting around, he broke his fall with his other foot, and gentled the cowboy from his knee to the ground.

"Charlie!" he cried. "Come on, boy, come on . . . !"

He could tell from the sweat-soaked shirt and the stiffening limbs that the young man was gone. Nordstrom checked his neck for a pulse. Finding none, he listened to Charlie's chest, but there was nothing there, either.

His own heart racing and his stomach tumbling, Nordstrom sat back on his haunches and looked at the young man with his face creased with grief. Charlie's head was turned to the side, chin dipped to his shoulder; Nordstrom knew his neck was broken. From the chill, the rancher could tell the lad had been dead for several hours.

Charlie's upbringing on the rugged frontier had made him look older than twenty-three, but death had ironed his features so he seemed even younger. His face, drained of color, was the hue of old porcelain, and his green-brown eyes stared from half-open sockets, lightless and unfocused. His Indian-dark hair curled flatly across his skull and over his forehead and ears. His teeth were white and uneven behind his pale, slightly parted lips.

Nordstrom dropped his gaze to the young man's torso covered with a thick, black porridge of jellied blood—so much of it that it was hard to tell how many times he'd been shot.

They'd filled him full of lead, then hung him for show.

Nordstrom gritted his teeth in anger, swiped his hat from his head, and threw it down. He stood and turned away, running his hands over his head and pulling at his hair. All around him sprawled dead horses, strewn as though fallen from the sky.

The air was heavy with the smell of burning timber and blood. The heat from the smoldering cabin seared his face.

"You savages!" he yelled, turning to the cabin, where the flames guttered and snapped, and where nearly everything he owned, all he'd worked for, went up in the smoke lifting to the darkening sky. "You goddamn savages!"

His eyes dropped again to Charlie, and he fell to his

knees, unable to believe the young mustang tamer was
dead. Nordstrom had promised Clem Decker before he'd
died in the Patched Skin Buttes that he'd watch over the
lad. He never should have left him here alone.

He slowly shook his head, squeezing his glistening
eyes closed. ''Oh, Charlie,'' he sighed, ''what am I ever
gonna do with myself for letting them kill you?''

He could not have given voice to it just then, but he
knew what he was going to do. He ground his teeth at
the knowledge, then stood and pulled the limp body over
his shoulder.

10

Not long after Nordstrom left the wagon train, Imbert Kohl cantered the major's horse, Windjammer, back to the caravan. As the procession continued, each wagon about a quarter mile apart to keep from eating each other's dust, Kohl walked the horse beside the major's van.

"There's a buffalo trail leading into those northern hills about two miles ahead," he told the major, pointing north.

The major didn't say anything, only nodded and stared at the rumps of his mules. Kohl frowned and studied the man. The Southerner wasn't as smartly dressed today as he normally was—no silk tie, no jacket, not even a hat. And the sleeves of his white blouse had been folded carelessly up his arm. The top two buttons of his shirt had been left undone, revealing his floury-white throat and chest and wiry wisps of gray-brown hair.

Kohl turned the horse away and dismounted, and as the wagon continued, he tied the stallion to the Southerner's van. He turned to watch his own wagon approach, the mules hanging their heads and occasionally bending their lathered necks to nip flies. Wilomene handled the reins with a sour, vacant look. Ida Mary sat next to her, the twelve-year-old's small, round face pinched with boredom and fatigue under the faded brim of her blue polka-dot bonnet.

As the wagon passed, Kohl walked along beside the driver's box and asked Ida Mary to fetch him a water flask and a biscuit with bacon from the food pouch. Stiffly, the girl did as she was told, and when Kohl had the food and water, he stopped to devour the sandwich and wait for the Lang wagon about a hundred yards away.

Kohl could tell the teacher was alone in his driver's box; the man's stout wife must be napping in the back. Good, Kohl thought. They could talk.

"Mind if I climb aboard, teacher?" Kohl asked when the Lang wagon approached.

"Help yourself," John Lang said, and slowed the mules as Kohl climbed up and sat down with a grunt. Lang flicked the reins and the mules leaned grudgingly into the traces, resuming their three-mile-an-hour walk.

Kohl, who'd finished his sandwich, offered his hide-covered water flask to the teacher. Lang shook his head.

"What's with Townsend?" Kohl asked him.

"What do you mean?"

"I don't know—he looks . . . sick or somethin'."

Lang shrugged. "Probably just getting tired of the trail," he said.

"I s'pose. . . . Listen, I found a buffalo trail into those hills about two miles ahead." Kolh pointed northwest, where the sage-covered plain lifted into an oceanlike series of swells gradually rising toward the toothy line of mountains looming beyond them. "Prob'ly good cover in there."

Lang nodded, the subject of cover reminding him of Nordstrom's visit. Lang mentioned it to the farmer.

"What did he want?" Kohl asked.

"The renegades stopped at his ranch."

"What for?"

"Us."

"Oh, for the love of Christ!" Kohl turned to Lang. "What in hell do they want?"

"You know what they want," the teacher replied with uncharacteristic impatience.

"I reckon," Kohl muttered, running a hand down his coarse, whiskered face. "I've a mind to give him to 'em, too."

"That's ridiculous."

"That's not what you were thinkin' two seconds ago."

Lang flushed and stammered. He felt guilty for involving the unwitting rancher in their dilemma, and that's what bothered him. "Sorry, Kohl. This is just getting to be a hell of a lot longer trip than I expected. No point in us going for each other's throats, though." There would be little point in sharing his true feelings with the farmer, he knew. Kohl didn't have Lang's conscience, and could not have empathized.

They rode in silence. Lang watched the trail rising beyond them, cut by thousands of wheels over the past twenty years, until the two tracks dwindled into one gray line snaking around low hills and disappearing in ravines.

Two hawks hunted high overhead—shaggy, winged shadows turning slow circles in the late-afternoon sky which had turned the color of spring timothy.

" 'Spect you wish you were still teachin' school back in Indyany, eh?" Kohl said at length, a humorless smile touching his lips.

"I have to admit the thought crossed my mind."

"We'll make it," Kohl said, though his tone was not reassuring. "Like the major said, there's only four of them, and five of us."

"I doubt we're as well armed as they are, or as knowledgeable about how to defend ourselves."

Kohl smiled wistfully. "No, but we got the fear."

Lang looked at the farmer, who turned to scan the buttes and shelves rising southward. Grass seeds and trail dust clung to his beard, and the sunburned skin on his cheeks was peeling, forming white patches of new amid the old.

"How's that?" Lang asked.

"You ever trapped a mink?"

Lang shook his head.

"Well, a mink is just an itty-bitty thing, right? I trapped one once and she 'bout took my arm off. I was twenty times her size, even had me a knife and a gun. But she had the fear."

Lang regarded Kohl's shrewd expression and nodded warily. He wasn't sure if Kohl was serious or if he was just putting on a brave face. He suspected the former, which troubled him. An honest assessment of their weaknesses was essential.

Lang smiled, humoring the farmer. "Well, I'm glad there's something in our favor."

Kohl sighed. "Well, I best relieve the wife," he said, and climbed down the moving wagon, careful not to stumble and fall under the heavy steel-rimmed wheels that could cut a man in two.

When he'd left, Grace Lang poked her blond, bonneted head out of the canvas behind her husband, her face marked by the pallet on which she'd lain. She climbed heavily onto the seat beside him, breathing hard, then gave him her angry blue eyes.

"John, I want to know what's going on, and I want to know now!"

The caravan pushed on for another two hours, following an old buffalo trail north through a series of shallow ravines and coulees. Over their left shoulder, the Big Blue Mountains rose in a toothy line, appearing near enough to touch. Their cool blue was a welcome sight amid the sweltering, mid-summer heat and the nose-drying musk of sun-baked grass and sage.

The wagons stopped for the night in a wide, rocky draw. The men unharnessed the mules and released them within the circle of wagons. When John Lang went off to relieve himself behind a knoll, he was startled to find a mounded grave.

In the rough board marker were scratched the words

"This man kilt by Injuns—July 3, '64. R.I.P. Watch yurselfs."

Feeling fear prick his spine and a deep ache in his loins, Lang hurried back to the wagons and busied himself laying out his camping gear. As he worked, he kept an eye on Grace, who set out a pot of pickled beef for sandwiches. He'd told his wife about their fix, and after her initial hysteria, she'd settled into a troubled silence.

He'd had to tell her. She, like Nordstrom, had every right to know of the danger they were in.

"What's the matter, John, did you see them?" she said, coming up behind him with a sandwich and a cup of water. Taking Nordstrom's advice, they'd built no fire, for the smoke could give them away.

Lang frowned. "No. . . . What? No, I didn't see anything."

"That look on your face—"

"I'm just tired, Grace," Lang said, pulling down a leg of the folding table.

"Of course you are, poor dear," Grace said patronizingly. "You sit down and eat, read your book for a while, and turn in early."

"I can't turn in early; I'm keeping the first watch tonight."

Grace sat down on the chair across the table from her husband. "What happens if you see them?" She still had a patronizing cast to her eyes, mixed with fear.

"Then I alert the others," Lang said, irritated.

"And then what?"

Good question, he thought. Then what?

He hesitated, feeling insulted, confused, inadequate . . . afraid. "Then . . . then we gather our weapons and make a stand."

Grace's eyes widened and her cheeks flushed. "A stand? You? Oh, for heaven's sake!" She lifted her double chin and cackled, rolling her eyes.

Attacking him was her way of handling her own fear, Lang knew, but at that moment he felt like standing and slapping the big woman's fleshy face. He couldn't un-

derstand why he'd let the woman's father, a saddlebag
doctor with a predilection for ginger beer, talk him into
marrying her.

Anyway, there was no time for such regrets. Keeping
the lid on his anger, he stood and stalked away from the
wagon, heading for a rocky hollow in the ridge where
he could be alone and think, try to gather his wits and
decide what kind of action he was capable of taking
against the men who wanted to kill them all.

In the bed of the Kohl wagon, Corrine lowered her head
to her upraised knees and stifled a sob. She hadn't meant
to eavesdrop, but the Lang wagon was parked beside
hers, only a few feet away, and she had overheard the
Langs' conversation. It wasn't so much what the teacher
and his wife had said that bothered her; it was the fear
she'd heard in their voices.

After Nils had told her he'd killed one of her attackers, she'd been afraid they were stalking the wagons,
and she'd watched for them every day, expecting to see
four ragged men on horseback suddenly appear out of
nowhere and storm the caravan. It was worse than a
nightmare; the fear reached her very soul and dropped
a dark veil over her eyes so that in everything she saw,
she saw them—sweaty, dusty, whiskered faces, lewd
smiles pulling the corners of their mouths and narrowing
their lightless eyes.

She couldn't help remembering their stench of alcohol
and rancid sweat, their hot, sour breath, their rough-
callused hands raking her bare skin. Their animal grunts
and whoops.

She trembled again as if chilled to the bone. Her worst
fear had come to pass. Her attackers were still out there.
From the terror she'd heard in the Langs' voices, she
knew someone from her party had seen them, and now
they were all afraid. Though not as afraid as she was.
Corrine knew firsthand what kind of men they were.

She lifted her head suddenly, eyes wide. A thought
had struck her. She scurried forward across the wagon

bed and pulled out a small, hide-covered chest of Mrs. Kohl's keepsakes. She opened the lid, removed the top tray covered with yellowed letters, ribbons, and hair swatches, and fished through the trinkets and old embroidered doilies on the bottom until she found what she was looking for.

It was a small pistol with a battered ivory grip and a short, scratched barrel. Corinne had seen Mr. Kohl give it to Mrs. Kohl for safekeeping, and had seen Wilomene stash the weapon in the box.

Several days ago, while riding in the box and trying to hold her fear at bay, Corinne had spied the trunk under a flour sack, and opened it. Beside the gun, Wilomene had placed several bullets wrapped in a knotted handkerchief. Corinne had untied the handkerchief and, studying the gun for some time, figured out how to load the weapon, snugging the stubby, brass-encased bullets into the cylinder.

Now she hefted the loaded pistol in her hand. Heavier than it looked, it was cold and smelled like oil and gunpowder. Corinne clicked back the hammer. That's how you fired it, she'd discovered. The trigger curved forward until the hammer locked.

Then all you did was aim and pull the trigger, snapping the hammer forward and exploding the shell.

She stared at the weapon for a long time before she lifted it to her face, opened her mouth, and slid the barrel inside. The chill of the steel numbed her lips and the taste of the oil made her gag. Her hands shook.

Her eyes wide and tearing, she thumbed back the hammer. Then she squeezed her eyes closed and poked her finger through the trigger guard, resting it against the curved trigger.

All she had to do was pull her finger back just a little ways . . .

On impulse, she pressed her finger lightly against the trigger, felt her heart thump against her breastbone. She knew if she increased the pressure just a little more, the hammer would slam home, the shell would explode, and the bullet would rip through the barrel, into her mouth, and through her skull.

The hurt, the shame, and the fear would all be gone.

She opened her eyes and slid the barrel from her mouth. Holding the hammer with both thumbs, she pulled the trigger and felt the hammer die. She rubbed the oil and spittle from her lips with the back of her hand. Leaning forward, she replaced the gun in the chest, set the tray in its cradle, closed and latched the lid, and slid the chest under the flour.

She leaned back against the wagon box, crossed her arms over her breasts, and heaved a long, resolute sigh. She could stick the barrel in her mouth and pull the trigger if she had to.

And when the men came again, she would have to. . . .

11

The shovel rang as it stabbed the flinty soil. Nordstrom tossed the dirt on the growing mound beside the deepening hole, and shoved the spade once more into the earth with a powerful push of his booted foot.

He'd started digging Charlie's grave at dawn. It was now nearly full morning. The work was hard but Nordstrom lost himself in it, barely aware of the climbing sun and growing heat and the sweat that soaked his hat band, stung his eyes, and slid down his cheeks, gathering in a point at his chin before it dribbled onto the hard, sandy ground in which he toiled.

Sweat stains grew under his arms and pasted his shirt against his back. Above him, a prairie thrush prattled in a cottonwood limb. Behind, the gray ashes of his cabin lay mounded like snow around half-burned logs and the exposed chimney poking skyward.

When the rancher was satisfied with the grave's depth, he tossed out the shovel, raised himself from the hole, and lifted his eyes. Charlie's body lay suspended above the ground in his Navajo saddle blanket. Last night, Nordstrom had tied the body to a stout cottonwood branch, safe from predators. This morning, its prone shadow slanted across the grave and Nordstrom's grim countenance.

"I'm gonna get 'em, boy," he said through gritted

teeth. He wagged his head. "Don't you worry. I'm gonna get every last one of 'em. They're gonna be sorry for what they did to you."

Nordstrom stepped forward and untied the ropes from the cottonwood's trunk. Using his broad back for a pulley, he lowered the body to the ground, then gently into the grave, crouching and grunting with the effort. Retrieving the shovel, he started returning the loose soil to the earth. An hour later, the grave was filled, mounded with stones, and marked with a cross fashioned from two green branches and rawhide.

The rancher tipped back his hat, planted his hands on his hips, and regarded the grave soberly, shot through with guilt. Charlie should have been burying *him,* instead of the other way around. The young cowboy had had his whole life before him, and if anyone knew how to live with brazen style, it was Charlie.

Nordstrom shook his head at the senseless waste of it all, feeling sadness and rage nearly equal to that which he'd felt when he'd lost Heather. There'd been no one to account for her death, however.

Four scoundrels in greasy buckskins would account for Charlie's.

"When I get back, I'll fix you up a headstone proper," he said to the grave. "In the meantime, I got business to tend to."

He turned to his wife's headstone only a few feet from Charlie's plot and squeezed his eyes closed against the fresh wave of sorrow washing over him. Feeling more lonely than he'd ever felt before, he wheeled around and strode past the still smoldering rubble of his cabin, which he considered only fleetingly. He'd given little thought to rebuilding. He'd lost so much here, only time would tell if this ground could ever be home to him again.

An hour later he sat high in the leather of his fleet-footed grulla mustang, cantering across a wide, grassy shelf, following the trail of four riders following the trail of five wagons.

He wore buckskins with fringed leggings, a cartridge belt and Colt .44 positioned for the cross draw, and a white Stetson with a slightly curled brim. His Winchester was snugged in his saddle boot so the stock rode just below his saddle horn on the horse's right side. His canteen was filled with water, his saddlebags with jerky for himself and with oats for his horse. A bedroll was strapped to his cantle.

It could be a hard ride, and it would not be over until he'd fixed the renegades' flint but good.

They were probably a good half day's ride ahead, he figured. But they'd slow down when they caught up to the wagons, if they hadn't already done so. Nordstrom doubted they'd worry about their backtrail, so he'd have the advantage there, at least. His only real concern, aside from being outnumbered, was reaching them before they attacked the pilgrims.

When he came to Long Shot Creek on the east side of the Lone Wolf River, he found a fire ring with warm ashes in an old buffalo wallow. The renegades had apparently spent the night here. The bones flung about the wallow told Nordstrom they'd shot grouse for supper, and from the ashes he could tell they'd headed out late in the morning.

Apparently they were taking their time. Why, Nordstrom couldn't figure. Maybe they were lazy. Maybe their aim was to stalk the wagons slowly and enjoy every second of the pilgrims' fear. Whatever the reason, Nordstrom was gaining on them faster than he'd figured he would.

He followed the creek to the river sliding between grassy cut banks. Splashing across to the other side, he lost the cutthroats' tracks in a wide, hard-packed swath gouged by herded cattle.

He trotted his horse in a circle, studying the ground, a furrow spreading across his forehead. Finally, he stopped and slapped his hat against his thigh.

"Piss on it, goddamnit, anyway!"

Finding the renegades' tracks in the cattle trail would

be like looking for a needle in a haystack.

"Shit."

He scoured the prairie on both sides of the cattle trail, and after a good hour, he came upon the tracks of four horses moving northwest. Nordstrom couldn't believe his luck. Happy to be back on the renegades' trail, he secured the hogleg on his hip and spurred the mustang over a tawny ridge.

An hour later he was cantering along a dry creek when, scanning the distance, he spied movement in a grove of trees about a half mile ahead and to his right. As he drew within a hundred yards of the grove, a horse defined itself between stout cottonwood trunks, swishing its tail at insects.

Nordstrom halted the mustang, his heart thumping and adrenaline rushing. Keeping an eye on the grove and reaching for his Winchester, he made out the tail-swishing rumps of two more horses, nearly hidden by the trees.

He jerked his head around, looking for cover, then spurred the grulla toward a knoll poking up on his left. Reining to a sliding halt, he jumped down and ran, crouching, up the knoll, confident that nothing short of a wildfire could make the mustang stray from where Nordstrom had dropped his reins.

Several feet shy of the knoll's round top, Nordstrom dropped to his belly, removed his hat, and lifted his eyes over the sandy brow. The grove lay a hundred yards ahead and to his right. All seemed quiet.

Damn lucky, he told himself. *I could've got myself bushwacked for sure.*

Evaluating the flat ground between him and the grove, he pursed his lips and narrowed his eyes in concentration, knowing that the wisest move would be to wait until the renegades mounted up and continued traveling, to trail them until he had the tactical advantage. But when you were one against four, there was no such thing as a tactical advantage, he thought, levering the breech of his Winchester open to make sure it showed brass.

Setting the rifle down, he sat up, palmed his revolver, plucked a shell from his cartridge belt, and loaded the empty chamber beneath the hammer. His blood roared in his ears; the heat of anxiety and eagerness spread up between his shoulder blades. He'd been a fighting man only when the situation had called for it, and he'd never enjoyed it.

But he'd enjoy this, he thought, tightening his jaw until his cheek dimpled. He donned his hat, holstered his pistol, and lifted his rifle.

Slowly, he moved out from behind the knoll, keeping his eyes fixed on the grove and holding the carbine up close to his chest until he was relatively sure no one was watching. Then he bolted, traversing the sage-pocked ground between the knoll and the motte quickly, running with his head down and eyes on the trees, watching for movement and listening for gunfire, careful to stay up-wind so he wouldn't startle the horses.

He circled around and entered the grove opposite the tethered mounts. Moving stealthily through the trees, he stopped when a camp appeared thirty feet before him, in a slight clearing cluttered with deadfall. Four men lay near a smoldering fire, heads propped on a log, hats tipped over their eyes, asleep.

With his right hand Nordstrom loosened the Colt in his holster, making it easier to draw, then stepped forward and levered a shell into the Winchester's breech.

"All right, everybody just keep your hands away from your sidearms and stand up nice and slow or I'll grease you where you lay!"

The men came awake quickly, turning stiffly and peering over the log to see Nordstrom bearing down on them with his Winchester.

"If I see one hand so much as twitch toward an iron, I'm gonna blow its owner to kingdom come!" Nordstrom said.

The men came to their feet, blinking groggily, mumbling curses and raising their hands above their waists.

It didn't take Nordstrom long to see that he'd captured

the wrong four men. These were drovers, dressed for the
trail in wool shirts, vests, and colored bandannas, with
.45-caliber Colts strapped around their waists.

Nordstrom scowled. "Who the hell are you?"

"Who the hell are you?" echoed a slack-jawed cow-
poke with a handlebar mustache and a sugarloaf sombrero.

"I'm the one with the gun," Nordstrom snapped.

That reminder got the short drover with the batwing
chaps and free-ranging left eye to pipe up with the information Nordstrom had asked for. "We're Tin Cup
riders from Weed Creek north of here about a hundred
miles," he said, wide eyes on the Winchester.

"What are you doing here?"

"We're herdin' cattle to the Red Cloud Agency in
Dakota." The short man spat and tipped his head to
indicate east. "We were about to cross the river back
yonder when four smart asses wandered up out of nowhere and shot their pistols over the herd. Caused a hell
of a goddamm ruckus, they did. Kilt one of our outriders
and toppled the chuck wagon."

"Four men in buckskins armed to the teeth?" Nordstrom inquired.

"That's right," a bull-chested cowboy growled.

Nordstrom dropped the Winchester's barrel, and the
cowboys lowered their hands. "Those are the four I mistook you for. I've been on their trail since yesterday.
They burned my cabin and killed my partner."

The drover in the sugarloaf sombrero said tightly,
"Crazy damn bastards need the California collar is what
they need."

"You goin' after 'em?" Nordstrom asked.

"We were, but we lost their trail," the short drover
said. "They're sneaky sons o' bitches and we ain't
trackers. Besides, our twenty-five a month don't cover
gettin' drygulched."

Nordstrom thought they'd probably made the right de-
cision. "Which way'd they head?"

"North," the short man said.

"Prob'ly headin' for Henry's Crossing on the Deadman," the drover in the sombrero added.

Nordstrom rubbed his bristly jaw, wondering what in hell the renegades were up to, stampeding cattle and calling a passel of angry drovers on their trail. They were an unpredictable bunch, he'd give them that.

He asked the drovers if he'd seen the emigrant train. They looked at one another and shook their heads. Nordstrom cursed. What the hell was going on?

"I reckon I better make tracks," he said with a sigh. "Sorry I interrupted your snooze."

The barrel-chested cowboy frowned warily. "You alone?"

"That's right."

"You ain't long for this world if you're trackin' those uglies all by your lonesome," the drover in the sombrero warned.

"That's all right," Nordstrom grumbled, heading through the trees toward his horse. "It ain't much of a world, anyways."

12

Riding northwest, Nordstrom decided to postpone his pursuit of the renegades. After the stampede, they'd no doubt lit a shuck out of the country.

They were probably expecting trouble from the cowboys. Stampeding a herd was akin to rustling, and the punishment was a California collar, a stretched neck, and a dead carcass left for the crows. The renegades were lucky the four cowpokes Nordstrom had run into weren't up to the task.

The rancher warned himself to keep his eyes peeled and his ears open for anything. For that's just what those men were capable of—anything. As the cowboys had pointed out, they might be headed for Henry's Crossing on the Deadman, but they could just as easily be following the wagons or lying in wait on a rimrock for an ill-fated pursuer to happen by.

Nordstrom decided to try and catch up to the wagons. The pilgrims wouldn't have a chance against the renegades. While Nordstrom felt none too kindly to the men of the group, he felt an instinctual need to keep the women from harm. If the renegades didn't show, Nordstrom could always track them later. Men like that cut a broad swath.

The rancher rode through a crease between the buttes west of the Lone Wolf River and picked up the wagon tracks along an old freight road angling northwest and following the valleys between watersheds. It was a big, empty region cut by tributaries of the Tongue and Dead-man Rivers and broken here and there by badlands, grim and forbidding but with an eerie beauty in the softly blended blues, grays, and duns of the sandstone rimrocks shouldering above the plain.

Wolves hunted here, and grizzlies, and Nordstrom saw tracks of the former around a seep lined with scoria. The ever-thinning buffalo herds had left the earth gouged and scraped in their search for forage, and they'd dug deep wallows along creeks and streams. Hawk cries punctuated the eerie silence, and prairie dogs stood on their hind legs, chortling and wringing their front paws as the horseman cantered past.

Late in the afternoon, Nordstrom rode around a high, gently rounded butte covered with vetch and sage and saw the white glow of a wagon cover two hundred yards ahead. The wagon was about a quarter mile behind the rest of the company and tilted at a curious angle. Nord-strom's first thought was that the renegades had hit the group, running one of the vehicles off the road, and as he galloped toward the Conestoga the rancher shucked his Winchester and touched the grips of his Colt to make sure the sidearm was still on his hip.

As he approached, he saw Kohl, Major Townsend, and John Lang on their hands and knees peering under the wagon. Kohl's son flanked them with a sheepish look on his face. The Norwegian girl sat on the ground near the mules, gazing off as if imagining herself far away from here.

Kohl was grumbling and swearing by note and rhyme so loudly that Nordstrom could hear the farmer from a half mile away.

Nordstrom yelled and waved to make his presence known, and cantered his horse up to the wagon. "What happened?"

Kohl straightened and ran his shirtsleeve through the sweat on his brow, dragged a ragged breath into his lungs. He jerked a thumb at the boy. "Goddamn boy here let the wheel slide off the trail, left the felloe back there in the bank."

Kohl snarled and cuffed the boy on the back of the head. The boy accepted the blow stoically, barely wincing. Standing, the girl moved as though to intervene, then caught herself.

"Oh, Uncle Imbert!" she pleaded.

Kohl turned his furious gaze on her, jabbing an arm. "You shut your mouth, girl!"

Nordstrom regarded the boy and the girl sympathetically. "Easy, Kohl," he said, repelled by the display. "That won't fix your wheel."

Kohl dropped his gaze to the spokeless felloe propped along the side of the ravine, and shook his head. "That was my only spare." Turning to rake the boy again with a scowl, he added, "He ruined the other one back aways. I don't know what in the hell we're gonna do."

Appraising the felloe, Nordstrom saw that every spoke in the hub had been snapped like kindling. Dismounting the grulla, he said, "Let's get the wagon unloaded."

"What are you gonna do?" Townsend asked.

"We'll have to build a crutch."

"A what?"

"I'll show you, but first we have to unload the wagon." Nordstrom wasted no time moving to the back of the old Conestoga and dropping the tailgate. He knew how quickly the sun fell when you needed it high.

When he and the others had shuffled the heaviest plunder to the front of the wagon box and had unloaded the rest, Nordstrom retrieved the jack from where it hung beside the tar bucket on the rear axle, and jacked the back of the wagon two feet off the ground. That done, he and the other men took an ax and walked out to a stand of trees marking the course of a distant creek.

Nordstrom picked out a young box elder as straight as any he could find, and chopped it down. Then he and the others dragged the twenty-foot length back to the lame vehicle, where, as the others stood over him watching with curious expressions on their tired faces, he knocked the spokes off the ruined wheel, cut a notch in one end of the box elder, and lashed the notch over the wagon's front axle so that the other end of the pole trailed out behind, like half a travois frame.

When he was satisfied the pole was secure, he lowered the hub of the broken wheel onto it, took a rope from the wagon's coupling, and noosed it over the crutch.

"What's that for?" Townsend asked, frowning skeptically.

"Should keep the crutch from slipping off the hub when the wagon turns left."

"Will it work?"

"Should," Nordstrom said, nodding.

Admiring the rancher's handiwork, John Lang said, "Where did you learn how to do that?"

Nils answered vacantly for the rancher, "The overland trails." He'd been so quiet that everyone turned to look at him now.

"That's right," Nordstrom said, brushing off his breeches and smiling at the boy. Turning to the men, he asked, "Everyone OK? Any sign of the riders?"

"Not yet," Lang said.

Nordstrom sighed, weary from the exertion of the past hour. "You might have gotten lucky. They made the mistake of harassing some drovers back near the Lone Wolf. Four men started after them before they got the jitters and turned back, but it's possible the renegades think they're still being dogged. They might be making a run for Henry's Crossing on the Deadman."

Just as Nordstrom said it, a problem occurred to him. Apparently, it showed on his face.

"What's the matter?" John Lang inquired darkly. "I thought you said we got lucky."

Nordstrom lifted his hat and scratched his head. "I may have spoke too soon. You're gonna have to get that wheel fixed, and the only blacksmith and wheelwright within two hundred miles is at Henry's Crossing."

Lang dropped his eyes and pursed his lips. "I see. . . ."

Kohl turned to cuff the boy again, but Nils was gone. The girl stood by the mules frozen, eyes on the ground.

"You best get that tire and felloe lashed to the wagon and get a move on. Night's coming fast and you'll want to find a camp."

While Kohl and Lang got the wagon ready to pull out, Nordstrom went to his saddlebags for a handful of grain to feed his horse. Townsend approached him with a grave expression.

"You're not here out of the goodness of your heart, are you, Mr. Nordstrom? Something happened."

Eyes flat with suppressed emotion, Nordstrom turned to the man while the grulla munched the oats in his palm. "No, I'm not, Mr. Townsend. And yes, it did."

The rancher dropped the remaining oats, turned, mounted his horse, and reined away, leaving the Southerner standing there looking grave.

As Nordstrom galloped past the wagon, he caught a glimpse of the girl. She sat on the seat with her hands in her lap, staring straight ahead. He halted the grulla, turned him around, and rode back.

The girl turned to him as if seeing him from far away. The grulla stomped and blew. Nordstrom leaned on his saddle horn and spread his lips in a thin smile. He wasn't sure if it was the girl's beauty or her mysterious reserve, but he'd felt drawn to her from the moment he'd first seen her.

"I'm Glenn Nordstrom," he said.

The girl's eyes widened and she stared at him for several seconds. She brushed a lock of tawny hair from her perfect face. Her expression softened, but she did not smile.

"I am Corinne," she said, flushing and lowering her gaze.

Nordstrom's smile grew; his eyes narrowed kindly. He tipped his hat, reined the grulla around, and galloped away.

Corinne watched him go.

• • •

Henry's Crossing was a little mushroom village on the Deadman where freighters, bullwackers, drovers, and drifters stopped for a drink and a shave and to get their mounts reshod. Most of the structures were made of dirty white canvas, though log buildings with false fronts and sashed windows appeared here and there on either side of the deep-rutted main street.

Large bull trains clattered through, trace chains jangling, blacksnakes spanking the rears of bellowing oxen, hoarse-voiced freighters spewing epithets in German. Bales of dried buffalo hides, shaggy and rank, waited on docks to be loaded onto stern-wheelers and shipped east.

It was a colorful little place where a man could quench his thirst on good, clean whiskey, minus the gunpowder and strychnine served up elsewhere, and frolick with one of the soiled doves of the Antelope Inn. This was the place J.L. Wood and the boys headed when they cantered into town on a balmy August afternoon shading toward dusk.

"Ah . . . women," Pete Hill said as he tied his horse to the hitching post.

J.L. dismounted his roan stiffly and turned to see what the wiry Hill was ogling across the street. Two Indian girls in red calico sat cross-legged before a stack of blankets similar to those they wore, under a blue and white striped awning and a sign which read "Teeth Pulled 25 Sents." Their round, dark-eyed faces were expressionless.

J.L. smiled darkly and nodded. "I gotta tell ya, I have always had me a taste for squaw flesh."

Stepping up behind him, Sonny Laagerman put his hand on his shoulder and said, "Now, ain't you glad we came here, J.L.?"

"Yeah, Sonny, I'm real glad we came here," J.L. said tightly, showing a wry, lipless smile. "I'm real happy now you shot over that herd to get 'em stampedin', and put those drovers on our trail. I'm just pink with joy over lettin' those wagons go after that cocky little bastard cut Dew's throat.''

He stepped forward slowly, backing Sonny up against the hitching post, drawing his knife.

Both hands on the hitching rack behind him, Sonny watched the knife move up to his throat, his eyes brightening with fear. ''D-don't, J.L.''

Jim McCluskey was standing on the boardwalk behind the hitching post. ''Those wagons'll show here in a few days, sure enough, J.L. This is the best place to cross the Deadman in a hundred miles.''

J.L. stared intently at the knifepoint drawing a bead of bright red blood at Sonny's throat. ''Sonny hopes you're right—don't you, Sonny?''

Sonny nodded almost imperceptibly, not wanting to move his neck against J.L.'s skinning knife.

J.L. drew the knife away from the terrified man's throat and sheathed it at his waist, saying, ''If you ever pull a stunt like that again, Sonny, I'm gonna carve a hole in your head. Understood?''

Sonny touched his thumb to his throat, then drew it away to look at the blood. ''Sorry, J.L. I just wasn't thinkin'. After Pete and I got to talkin' about how we ain't never seen a stampede before, I just lost my—''

''Understood?''

Sonny jerked his head, nodding. ''Understood, J.L. Understood. Let me buy ya a drink.''

Ignoring him, J.L. turned and headed for the tavern's louvre doors.

Inside the long, dark saloon, games of chance were being played by drovers in back-tilted sombreros. Fallen angels in bright gowns sipped whiskey at the bar waiting for trade. A scrawny, middle-aged man with a pinstriped shirt and a nervous twitch played an almost unrecognizable version of ''I'll Take You Home Again, Kathleen'' on a bullet-scarred piano shoved against the wall.

''Well, J.L. Wood—long time no see!'' exclaimed the man behind the bar, a round, hard-bellied fellow with bushy black muttonchops and pockmarks marring his face, like a dented coffee can.

J.L. didn't care for the man, and knew the man didn't care for him, so the bartender's phony friendliness chafed. He imagined taking out his Colt, thumbing back the hammer, and firing a slug between the two lying eyes. But that would have been more trouble than the apron was worth, so J.L. just pushed up to the bar, scowling, and said, "Etta still servin' drinks here, Ed?"

Ed's smile faded. He picked up a glass and began toweling it dry. "No . . . Etta don't work here no more, J.L."

"Where'd she go?"

"Fort Reno, I heard."

"You don't say."

"What'll you have?"

J.L. ignored the question and pursued the subject of Etta. "Who's servin' drinks these days?"

A thin smiled plucked at the apron's heavy lips and a bead of sweat popped out on his forehead. "Just me."

Impatiently, Jim McCluskey leaned on the bar. "Well, you can serve me up a shot of the best whiskey you got."

Behind him, Pete and Sonny chimed in, agreeing.

Ed set three shot glasses on the bar, uncorked an amber bottle, and filled each glass to the rim. He cocked an eyebrow at J.L. "What's yours, J.L.?"

J.L. sneered. "She ain't workin' upstairs, is she, Ed?"

"No—I told ya, J.L. Etta moved on."

Slowly, J.L. relaxed his scowl. "Give me a bottle o' apple jack, then."

The man turned and retrieved a bottle from a low shelf under the mirror. He set it on the bar, squinting his eyes as he figured the tab. "Let's see . . . that'll be two dollars, all told."

"Pay the man, Jim," J.L. ordered, grabbing the apple jack and heading for a table.

He was halfway across the room when he heard footsteps on the open stairs leading down from the rooms on the second floor, where Ed kept a passel of girls. J.L. did a double-take. The red hair and matching red dress with a puffed bustle and dangerously low-cut bodice bespoke Etta.

She saw him just as he saw her. She stopped midway down the stairs and froze. Her eyes widened and her face flushed. Then she jerked her gaze to the bartender as if for counsel. Finding no help there, she turned and ran awkwardly, grabbing at her skirts, back up the stairs.

J.L. gave an unintelligible yell and turned to the apron, whose face had turned white. "Thought you said she left, ya fuckin' liar!"

Deciding to deal with the bartender later—Etta was getting away—he bolted across the room, knocking over chairs and tables, and thundered up the stairs two steps at a time. When Etta stopped, turned at top of the stairs, and saw him coming with the bottle clenched in his right hand, she gave a short, drum-rattling scream.

"No, J.L . . . *please!*"

13

The girl turned left and ran screaming down the upstairs hall between closed doors.

"Daddy's home, my flower!" J.L. whooped, having fun.

He chased the girl down the hall. She turned into the last room on the left, but before she could get the door closed and locked, J.L. shouldered through it, throwing it wide and nearly tearing it off its hinges. The girl sprawled backward onto the floor.

"J.L. . . . *no!*"

The girl's screamed plea was followed by a thick "What the hell . . . what the hell's goin' on?"

J.L. turned away from the girl. On the bed, a man pushed onto his elbows and looked groggily around at the commotion, the sheet sliding down his pale, bony chest to his soft belly. He looked about thirty, with a neatly trimmed mouse-brown beard and short dark hair with a mussed middle part. The room was dusky red, with the late-afternoon light pushing through two windows over which shades had been drawn and mauve-colored curtains pulled.

J.L.'s grin faded. His eyebrows straightened, and the lines around his eyes disappeared. He'd been delighted to see Etta on the stairs, and her running had delighted him even more. His women—and there were many women J.L. considered his own—often reacted that way to the hunter's sudden reappearance. While most men would have taken offense, J.L. saw it as all part of the game.

Like the predator he was, he enjoyed running his women down and taking his rough pleasure by force. He believed that, after the initial shock and surrender, most of the girls even enjoyed it—though of course they wouldn't admit it.

But finding one of his girls with another man was not part of the game.

Turning from the man on the bed to the girl on the floor, J.L. said, "Who the hell is that? I told you I didn't want you workin' upstairs no more. I told you to wait tables down in the saloon—that's all!"

Scuttling on her butt across the floor, pushing with her feet, the girl returned J.L.'s glare with one of her own. "Who're you to tell me what to do? I gotta make a livin'!"

"You'll make your livin' *downstairs*!"

"No, I won't!"

"Yes, you will!"

"You can't make me!"

The man on the bed interrupted the verbal fusillade by pushing his back against the headboard and thrusting his arm and finger at J.L. "I paid for the whole night, ruffian. Get out of here!"

Silence.

J.L. turned to the man slowly. His eyes were cool. "Who are you, slick?" he asked quietly.

A low, clipped moan fluttered across the girl's vocal chords and caught in her quivering lips. J.L. ignored her.

"I'm Dr. Lyle Huseby."

"Sawbones, huh?"

"Dentist."

While his face remained calm, J.L.'s voice rose slightly, taut as razor wire. "Well, Mr. Dentist, get your ass outta that bed and get your duds on. You're outta here. This is my woman. I bought and paid for her.

You're stealin', an' if I ever catch you stealin' from me again, I'm gonna cut your ears off.''

Outraged, the dentist's eyes narrowed. Before he could say anything, the girl yelled, "You did *not* buy me, J.L. I'm my own girl!''

"I gave you a hundred dollars, whore!''

"You're sick!''

Growing bored with the exchange, J.L. sighed and turned to the man on the bed. "Get your clothes on,'' he ordered. Then turning to the girl, who stood now in front of a window looking harried, he said, "You . . . off with yours.''

"This is outrageous!'' the man yelled. He turned and fumbled in his clothes neatly folded on the chair beside the bed. From beneath the pile he pulled a silver-plated derringer with pearl grips, but before he could bring it to bear, J.L. grabbed his wrist and squeezed, twisting, until he heard the quiet grinding and cracking of bones. The pistol clattered to the floor.

The man screamed, grabbing his wrist with his other hand. Face pinched with mute anger, eyes on fire, J.L. shoved the man's head down between his knees, got him in a headlock of sorts, and unsheathed his skinning knife in one quick motion. Quickly, he held the dentist's head steady by a handful of hair and, as though trimming fat from a roast, lopped off the man's left earlobe.

The man cupped his bloody ear with his uninjured hand and wailed.

The girl screamed.

Pinching it between his thumb and index finger, J.L. held up the pale, round lobe like a trophy, grinning. Blood dribbled onto the sheets. "Lookee here—the ear of a tooth fairy!''

Paralyzed with horror, the girl clutched her face in her hands and screamed. The man wailed. J.L. tossed the lobe on the floor, grabbed the man behind the neck, jerked him off the bed, and sent him staggering into the hall.

Clutching his head from which blood spurted, the na-

ked dentist bounced off the wall. "My ear!" he
screamed. "My ear!"

J.L. cupped his hands around his mouth and called
down the hall, "The dentist here cut hisself shavin'—
somebody get a sawbones." Then he turned back into
the room and shut the door. He regarded the girl calmly.

She stood against the window, looking ashen. Little
moans rose up from her throat. "No . . . ," she said,
wagging her head slowly.

Absently stropping the bloody blade of his skinning
knife on the thigh of his buckskin pants and ignoring
the commotion growing in the hall, J.L. grinned.

"Now, my flower . . . where were we?"

For the next several days, Nordstrom accompanied the
caravan northwestward, toward Henry's Crossing on the
Deadman, but kept his distance from the wagons. Thinking that he could better protect the emigrants from the
perimeter, he ate and camped alone, never quite a part
of the group, never quite apart from it.

During the day he scouted the trail ahead and hunted,
shooting antelope and deer, quartering and dressing the
carcasses and delivering the meat to the caravan when
the wagons had stopped for the night. Several times Mrs.
Kohl and Mrs. Lang invited him to join them for a meal
around their fire, but he only smiled politely, tipped his
hat, and rode away.

He avoided Cynthia Townsend as much as possible,
though once or twice, when he was talking with the men,
he saw her watching him and smiling wistfully, as
though amused by his embarrassment and guilt. Nordstrom wondered how many other "amusements" she'd
left back in South Carolina.

At night he circled the wagons atop the grulla, whose
hooves he wrapped in deerskins to keep them quiet. He
rode the bottomlands, dry washes, and rocky draws—
anywhere the renegades might camp—looking for the
telltale glow of a fire and the smell of smoke.

As he rode, staying low to keep his silhouette from

showing against the starlit sky, he replayed in his mind's eye the image of Charlie hanging from the rail over the front gate of the ranch, and his cabin burning down to dust and glowing cinders. He imagined killing each of the renegades whose faces he remembered clearly from the day they showed up at his verandah—smirking and scowling with the malignant arrogance of the truly evil.

But when he'd seen no sign of the riders by his fifth day with the caravan, he was certain they'd gone on to Henry's Crossing—where they'd either forgotten about the emigrants or were waiting for them. Eager to settle the score, Nordstrom cursed his luck, though he knew it was good luck for the pilgrims.

In the late afternoon he crossed a grassy finger of land and descended to where the wagons clattered around a brush-choked ravine. He raised a hand, and Major Townsend pulled back on the reins, bringing his mules to a sudden halt. The animals dropped their heads and nipped at the ragweed growing along the trail and filling the air with its unmistakable musk.

"Trouble?" Townsend asked.

Nordstrom shook his head and waited for the other wagons to move up next to the major's. When they had, the men and women regarding him curiously, he pointed to a notch in a grassy ridge a quarter mile south and said, "You'll want to pull up there for the night. There's a seep in the side of that ridge, and the notch will hide a fire."

"Why we stoppin' so early?" Kohl asked.

Nordstrom shrugged. "Why not? By noon tomorrow we should be at the crossing."

Kohl leaned over the side of his wagon and spat a coffee-colored stream of chewing tobacco. "Why not keep movin'?"

Incredulous lines spoked around Nordstrom's eyes. "I just told you."

Mrs. Lang cleared her throat. "You think they're waitin' for us there, don't you, Mr. Nordstrom?"

"They could be, ma'am."

"And you want us to be fresh for them, is that right?"

"That's right." It was the truth, but Nordstrom also wanted to be fresh for them himself. And while riding into town under cover of darkness would have its advantages, it would also be foolhardy.

John Lang said, "There must be some law at Henry's Crossing, isn't there, Mr. Nordstrom?"

"Not the last time I was there, there wasn't. Even if there is now, I don't think we should depend on it."

Douglas Townsend squinted his soft blue eyes against the west-falling sun. Cynthia sat beside him, looking lovely as ever—dust-streaked sweat on her face, and all. "Why don't we split up?" her husband asked. "No reason why we all have to go to the crossing, is there?"

Kohl sneered. "You mean, why not throw the Kohls to the wolves alone, eh?"

Douglas craned his head around to look at the farmer. "Why not? It was that *girl* and your *boy* who antagonized them, wasn't it?"

"Why, you little pecker!" Kohl growled.

Cynthia turned to her husband angrily. "Douglas!"

"All right, all right," Nordstrom broke in. "That's enough. It's best for all of you if you stick together."

"Why should we listen to you?" Douglas said, swinging a haughty look at the rancher.

Nordstrom gave him an icy stare, controlling his impulse to pull the squirrely little aristocrat down from his van and slap the shit out of him. At length, he wagged his head and sighed, reining away.

"That's my advice. Take it or leave it," he said.

He camped that night on the other side of the grassy finger, only a hundred yards from the circle of wagons. The grulla cropped fodder along the bank behind him while Nordstrom nibbled dried beef, waiting for his coffee to boil on the campfire before him—the first such fire he'd allowed himself since he'd begun hunting the renegades.

He was sipping a second cup of coffee and cleaning his revolver when he heard shoes tearing grass and kick-

ing an occasional stone beyond the firelight. Dark had
come down, and stars had dropped over the broken
plain. Nordstrom slapped the pistol's cylinder closed and
rolled into the darkness beyond the sphere of light.

"Who's there?" he called, thumbing back the hammer.

"Corinne," a soft voice said.

"What?"

"I brought you somet'ing hot for supper." She grew
from the shadows to stand near the guttering flames, a
plate in her hand. "Where . . . where are you?"

Nordstrom stood and walked into the firelight, surprised at the girl's presence, and warmed by it, but afraid
for her safety. "Did you come here alone?"

She nodded, meeting his gaze shyly and holding out
the plate of pan-fried antelope, potatoes, and two gravy-
covered biscuits. The food made his mouth water, but
he said, "Do the others know you're here?"

She shook her head. "No, but they would not care."
She reported the information matter-of-factly, without a
trace of self-pity in her Norwegian-accented English.
"Nils brought it to the wagon for me. I wasn't hungry,
but I thought you probably were. Here—take."

He accepted the plate she'd thrust out at him in her
fine-boned, long-fingered hands. "You shouldn't have
risked it."

"I don't care," she said flatly. "I don't care anymore
what happens to me. Besides, I have this." She stuck
her hand in the deep right pocket of her skirt and pulled
out what looked to be an old Smith and Wesson pocket
pistol.

"Where'd you get that?"

"It is Mr. Kohl's. Mrs. Kohl hid it in the wagon. I
found it."

"Can I see it?"

Hesitant at first, she stepped forward and handed him
the pistol. Sitting on a rock with the plate resting on his
knees, Nordstrom studied the little cannon, thumbed
back the hammer, tested the trigger, then gave it back

to the girl, who stood over him, making damn sure he returned it.

"You know how to use that thing?" Nordstrom asked.

"I figured it out," Corinne said, returning the gun to her pocket.

"Unless you're Annie Oakley, it ain't gonna do you much good against those four."

The girl turned, found a place on the bank sloping up behind the fire, and sat down, drawing her knees up and smoothing her skirt over them. The firelight danced on her velvety skin, as soft and pink as a child's. "It is not for them; it is for me."

"What are you saying, you're gonna shoot yourself?"

"If I have to."

Nordstrom studied the girl across the fire. She wasn't mad, just practical, he decided. Her eyes, though downcast, betrayed an inner strength born of horror and loneliness. He wanted her to know he understood, but then he realized, from her seeming comfort at his fire, that she already did. That's why she was here.

He didn't say anything, just let her sit there quietly, staring into the fire as he ate. Even after all that had happened to her, she was lovely—a tawny-haired, full-lipped, deep-bosomed goddess out of some old Norse legend. Hers was a singularly tranquil presence—not at all unlike his dead wife's—and Nordstrom was enjoying every minute of it.

Finally, when he was through with the meal and set his plate down at his feet, she said, "What happened? Why are you here?"

"They attacked my ranch," he said. "They killed my partner, Charlie, and hung him from the front gate post." He knew he didn't have to mince words with her, and he saw from her eyes, which never wavered, that he was right.

She frowned and said, "And you are here because they are after us."

"That's right."

"We are the ..." She looked around, searching for the word, then swung her gaze back to his. "The bait."

He winced a little at her directness. "I guess you could say that." He gestured at the coffeepot gurgling on a rock in the fire. "Would you like a cup of coffee?"

"No. I better get back to the wagons." She stood and brushed off her dress. "Nils will be worried," she said with a trace of irony.

"The boy likes you."

"Yes, and I like him, though ..." Her voice trailed off.

"Not in the same way," Nordstrom finished for her.

"Nils is a goot boy, goot friend," she explained, as if defending the lad. She dropped her chin and crossed her arms, and said thoughtfully, "His father treats him bad. ..."

"Kohl's a hard man," Nordstrom agreed.

"I better go." She picked up his plate and fork and started away.

"Corinne ... ," Nordstrom said, not wanting her to go. His mind was a nest of mixed emotions. He knew only that he wanted to hold this girl for a very long time, and the desire was only partly physical.

She turned back to him and smiled, as if she understood, then walked away.

Nordstrom rolled a cigarette and lay smoking with his head against his saddle, watching the stars. When he'd smoked the cigarette down, he tossed it in the fire, which had burned down to nearly nothing, then pulled up his blanket and tipped his hat over his eyes.

He awoke later with a start, reaching for the pistol on his hip, but a soft hand covered his own right hand as it closed around the grips.

"It's OK," a female voice said, pushing him back down.

It was Corinne, he thought, smiling through the dusk of sleep. Corinne had returned to him because she shared his loneliness ... his pain. ... He half-opened his eyes, but clouds had moved in, turning the sky as dark as a cave, so he closed them again, and slid over, making room for the girl under the blanket.

She snuggled against him, breathing hard with her need, stripping off her clothes, then helping him out of his. It wasn't before she'd straddled him, pressing his hands against her hard-nippled breasts and giving a husky laugh, that he realized it was not Corinne at all.

It was Cynthia Townsend. He should have known from the heavy smell of perfume.

His heart sank and his body ached with disappointment, but as she ground her hips against his, moaning and quaking with passion, it became far too late to do anything about it.

14

Major Townsend lay his pallet under his wagon, hoping he could sleep better in the cool night breeze. But his back and seat hurt from the long trek overland, and although he was so tired that he could barely hold his eyes open, the pain and fatigue would not give him release.

"Cruel goddamn joke," he said with a sigh.

He turned his head to look around the wagon box at the sky, where stars hung brightly, winking like the Christmas ornaments his darling wife, Renda, used to hang every year on the red oak that drooped its mossy bows over the wide stone verandah of their manor.

Interrupting his reverie, muffled footfalls sounded down the ravine to the major's left. He lowered his gaze to peer into the shadows, reaching for the revolver by his pillow. As he pulled back the hammer, a moving object came together in the darkness—a cloaked figure with a lush silhouette of mussed dark hair. Perfume the fragrance of a Southern spring rain touched the major's nose.

Cynthia's perfume.

What in the hell was she doing? His heart drummed and his stomach rolled. Nordstrom's camp was that way, only a hundred yards or so, probably fairly easy to find in the starlight. The major remembered the person he'd seen leaving the rancher's cabin, and, too weary to deny his suspicions about his daughter-in-law's infidelity any longer, he slid out from under the wagon and pushed himself to his feet.

He wheeled furtively around the wagon tongue. Moving as quickly as his stiff old legs would carry him, he cut the person off just as she stepped around a thicket about twenty yards down ravine from the wagons.

Close enough to see that it was indeed Cynthia, the major grabbed his daughter-in-law's wrist and jerked it harshly. Startled, she muffled a scream.

"Where have you been, woman?" the major hissed, keeping his voice low and baring his teeth like a feral cur.

"Ouch—you're hurting . . . ," Cynthia complained, struggling against the major's grip.

"What have you *done*?"

Fighting free, Cynthia stepped back, feigning ignorance. Keeping her voice down, she said, "What are you talking about?"

"You don't have to tell me—I can smell it on you . . . you . . ." The major shook his head as he dredged up the salt to tell the woman what she really was.

"You *what*?" Cynthia challenged him with a look that told the major she no longer cared what he thought, that she had no more respect for him than she did his son.

"*Whore!*" the major rasped, straining his vocal chords.

"Major Townsend!" Cynthia started theatrically, pulling the nightcape closed at her throat. "What a thing to call your daughter-in-law!"

"You don't care anymore—that it? You used to be a little more discreet, when I had land and money."

"Why, Major, you've gone mad," Cynthia said, meeting his angry gaze with a cool, haughty one of her own.

"You've blackened your family name. What would your father—what would Henry—?"

"What name?" Cynthia said with a mirthless laugh.

"What name do any of you rich Southern gentlemen have anymore?" She watched him, as if waiting for an answer. When none came, she continued. "It's all rubble—your plantations and your names—and none of you can put them back together again because you wouldn't lift a finger to pound a nail, and all your slaves are gone."

"We have our dignity," the major said. "That's more than you have."

"Is it?"

As she started away, the major said, "I'll tell him," meaning Douglas.

She turned her fearless eyes on him again. "After the way you've belittled him all his life, keeping him a child? He won't believe you, but he'll sure hate you. Remember? He thought I was his idea, not yours." She punctuated the thought with a lifting of her lovely brows, turned on her heel, and headed for her wagon, where Douglas slept like a lamb.

The major watched her, scowling, hating her even more now because he knew she was right. He was weak, and Douglas would not believe him—wouldn't allow himself to take his father's word over his wife's. Even if Douglas did believe him, he'd still hate the old man for knowing . . . and for telling him what he was happier not learning.

But something had to be done, the major thought, walking as if in a trance back to his wagon and imagining closing his hands around the bitch's skinny neck.

Nordstrom rose the next morning feeling stupid, though again he couldn't help admitting to himself that his visit from Cynthia had been refreshing. But it was the very thing he'd always avoided on his previous overland trips. Getting emotionally or physically entangled could only lead to trouble.

He'd heard once about a wagonmaster who'd gotten involved with the wife of a Kansas farmer. One night the farmer and his two beefy brothers crept into the wagonmaster's camp to find the man and the farmer's wife going at it like a couple of dogs. They separated the two, beat the wagonmaster senseless, tied him to a tree, and whipped him with a blacksnake until his back split open like a roasted sausage, blood frothed from his lips, and his heart gave out.

The wife was whipped, as well, though not as severely. Then she was made to walk, tied, behind the wagon until the caravan met up with a Shoshone hunting party. The farmer sold the woman to the braves for half an antelope, and never saw her again.

No—fooling around with another man's wife was an ugly business that almost always ended in tragedy, Nordstrom told himself. And by the clear light of day, he saw that getting involved with Corinne would be a mistake, as well. He was at least ten years older than she, and the boy, Nils, had taken a fancy to her. Besides, Nordstrom had a job to do, and he didn't have time to fawn over a girl.

For chrissakes, what had gotten into him?

After drinking some coffee, he saddled the grulla and rode over to where the caravan was preparing to move out. His dusty frock coat hanging open and his wool pants showing their wear, the major was tightening the last cinch on his team.

Nordstrom asked him if he was ready to move out, but the major acted as though he hadn't heard.

Nordstrom repeated the question.

The major ignored him.

"Everybody set?" Nordstrom said again.

Still silent, the major pulled on the halter to make sure it sat evenly on the mule. He turned, and Nordstrom saw that his face was grim, almost ashen. His shoulders drooped.

"We're set," Townsend mumbled tightly beneath his heavy gray mustache, turning away and climbing up to his seat.

Nordstrom appraised him, frowning. "Everything all right, Major?"

"Ha, there," the major called to his mules, flicking the reins.

Nordstrom turned his horse to watch the wagon pass, water gurgling in the barrels latched to its side. Douglas and Cynthia's vehicle came up next. Cynthia sat beside her slouch-hatted husband, in a white blouse, her hair blowing free, face as pink as a Western dawn.

"Good morning, Mr. Nordstrom," she said cheerfully.

Nordstrom tipped his hat and pursed his lips, trying to fashion a smile. Watching the wagons dwindle in the distance, he cursed.

Townsend knows, he thought, with a sinking sensation in his bowels. He knows, you stupid goddamn jackass son of a bitch.

He knows.

Nordstrom in the lead, the caravan followed the sluggish Fairibeau Creek until it petered out in an alkali flat. There they picked up a freight road Nordstrom didn't remember seeing before. He hadn't been far from home in the past three years, and the West was filling up. Deep-rutted from heavy, two-inch steel tires, and littered with mule and bull droppings, the trail split the benches tilting toward the Deadman.

It was about eleven-thirty in the morning when Nordstrom halted his horse on a knoll a good half mile ahead of the wagons. He'd been keeping his distance to scout ahead and to keep from getting backshot by the major, which, under the circumstances, Nordstrom thought all too possible.

He couldn't wait to rid himself of this bunch, and he figured to do just that once they got their tire fixed and had crossed the Deadman.

Good-bye, Major. Good-bye, Cynthia. And yes, good-bye to you, too, Corinne. The last thing you need is a sour ex-rancher with only a burned-out cabin and two graves to his name.

If all went as he expected, he'd settle his score with the four renegades on this side of the Deadman. He had no idea what he'd do after that, where he'd go, and at the moment he didn't care.

Loosening his grip on the reins to let the grulla crop the few scattered spokes of grama and bluestem beneath him, he fished around in the pocket of his buckskin tunic for his tobacco and rolled a smoke. He gave his back to the wind and cupped a match to the twisted end of his cigarette.

When he'd gotten a good draw, puffing smoke, he peered down the grade gentling northward between dikes thrusting their rock-strewn heads above the rolling prairie, like the battered hulls of overturned ships. About two miles away, buttes and cottonwoods traced the Deadman's course.

In a horseshoe under skirmishing geese sat the town— if you could call it a town—of Henry's Crossing. It had grown some since Nordstrom's last visit. Only a handful of canvas lean-tos then, now it appeared to boast several log shacks and false-fronted clapboard stores. There was even a good-sized stockyard, its holding pens spilling down a tawny hill. The muffled pops of a hunter's shotgun pierced the wind, and isolated flocks of geese rose off the river to form shaggy V's under high, thin clouds.

Nordstrom smoked and waited for the wagons. When he heard them clattering within fifty yards, he turned to make sure the major wasn't drawing a bead on him, then sparked his cigarette out on his heel. He gestured for the emigrants to follow him, and he clucked the grulla down the grade between the dikes, heading for a grove of cottonwoods east of the town.

When he made the grove, he checked to make sure no other campers were in the area, then waited again for the wagons, which came on slowly, the mules straining with their loads and the weight of their tired feet, and nodding their weary heads.

Imbert Kohl's vehicle was the first to arrive, Kohl sitting with Ida Mary in the driver's box. Corinne was walking alongside the wagon, her hair blowing freely in the breeze. Gazing around her with a solemn expression on her lovely face, she appeared happier to Nordstrom . . . somehow more alive than when he'd last seen her. As she approached beside the wagon, she regarded him seriously for a moment, then curled her lip with a smile.

Nordstrom turned away. To Kohl, he said, "This will be a good place to camp until your tire's fixed. I don't remember where the smithy is, but you'll find him."

He reined his horse around and started away.

"Where you goin'?" Kohl asked.

Nordstrom stopped. "To check things out." He couldn't help sliding his gaze to Corinne, who pinned him with her keen blue eyes, curious.

He jerked away and urged the grulla toward town.

A few minutes later he cantered down the deep-rutted main street five times the size it had been three years ago, and ten times as busy. Threading his way around bull trains, lumber drays, and farm wagons loaded with mining equipment, Nordstrom looked around for the renegades.

They weren't going to stick out in this crowd, that was for sure. Every other rider he met or passed was dressed in greasy buckskins and armed to the teeth, the scarred stocks of their big-caliber rifles jutting up above their saddle horns. That's all right, Nordstrom thought.

They'd have trouble recognizing him, then, too.

When no rider in particular caught his eye, Nordstrom started checking out the livery barns, of which there were two. A blaze-faced black caught his eye in the paddock of the second one. He scrutinized the seven other mounts and thought he recognized a chestnut gelding and a mouse-brown dun, but he couldn't be sure.

"Help you, mister?"

Standing by the corral and holding the grulla's reins, Nordstrom turned to see a bearded man in gray overalls and knee-high boots approach, a short-haired mongrel at his heels. Nordstrom nodded at the blaze-faced black in the corral.

"Whose horse is that?"

The stableman chuffed and shrugged. "I don't know his name."

"Come in with three others four or five days ago?"

The big man squinted his eyes and cocked his head. "You law?"

"Nope. But I still want to know who belongs to that horse."

Head tilted to one side, the man studied Nordstrom. Nordstrom held his gaze. The hostler blinked. "There's four of 'em," he said finally.

"Hunters, would you say?"

"I'd say."

"That chestnut and the brown one part of his crew?"

The man slid his eyes over the top rail and said lazily, "And that buckskin over by the water trough. Why you wanna know?"

"Why's none of your business but I'll give you a double-eagle not to tell them I was askin' about them, and I'll let you stable my horse for me if you give him a good long curry and plenty of oats. Deal?"

"Let's see the double-eagle."

"One more thing. Where they stayin'?"

The man dropped his gaze and wagged his head. "Can't tell ya that, mister."

Nordstrom furrowed his brow. "Can't or won't?"

"Can't."

Nordstrom dug in his pocket and flipped the man the coin. The man studied it, tried bending it with fingers as big and red as sausages, and nodded. "All right; you gotta deal."

Nordstrom pulled his Winchester from his saddle boot, swung his saddlebags over his shoulder, handed the grulla's reins to the hostler, and started up the street. The mongrel nipped at his boot and slunk under the bottom rail of the corral.

"Ain't too friendly, is he?" Nordstrom remarked.

"He's about as friendly as it gets around here, friend," the man said with a grunt.

Nordstrom didn't doubt that at all.

15

Holding the big grulla's reins, Hyram Jorgenson watched the newcomer walk away, saddlebags slung over his shoulder, Winchester in his hand. Jorgenson fingered the double-eagle thoughtfully, biting his lip. When Nordstrom disappeared around the corner, the hostler led the mustang into the livery barn and dropped the reins in the alley between the stalls.

He called to the floppy-hatted figure on the other side of the barn. "Hey, Red, stall this peg pony, will ya? I got business uptown."

At the main drag, he turned left and trudged down the boardwalk with the set jaw and determined eyes of a man on a mission.

When he came to the Antelope Inn, he brushed past three burly freighters clenching soapy beer mugs and prattling in Swedish, and pushed through the saloon's louvred doors.

"Jorgy, you old bastard, what'll it be?" asked the apron.

All business, Jorgenson shook his head, continued on down the bar, and climbed the stairs to the second floor. He stopped at the last door on the left and knocked.

A cross between a grunt and a yell answered. It was followed by singing bedsprings and muffled voices—a man's and a woman's. Curious, Jorgenson turned his ear to the door.

"Who the fuck is it!"

Jorgenson jumped back, startled and stammering. "Hyram Jorgenson."

"Who?"

"The hostler over to the livery."

"Well, why the fuck didn't you say so?"

The door opened, and the smell of stale beer and cigarette smoke and perfume wafted over the liveryman, whose face colored.

The shaggy-haired, sharp-faced man who stood before him holding a pistol was buck naked. He had a chest and belly like a washboard. Sliding his gaze around the man, Jorgenson saw that a woman—Miss Etta, he believed it was—sat on the bed in only a thin, pink chamise, painting her toenails.

"Well, what is it?" asked the man the hostler knew only as J.L. Jorgenson could tell from his mussed hair and puffy eyes he'd been sleeping.

It took a moment for the liveryman to get over the shock of the man's nudity and the confusion over what to do with his eyes. "Uh . . . a man come askin' for you at the livery, just like you said there might be."

"How many men?"

"Just one."

"Were there wagons?"

"Nope."

The hunter frowned. "No wagons?" He seemed angry, and that made the liveryman even more nervous. This was a man you didn't want to rile.

"No, sir," Jorgenson said, shaking his head. "There were no wagons. He come in alone on an appaloosy— fine-lookin' horse."

The girl asked in a dreamy, drugged-sounding voice, "Who's lookin' for ya, J.L.?"

J.L. ignored her. "Describe him," he ordered the hostler.

Jorgenson shrugged. "Oh, I don't know . . . 'bout six

feet, broad-shouldered. He wore buckskins. . . ."

"Blond beard cut kinda short?"

"That's him," Jorgenson blurted with a nod of relief.

Absently, J.L. lifted his gunhand and caressed his upper lip with the barrel of his Colt revolver. "Well, I'll be goddamned," he said. "It's the rancher. . . ." His eyes brightened a little, as though cheered by the prospect of a new game with higher stakes.

"Is that good news, sir?" Jorgenson asked hopefully.

J.L. turned his eyes on him as though he'd forgotten he was there. "You didn't tell him anything about me and my friends, did ya?"

"No, sir, I surely didn't," the hostler lied, feeling the double-eagle in his pocket, round and firm against his thigh.

The hunter gave him a doubtful, sidelong look. "You sure now?"

"Yes, sir."

J.L. considered the man. The hostler was about as uncomfortable as a man could be with his clothes on. He found it impossible to return the hunter's gaze, for he'd never seen eyes so crazy. And he couldn't look down without seeing the man's red noodle.

"All right, then," J.L. growled at length. "I guess you deserve that double-eagle I promised you, don't you?"

"I guess so," the hostler said, like a truckling errand boy, happy to be almost out of there.

J.L. turned and stomped around the room cursing, looking for his pants, then returned to the door and gave the hostler a coin to match the one in his pocket. Jorgenson didn't bother to scrutinize the coin, but quickly shoved it in his pocket, tipped his hat, and hurried down the hall.

"Much obliged," he mumbled.

"Me, too," J.L. said with a dim smile, quietly latching the door.

•   •   •

After leaving the hostler, Nordstrom went into the Dead-man River Saloon. He bought a mug of beer, then took it out on the boardwalk to drink it and watch for the hostler. He'd been able to tell by the man's demeanor that he was lying when he told Nordstrom he didn't know where the renegades were. And Nordstrom would have bet his last good horse that the liveryman was also their snitch.

He would have made good on the bet, for he was sitting there on the boardwalk, his saddlebags and rifle piled at his side, when the hostler came up the street intersecting the main drag on Nordstrom's left. Nord-strom watched as the man crossed Main, limping a little as he hurried on his long, stiff legs. The dog followed close on his heels, head hanging, tougue out, staring at the man's boots.

The hostler walked about a half block east, then turned into the Antelope Inn. The dog stopped at the doors, looking in, then sat down to wait and snarl at passersby.

Nordstrom set his beer down on the boardwalk and rolled a cigarette. He knew the hostler could have been after a drink and nothing else, but the rancher didn't think so. The man's odd reaction to Nordstrom's ques-tions, and his scurrying off right after Nordstrom had left the livery, was just too much of a tip-off.

Nordstrom sat there and smoked and sipped his beer until the hostler reappeared on the boardwalk outside the Antelope Inn. Dog in tow, the man ambled across the street, half-running to get clear of a lumber dray storm-ing in from the east. He was heading back the way he'd come, which brought him within thirty feet of Nord-strom.

Nordstrom caught the man's eye. The hostler did a double-take. Nordstrom just smiled and raised his beer. The panting mutt sucked in its tongue and showed its teeth. Scowling and flushing, the hostler hurried on down the street toward the livery barn.

Nordstrom returned his beer mug to the saloon, then

went back outside, picked up his rifle and saddlebags, and headed across the street toward the Antelope Inn. Inside, it was cool and dark. Nordstrom stood near the door and looked around.

There were about a dozen men and two dolled-up pleasure girls inside. Most of the men looked like cowboys on a five-day binge: long hair, scraggly beards, Texas spurs. There were about five men in buckskins.

Nordstrom considered them from across the dusky room obscured by clouds of blue smoke and bright window light. He doubted he could have picked any one of the renegades out of a crowd without the others, but Nordstrom recognized the three. They sat, minus their leader, at a table between the windows, with three cowboys, playing poker.

Nickel cigars and loosely rolled cigarettes smoldered in ashtrays. Coins and whiskey glasses littered the table. All six men were too involved and probably too drunk to heed the stranger eyeing them from just inside the swinging double doors.

Nordstrom looked around for the other man—the lean, wiry firebrand with the snake eyes and killer's cool countenance. Not finding the man in the room, Nordstrom's eyes returned to the three others at the table, wanting them to see him, urging them with his eyes to turn their own toward his, so they could see him, remember him, and go for their guns.

Hatred boiled up from deep within him as he remembered the image of Charlie's bullet-riddled body hanging over the gate. Nordstrom gritted his teeth and lowered his shoulder so that the saddlebags began sliding down his arm toward the floor. He tightened his grip on the Winchester and slowly lifted it before him.

"What'll it be, mister?"

Nordstrom lifted his shoulder slightly to cease the saddlebags' decent down his arm, and eased his grip on his rifle. He turned to the barman, a thick-set, pasty-faced man with dark pomaded hair parted in the middle, who eyed Nordstrom expectantly.

It took a moment for Nordstrom to come up with a reply. Gathering his wits, he said, "Got a room?"

"With or without?"

"With or without what?"

"A girl," the man said, as if he'd never heard such a stupid question.

Nordstrom thought about it, deciding he'd be less conspicuous with than without. "With."

The barman said, "Be five dollars for an hour, ten for the night."

Nordstrom glanced at the three renegades at the card table. They hadn't noticed him and apparently weren't looking for him. Maybe the hostler *had* been out to wet his whistle. Or maybe he'd come to inform someone else who, if not in this room, must be upstairs.

"I'll go for the night."

"Any color preference?" the man asked. "We got a nigger fresh in from Mandan. She's extra, though."

"Just give me your standard girl and a room key."

The apron pursed his lips and lifted his hands aquiescently, reached under the bar, and slapped a key down in front of Nordstrom. Nordstrom dropped several coins on the counter, picked up the key, glanced back at the renegades, then headed for the stairs.

The barman looked across the room at one of the girls, and nodded. "Mona," he said, tipping his head at Nordstrom.

The rancher didn't bother to consider the girl he was about to spend the evening with. He was too busy eyeing the renegades as he made his way to the stairs.

They hadn't seen him, much less recognized him. For that reason there was no need to get hasty. Before making a move against these men, Nordstrom knew he should think it through. You couldn't just walk into a joint and pink three patrons without causing one hell of a ruckus, maybe getting backshot by the apron or a trigger-happy bystander.

There would be a better time and place. Besides, he

needed to find the other man, the leader, before he
showed any of them his hand.

Nordstrom climbed the stairs, hearing the footfalls of
the girl behind him. He didn't turn to look at her, just
noted the number on his key and headed for the room,
keeping his ears open for voices. There were several,
none recognizable or suspicious.

"Why, you're about as skittish as a—!"

Nordstrom wheeled sharply to the girl behind him,
cutting her off with a look. She froze, stared at him
quizzically, a little fearfully. Realizing covert action at
the moment could draw more suspicion than the sound
of his voice, Nordstrom smiled.

"Oh, it's just I'm stiff from ridin' herd—that's all,"
he said jovially, in the best aw-shucks drover's voice he
could fashion.

He turned and unlocked the last door on the right.
Tentative, the girl followed him in.

"So you been ridin' herd, have ya?" she said with
feigned ease, not yet sure what to make of this one.

"Yeah, I'm up from Oklahoma," Nordstrom said, not
sure how to end the game he'd started spur-of-the-
moment.

He dropped his rifle and saddlebags on the bed, then
went to the single window and drew the shade. At the
marble-topped stand behind the door, he poured water
from the pitcher into the washbasin and doused his face
and neck, groaning with the soothing feel of clean skin.

"Good Lord, I need a bath," he said with a sigh.

He removed his neckerchief, unbuttoned his shirt, and
scrubbed his chest. The girl watched him admiringly
from the other side of the room. Finally, he turned to
her. She was peeling her dress down her shoulders.

"Hold it, hold it," Nordstrom said, forgetting the
masquerade.

The girl looked up, her dark red curls falling flat
against her forehead and brushing her naked shoulders.
Studying her face for the first time, Nordstrom could see
that she was probably his age—too old for her occupa-

tion—and pretty in a hard, Western way, with red hair piled on her head, and lots of unfulfilled years behind her.

"What?" she said, half-surprised, half-annoyed.

"Why don't you go down and get us a bottle?"

She grimaced and dropped her shoulders. "Are you peculiar or just shy?"

Nordstrom shrugged. "Both."

Scowling, she drew the straps of her dress up and went to work on the buttons. She walked toward him, giving him a gaze of supreme tolerance, and held out her hand. "It's your night, chump."

He planted a dollar in her palm. She walked around him, still looking at him as though he were the queerest thing she'd ever seen, and left.

As the door clicked closed behind her, the door across the hall opened, and a voice rose. Nordstrom could make out only snippets of sentences. "Tell 'em . . . leave their fuckin' game . . . hurry your ass . . ."

The door closed. Bare feet slapped down the hall.

Nordstrom turned his ear from the door. His heart raced, nearly taking his breath. Sweat slicked his palms. It was him.

Snake Eyes was right across the hall.

Soon, they'd all be less than ten feet away.

16

Compulsively, Nordstrom fingered the butt of his Colt, his mind racing to come up with a plan. Back at the ranch and on the trail it had all seemed so easy. He'd simply track the renegades and kill them.

But he hadn't planned on close quarters with other people around. Suppose one of the girls got hit. . . .

An idea had only half-formed when he heard men's voices and boots clomping in the hall. A girl squealed. "Ouch—that hurt, you!"

"You keep your damn hands off Etta!" Nordstrom recognized the angry voice of "his" girl, who'd apparently gotten caught in the stampede up the stairs.

"Well, how 'bout you, Mona? You ain't busy tonight, are ya?"

"No—I'm gonna go suck this whiskey down all by my lonesome," Mona snapped back.

"Who you got in there?" one of the men asked, his face only inches from Nordstrom's door.

Nordstrom drew his pistol and clicked back the hammer. He swallowed, trying to suppress his racing heartbeat. If the men came through the door, he'd need a steady hand not to hit one of the women. He stepped back, pistol raised, and waited.

"None of your damn business. Now git away from

me!" Mona said, grunting as she struggled away from
the men.

The door across the hall opened as Mona opened
Nordstrom's door and stepped into the room, looking
harried, her hair in her eyes. She was clutching a bottle
of whiskey by the neck, like a weapon. In the moment
before she closed the door, Nordstrom caught a glimpse
of one of the renegades, black eyes feasting on Mona's
backside, whiskered cheeks bunched in a grin.

"Get in here, goddamnit!" boomed an angry voice
from the doorway across the hall.

"OK, J.L. Take it easy."

Mona swung the door closed behind her. "Here's
your goddamn whiskey," she said angrily, tossing the
bottle on the bed. Then her eyes found the drawn Colt.
"What—?"

"Shh. Get back. Be quiet." Nordstrom grabbed her
hand and pulled her to the back of the room, then
wheeled to press his ear to the door.

"What the hell—?" Mona said, thoroughly confused.

"Be quiet," Nordstrom rasped. "I'll tell you in a
minute." He winced with the effort of trying to hear
through two doors. The doors and walls were thin, but
too much noise rose from the saloon below. He picked
up muffled voices, but that was it.

Finally, he gave up, and turned to the woman who
stood watching him uncertainly. He gazed at her for a
long moment. She held his eyes.

"Can you keep a secret?" he asked her.

"It's my business to keep secrets, mister," she said.

"Those men raped an emigrant girl," he said. "They
shot my hired man and played cat's cradle with his head.
Then they torched my ranch cabin. I'm gonna kill
them."

She snorted a laugh. "J.L. and his crew? Good luck."

"You know them, I take it."

"Sure. Who doesn't around here? They're scum, but
they're no men to mess with. I can see how you'd be
mad if they did what you said, but getting yourself killed

won't fix your cabin or bring your friend back.''

Nordstrom ignored the warning. ''Who's in there with them?''

''That'd be Etta—J.L.'s favorite. Thinks he owns her. She's a sweet girl.'' Mona's voice rose sharply. ''Don't you let her get hurt. You do anything against those men, you do it outside—far, far away from here. We get enough trouble downstairs without you goin' an' startin' a shootin' spree up here where the girls are.''

Nordstrom turned back to the door and considered the woman's admonishment, knowing she was right. He'd do everything he could to keep lead from flying through these papery walls. He didn't want to have any blood on his hands—any except the renegades', that is.

He turned to Mona and raised his eyebrows, his face softening and his eyes brightening. ''You're the boss,'' he said.

Removing his hat and throwing it on the room's single chair, he sprawled out on the bed and laced his hands behind his head.

''What does that mean?'' Mona asked suspiciously.

''It means I wait 'em out, I guess.''

Smoothing her skirt beneath her, Mona sat on the edge of the bed and turned her brown eyes on him, her expression softening. ''What's your name?''

''Nordstrom.''

''You paid for me. I'm yours for the night, Mr. Nordstrom.''

Nordstrom shook his head, liking her and not wanting to hurt her feelings. ''Some other time. I'm a little too keyed up for that sort of thing, if you know what I mean.''

She brushed a ringlet of red hair from her cheek. Her voice turned playful. ''That's too bad. I'm very good at what I do.''

Nordstrom laughed. ''I bet you are.''

She frowned thoughtfully and cocked her head. ''You *are* a peculiar one, aren't you? You married?''

''Once.''

"End bad?"

Nordstrom lowered his gaze and pursed his lips. "I'll say it did."

A few minutes later the door across the hall opened and boots thundered above the din of harried voices. Nordstrom bounded from the bed, reaching for his Colt, and listened at the door.

"Son of a bitch!" someone said. "He followed us, that . . ."

"Sure enough, he followed us. We just gotta make sure we find him before he finds us."

"That shouldn't be too hard. . . ."

The voices faded as the men descended the stairs.

"I'll be right back," Nordstrom told Mona. "Will you wait for me? As long as they don't see you, they shouldn't get suspicious about this room."

She looked at him with an expression of mock anger. "I'm yours for the night, I reckon," she said with a sigh.

He retrieved his Winchester from the bed, started out the door, then turned back with an afterthought. "Where's the smithy?"

"Take a right outside. End of the next street."

"Obliged."

At the top of the stairs he listened until he was sure the men had left the building, then he went down, crossed the saloon, stepped outside, and looked around. Two of the renegades were moving up the street on his right, two on his left—one on each side of the street— looking around with their hands on their holstered guns.

Nordstrom tipped his hat low over his eyes, turned right on the boardwalk, and started west, staying one block behind the renegade on that side of the street. When the man stopped to peer into shop windows, looking for him, Nordstrom froze in his tracks and tried his best to look casual.

Just after the man passed the blacksmith shop, Imbert Kohl and his son appeared on the boardwalk behind him. Apparently, they'd just bought a wagon wheel.

"Good," Nordstrom said, nodding at the tire. "When you get that tire on your wagon, move the hell out, and move out fast."

"What about you?"

Nordstrom forced a wry smile. "I'm gonna keep them busy here in town."

Kohl grumbled something incoherent, then he and the boy climbed onto the wagon and moved off down the street and turned a corner, heading south. Just as they did, the man ahead of Nordstrom turned to say something to the renegade across the street. He froze as he saw Kohl's wagon disappear behind the wide, wooden dock of Kaufman's Mercantile.

"*Goddamnit!*" Nordstrom said aloud, lifting his rifle.

The renegade's eyes widened as he recognized Kohl's wagon. Lifting his arm to point, he yelled to the man across the street. "Hey, Pete!"

The report from Nordstrom's rifle cut him off. The slug caught him in the right shoulder and twisted him around so that he faced the rancher, about a block and a half away. The echo of the first shot hadn't died when Nordstrom jacked another shell into the chamber and squeezed off the round.

The man bounced back with the force of the bullet slamming into his chest, staggered against a building, and slumped into the dusty street.

Seeing that the man was finished, Nordstrom peered across the street, where the other man was crouching, pistol drawn, trying to get a bead on him. Nordstrom lifted his Winchester, but before he could get a bullet off, three riders on jittery mounts entered the field of fire.

Nordstrom lifted the Winchester and yelled, "Get the hell out of the way!"

Before the men could figure out what was happening—they were jerking their heads around bewilderedly and trying to maintain control of their dancing horses—the man across the street shot through them. One of the horses fell forward on its chest, screaming, the rider sailing over its head with an angry yell.

Seeing the wounded horse, the other two went for their pistols and began throwing lead the renegade's way, though their mounts were moving around so much that hitting their mark would have been nearly impossible.

Nordstrom swung a look westward. The other two renegades, having heard the gunfire, were running toward him, one next to the buildings and one in the street, both with their pistols drawn.

Nordstrom squeezed off an errant round in their direction, trying to slow them up, then turned and ran down the empty lot between buildings. Behind the shops were trash piles, outhouses, and several stacks of cordwood. He dove behind a woodstack and peered over the top, bringing up his rifle.

He would have loved to end his hunt right here, and he thought it possible if all remaining three renegades stormed out from between the buildings just a few feet away and into the open where he could give them the lead-riddling they deserved.

But it was too much to hope for. They hung back behind the corner of one of the buildings, and one of the men jerked his head out for a peek, quickly surveying Nordstrom's position before drawing back.

Cursing his luck, Nordstrom stood and, bringing the Winchester to his hip, snapped off a fury of lead into the buildings and the gap between them—hitting nothing but wood and air. Hoping he'd at least bought himself some time by pinning the men down, he turned and ran north along the building flanks, weaving between outhouses, woodstacks, trash piles, and derelict wagons.

From the sound of the gunfire behind him, he knew he'd bought himself some time, so he ran back to the main drag, crossed it, and headed for the livery barn. He found the hostler in the corral, pouring oats from a wooden bucket into a trough. Nordstrom snuck up behind the man, raised the rifle, and snugged the barrel against the man's hairy collar.

The man stiffened and raised his head.

"It's the man you double-crossed—what do you think of that?"

"I . . . I—"

"Shut up. I'm gonna give you a chance to make it up to me. I want my horse saddled and waiting for me in the trees back behind the Antelope Inn in one hour. Make sure the men lookin' for me don't see you. Swing around the edge of town and tie the horse out of sight. Do you understand?"

The man jerked a nod.

"If I find he's not there, you're gonna find out how much a double-eagle's really worth. Understand?"

The man jerked another nod.

Nordstrom turned, looking around cautiously, then ran back in the direction from which he'd come, taking cover behind wagons. Approaching the Antelope Inn, he pushed through the doors and looked around. The saloon was empty, everyone apparently having cleared out to find out what all the hubbub up the street was about.

Nordstrom went upstairs and knocked on the door of his room.

"Who is it?" Mona asked quietly.

"Your favorite customer."

She opened the door and Nordstrom brushed past her. Mona watched him curiously. "I was just about to leave. After all that gunfire, I figured you were dead."

Nordstrom swept the hat from his sweaty forehead and heaved a sigh. He pulled the shade away from the window and peered down at the street. "Not yet."

"Soon, though," Mona said regretfully. "Real soon, I'm afraid, honey."

17

"I want that bastard found, goddammit!" J.L. howled at the top of his lungs, his face flushed and his body shaking with rage.

He and Pete Hill and Jim McCluskey had searched the area behind the businesses and had come up with nothing. The rancher had slipped away.

Pete Hill mumbled sullenly, "One o' us better go check on Sonny. He got hit pretty good, I think."

"Fuck Sonny," J.L. snapped. Aiming a hot gaze at Pete, he said, "I want you to mount up and circle the town—make sure he ain't ridin' away. Jim, me and you are gonna search every fuckin' store and saloon and livery, and every goddamn hotel room in town, and we ain't gonna stop till we find that sumbitch!"

Splitting up, Pete loped off for his horse, Big Jim began searching the east side of town, and J.L. started at the livery barn on the west.

He asked Hyram Jorgenson if the rancher had been back for his horse. Pumping water into a stalk tank in the corral behind the barn, Jorgenson regarded J.L. white-faced and didn't say anything.

"Well, has he?" J.L. urged.

Jorgenson cleared his throat, thoroughly befuddled and exhausted by the tumultuous swing his life had suddenly taken. He was a simple man, pulling an honest day's wage, and he wished all these damn gunwhips would just leave him be. "Wh-who did you say?" he stuttered.

"Are you deaf or just stupid?"

"Couldn't hear ya over the pump," Jorgenson explained, cupping a hand to his ear.

J.L. gave a hot grunt. "The rancher you told me about earlier!"

Jorgenson looked at the wiry no-account, offended. He didn't cotton to be talked to like he was just some everday shit shoveler. "No," Jorgenson said, lifting his head defiantly. "I ain't seen him for hours."

"There—that wasn't so hard now, was it?" J.L. said wryly, turning and heading back up to the main drag, where he started pushing through doorways, stomping across saloons, and kicking in the door of every hotel room on the west side of town. It was when he'd kicked in the last door, finding only a Negro soldier and an Indian girl naked and too busy to notice the intrusion, that it occurred to him the only hotel he hadn't bothered to check was his own.

J.L.'s eyes deepened, gaining a haunted cast: the Antelope Inn!

Drawing his revolver, he ran back outside and up the street. Seeing Jim, he waved for the big hunter to follow. He pushed through the doors of the Antelope Inn and took the staircase two steps at a time, blowing breath through his gritted teeth and cursing.

He knew the rancher had to be here. It was the only place left to hide in town, the only place J.L. and the others wouldn't think to look. Not right away, at least.

Subconsciously, J.L. had thought there was something suspicious about that closed door right across from his. Most of the doors up there were opening and closing all day and all night long. He couldn't remember one staying closed for much over an hour.

No—the room had been too damn quiet, and now he knew why. That rancher was more savvy than J.L. had estimated, since most of the ranchers J.L. knew were little brighter than the stock they wrangled. The son of a bitch had been hiding out right under J.L.'s nose, probably having him a good laugh, too!

Not for much longer.

J.L. pounded down the hall, barely able to keep from shouting every curse in his vocabulary, his eyes brightening with a self-satisfied grin. When he came to the last room on the right, he stopped and lifted his revolver, curling his lips in a snarl and dragging a deep breath into his chest.

"Church is over, friend!" he howled as he kicked in the door.

The door pounded back against the wall, splinters flying from the casing around the latch, and J.L. swung his pistol toward the two figures on the bed, pulling back the hammer.

A woman screamed.

A man yelled, "What the hell?" and turned his startled eyes at the man hovering over him aiming a raised pistol with a cocked hammer. "Don't!"

J.L. scowled, the furrows in his forehead flattening. There was a man on the bed lying between a woman's naked knees with his trousers down around his ankles. He was at least forty, with thinning dark hair and deep lines around his eyes and mouth. The sweat of his toil glistened above his lip.

It wasn't the rancher.

J.L. slid his gaze to the woman looking up at him with an expression of startlement and annoyance. "J.L., get your ass outa here—I'm workin'!" Mona screamed.

"Where is he?" J.L. screamed back.

"Where's who?"

"You know who. . . . Oh . . . goddamnit . . . !"

Boiling, J.L. stormed back out of the room, saw that the window at the end of the hall had been pushed open about three feet, and looked out. Directly below sat a supply wagon loaded with buffalo hides. Beyond it about two hundred yards, a man was running through the stunt willows on the bank of the Deadman.

McCluskey came up behind J.L. breathing heavily.
"What's up, J.L.?"

J.L. turned and bolted down the hall. "He's gettin'
away!"

His ankle tender from his jump from the hotel window
to the supply wagon, Nordstrom slipped and cursed his
way down the bank toward the Deadman, which slid,
wide and green and rocky, between low bluffs.

His saddled mustang was tethered to a sapling near
the water. Seeing it standing there with its head down
and its flanks rippling at pesky monarchs, Nordstrom felt
relieved. If the hostler hadn't taken his threat seriously
and shown up with the horse, the rancher's goose would
have been cooked.

Gaining the horse, Nordstrom untied the reins from
the tree and threw them over the saddle horn, then lifted
his injured left ankle tenderly into the stirrup. Wincing
against the pain—he hoped the ankle was only sprained
and not broken—he heaved himself into the leather and
started the grulla across the river.

He decided to head north and then west and to lead
the renegades as far from the pilgrims as he could. He'd
rely on the grulla's speed and agility to open enough
turf between him and his pursuers to allow him time to
arrange an ambush. He wasn't a backshooter and he
never would be, but he aimed to sweep the element of
suprise onto his side of the table.

The water was only about knee deep here at the
crossing, and the grulla splashed through it easily, only
once slipping on rocks. Nordstrom cast several glances
over his shoulder to see if the savages were back there
yet, but all was quiet so far. He figured it would take
them several minutes to get their mounts ready to roll.

That's why the crack of the rifle behind him was such
a surprise. Even more of a surprise was the sudden hot
pain in his side. He gave a grunt and jerked forward
with the impact of the bullet.

Glancing behind, he saw a mounted rider on the riverbank, with the log and clapboard buildings of the town behind him. He was aiming a rifle toward Nordstrom. Smoke puffed and fire geysered from the barrel, and the crack of the Henry echoed off the water.

The round whined so close to Nordstrom that he could feel the hot wind on his cheek.

Holding his side where a thick wetness spread, pasting his shirt, he spurred the grulla onto shore and up the bank, keeping his head down. When he gained the ridge, he heard another crack and urged the mustang into a gallop. He knew he was out of the Henry's range now, but he wasn't taking any chances.

"Go, horse, go!" he yelled, wincing with the pain of the hot lead in his side.

He rode a twisting course through the sage flats and ravine-cut tables of the high desert country north of the Deadman. Buttes rose up around him, purple-shadowed in the gathering dusk. He rode between them, cutting this way, then that, and back again, not wanting to lose his pursuers but wanting to give them a damn hard time of tracking him.

He didn't think the wound was serious; the bullet hadn't seemed to hit anything vital, and it had gone all the way through. The pain was bad enough to water his eyes and tickle his loins, but the biggest problem was the bleeding. He knew he had to get it stopped before he grew too weak to ride.

After a half hour he stopped at Muggins Creek. Dismounting, he walked into the shallow water that rippled between thick stands of cattails and sawgrass, and opened his shirt, gently peeling the deerhide away from the soupy red wound.

"Nothin' serious," he told the grulla drinking nearby. "Just enough to hold me up and bedevil me, that's all."

He scooped water into the wound, brushing the jellied blood away with his fingers. When he'd cleaned it as well as he could without alcohol or whiskey, he padded the small, round hole in his left side and about six inches up from his belt with moss, then twisted his shirt and tied it aroung his waist, covering the wound. He figured a good, tight knot would apply enough pressure to stop the bleeding.

He'd been hit worse than this, he told himself, not acknowledging the fact that he was growing dizzy and his vision was dimming.

An odd picture of a man with a shirt banded around his waist and torso clad in only the tops of his longjohns, he mounted awkwardly, favoring the bad ankle and the hole in his side. He urged the grulla forward with a groan, fighting the growing weight of fatigue pushing his head down, and rode up out of the creek, mounting the cut bank.

But the horse had gone only about fifty yards when Nordstrom finally succumbed to the nausea and light-headedness and fatigue, and fell out of his saddle. He didn't feel the impact of his crippled body hitting the ground.

He was unconscious before his feet left the stirrups.

Only the horse noticed the riders approaching on the rim of the canyon above the creek—five barechested Indians in breechclouts and moccasins silhouetted against the salmon western sky.

Instinctually suspicious of strangers, the horse gave a start, bolting several steps forward. But it did not leave the prostrate body of its master.

It dipped its head, laid back its ears, stiffened its tail, and watched the strangers approach.

Nordstrom rose slowly out of a deep black pool. It was several minutes before he realized the pool was uncon-sciousness and that he was now half-awake. It was sev-eral more minutes before he realized the jolts he was feeling were due to movement.

He was moving. He was being moved.

The scraping against his left hand was rocks and tufts of sage. His hand was sliding along the ground.

Then the pool rose up again to swallow him in its

infinite black, and he was grateful. The burning pain in his side was nearly unbearable.

He woke again later to the warmth of a fire pressing against his cheek, the stench of raw alcohol, and the flavor of roasting meat. Opening his eyes, he saw that the sky above him was black and that glowing embers from a nearby fire were swallowed by it.

He lifted his head and saw four Indian braves in breechclouts sitting across the flames, legs crossed, sticks of roasted meat in their hands. They were passing a bottle.

Nordstrom felt his stomach sink. His first thought was that he'd been caught by rampaging Indians, and they were getting ready to torture and burn him.

Then another face floated into his field of vision. It was a familiar face, though Indian. He studied it, squinting.

The man knelt next to him and pulled the wool blanket down to Nordstrom's waist. The smell of the liquor was harsh in the rancher's nose. He saw that his shirt had been removed, and a thick mound of something wet and sticky had been placed over the wound in his side.

"Someone musta mistook you for a buffalo, Nordstrom. They stuck you good."

The rancher grunted a sardonic agreement to the comment, trying to place the voice, the big round face hovering over him with its ironic eyes and skin as red and weathered as old cedar. His long black hair was drawn tautly back from his temples. There was a necklace of grizzly claws around the thick neck, and lines had been painted high on the fleshy cheeks. Etched with battle and ceremonial scars, the man's raw-boned torso and rounded shoulders were bare.

He stuck a twisted shuck between his lips, squinting around the smoke, and fingered more of the sticky substance onto Nordstrom's side.

"Looks to me like a woman's work. Did a woman shoot you, Nordstrom?" The big Indian glanced at his compatriots across the fire.

"You're a real hoot, Hawk," Nordstrom grunted. Hawk Flying High, also known to the soldiers at Fort Phil Kearney, for whom the Indian once scouted, as Hawk Talking Too Much. Nordstrom once worked with the Indian on a government survey west of Fort Hall in Idaho.

Pushing the substance into the wound against Nordstrom's protestations, the Indian continued. "Squaws shoot their men when they aren't satisfied. Maybe white women, too, eh, Nordstrom? Maybe you didn't satisfy your woman and she shot you. Maybe aiming for your white balls, eh?"

Not all of the other four Indians seemed to understand their comrade's English, for only one was laughing. The others were smiling, though, apparently getting the gist of the ribbing if not the details.

"Leave it to me to get gutshot and saved by the windiest Indian north of the Bighorns."

Hawk set the pouch down and pulled up Nordstrom's blanket. The rancher realized for the first time that he was lying on a travois the Indians must have rigged up when they'd found him.

"Where's my horse?" he asked.

"Tied with ours in the trees. How you feelin'anyway, white man?"

"Been better."

"Who shot you?"

"An ornery hide hunter with a Henry rifle. Somethin' sure smells good and it ain't that concoction you're dressing me with, neither."

"This is an old Crow remedy for men shot by their women—fresh buffalo shit and firewater."

One of the men across the fire snorted a laugh.

Hawk plucked a stick out of the fire and held the rabbit skewered on the end out to the rancher. Nordstrom removed a piece of meat, burning his fingers but too hungry to care.

"Eat, my friend," Hawk said. "You want a drink of Happy Dancer's firewater?"

"Thought you'd never ask."

Hawk pointed at the bottle sitting at one of the brave's knees. When the brave had handed it over, Hawk gave it to Nordstrom after tipping it back himself.

Nordstrom took a conservative swig, knowing that if this was typical Indian firewater, he could be taking his life in his hands. But the liquor would help kill the pain, he figured.

Not bad. He took another, longer pull from the bottle, until one of the braves objected with a growl. He smacked his lips, corked the bottle, and returned it to Hawk, who tossed it across the fire.

"Good stuff," Nordstrom said, surprised.

"Happy Dancer knows a rich white woman who gives him her husband's liquor after Happy Dancer makes her happy. Rich white woman from Milestown, but she has no tits compared with our Crow squaws."

Hawk translated for Happy Dancer, who curled his nose and tipped back the bottle.

Hawk turned back to Nordstrom. "Get your strength back. They winged you good. If we wouldn't have come along, you would have bled dry. Wide Nose over there wanted to take your scalp and leave you, but I said no, that's Nordstrom. Me and him go back a ways. Him a good white man, and there aren't many good white men."

"No, there aren't, Hawk," Nordstrom agreed. "Where you headin', anyway?"

"South. The village moves. We are going ahead of the others and caching meat along the way."

"I reckon I owe you one."

Hawk looked at Nordstrom and grinned wistfully. "Happy Dancer thinks so, too. He wants your horse. I told him to settle for your tobacco." The grin broadened into a smile as Hawk brought the quirley to his lips and inhaled deeply.

Nordstrom returned the grin. "Tell him to stop by my ranch sometime. You know where it is—valley of the

Little Blue. I'll fix him up with a mustang that'll ride him to hell and back.''

Hawk turned to the men across the fire and spoke in Crow. When he finished, one of the brave's eyes brightened and he gave an excited howl, then muttered something in his tongue.

Hawk frowned and turned to Nordstrom.

"He said it would be better to steal it from you.''

Nordstrom grunted. "Tell him to save his vinegar for the men trackin' me. They might pay us a visit tonight. You'll all want to keep your eyes peeled. Pickin' me up, you picked up trouble for yourselves.''

In a sudden gesture, Hawk pulled his wide-bladed skinning knife from the scabbard hanging on his thigh and held it out for Nordstrom's inspection. "You forget what kind of fighter Hawk is, Nordstrom? No white man will dare enter my camp unless he wants one of my women to sweep out my lodge with his scalp.''

Nordstrom sighed and settled back on the travois. "Yeah, well, just the same—tell 'em to keep their eyes peeled, will ya? And tell 'em to leave my scalp alone, too.''

He tilted his hat down over his eyes and gave into the pain once more. The food had helped, and he hoped that by morning he'd be well enough to ride. He thought he'd be safe here with Hawk and the other hunters—as long as the men tracking him had a healthy fear of Indians.

And as long as the Indians didn't get too stinking drunk and turn on him.

He'd been in tighter spots, he told himself as he drifted off. Well . . . just as tight, anyway. . . .

18

Lang had been feeling edgy all morning.

He and the other emigrants had replaced the wheel on Kohl's wagon and they'd crossed the Deadman without incident, but Kohl's story about the shooting that had broken out as the farmer was leaving town had lifted the hair on the back of Lang's neck.

It was still standing a day and a half later.

Kohl hadn't taken the time to check out who was doing the shooting; he'd been too busy getting the hell out of there. But he was almost certain Nordstrom was involved. And that meant the renegades were no doubt involved, as well.

That's why Grace Lang's coaxing her husband to turn around and return home was especially irritating this morning. Lang was almost afraid enough to do it.

It would have made sense. He could return to Oakville and get his schoolmaster's job back, and Grace could return to work in her brother-in-law's farm supply store, where she'd put her good business sense to work managing the accounts. Lang could spend his days lecturing on the aesthetics of Shakespeare and Pope to the yawning, torpid youths of Oakville, his nights grading their inscrutable themes, and his weekends hunting ducks with his patronizing brother- and father-in-law who thought Shakespeare and Pope were brands of shotgun shells.

It would have been so easy to turn back. That's why Lang vowed not to do it, though he couldn't have explained the connection to Grace. She would have thought his reasons for not turning back as opaque as his reasons for wanting to go west in the first place. Free land and a new start meant nothing to her.

"We can't abandon the others," he told her now, appealing to her Christian sense of brotherhood as they rode mid-morning through an endless expanse of hogbacks.

"We wouldn't be abandoning them, John," Grace said with an air of extreme frustration. "We'd invite them to turn back with us, and if they didn't want to go, they'd be abandoning *us*."

"They have nothing to go back to, Grace. The major lost his plantation in the war and Kohl lost his farm—"

"To ignorance," Grace chuffed, finishing her husband's sentence.

Lang scowled and rolled his eyes.

"Anyway," Grace continued, "what do any of them have out here? What do *we* have out here?"

"We have . . . ," Lang said, searching for a way to express what he was thinking in a way his wife could understand. "We have . . . possibilities. . . ."

"*Oh!*" Grace exclaimed, thoroughly confounded by her husband's uncharacteristic obstinence. "I've never heard anything so stupid in my life!"

Lang offered no rebuttal. He'd die before he returned to Indiana. If Grace wanted to go back, that was up to her; he'd put her on the first stage they found. But he was going on with the others.

Ignoring Grace's exhortations, Lang watched the rolling country around them, the Townsend wagon kicking up dust a quarter mile ahead, and thought about their plight.

Where was Nordstrom? Was he alive? Lang had

hoped they'd run into a lawman somewhere along the trail, but he realized now it had been too much to hope for.

This was truly a lawless land. People were still making their own laws out here. They enforced them if they could, broke them when they wanted.

No one was safe. . . .

The thought gave Lang a heavy feeling in his loins, and it was not all bad. It was a feeling, anyway—which was more than he'd had in Indiana.

At noon the wagons pulled up to a narrow creek that ribboned through the prairie. Barely a trickle this time of year, it bore the skunky smell of decay, but there was a big lone cottonwood offering shade. There the tables were set up and food displayed—bread, cheese, pickled beef, and canned tomatoes. Coffee was started on a small fire.

Restless and nibbling a sandwich, Lang strolled around the camp, only half-listening to Grace trying to convince the others to turn back. There was a large rock in the high weeds upstream. Lang headed for it. He'd sit and eat his sandwich and enjoy a little peace and quiet.

But then a horseback rider appeared on the low grassy ridge on his left.

"Hello the camp! We've been lookin' *all over* fer you!"

It was a high, shrill man's voice, filled with irony and folly. It didn't take Lang long to realize whose it was. The man's ragged buckskins, insolent demeanor, and the casual way he sat his saddle, as though he were waiting for a long train to pass, said it all.

Lang pulled his beat-up old Colt from the waistband of his trousers and confronted the man defensively, his knees turning to putty.

"Easy there, Jesse James," the renegade said, opening his hand before him, then nodding to indicate another rider making his way down the ridge across the creek. "You shoot me, my friend over there is goin' to shoot you."

The other—a big man with a beard and a big, round hat—came on slowly with a rifle butt planted on his thigh. He didn't stop until he got to the creek. Then he just sat there, tipped his head, and looked over the camp like he was picking out a horse to steal. His big chestnut dipped its head to crop grass.

Lang turned to the wagons. Everyone had frozen, looking around dumbfoundedly. They'd been afraid for so long of this very moment that its actuality was like a dream.

Finally Grace howled, "Oh, my god!"

"Get under the wagons!" Townsend ordered the women.

Kohl ran to his driver's box and retrieved his Springfield rifle and held it close to his chest, looking around as if not quite sure what to do with it. His son just stood between the wagons, squinting against the harsh noon light.

Finally, he turned to see the Norwegian girl standing beside him, looking as though she'd fainted on her feet. He put his hand on her shoulder and moved her to the nearest wagon, then gently pushed her down and under the box. She succumbed stiffly and crouched behind the wheel, looking around with her long hair down around her shoulders, her hands grasping the spokes of the felloe like a prisoner. Nils scuttled beside her.

Lang had taken in the scene in only a few seconds, turning then quickly to see another rider downstream, moving toward Lang and the wagons behind him. A knife blade glinted from a torn sheath strapped under his shoulder.

There were only three, Lang thought. Unless the fourth was still hiding. He and the others would have a better chance against three. But how much better?

Lang lowered the pistol to his waist. He glanced again at the wagons, feeling naked out here by himself.

Where was Nordstrom?

"Take it easy now, folks," the first rider said. "All we want is the boy. You turn him over and we'll be on our way."

No one said anything for a long time. There was only the sound of the breeze in the grass.

The man tipped his head until his ear nearly touched his shoulder. "You all deaf over there? ... Give us the boy and we'll let the rest of ya go."

"Not a chance," Lang heard himself say.

The man studied him with a frown.

"You want to die?"

"No," Lang said.

"It sure sounds to me like you do."

There was another long silence. The horses shifted their weight and cropped grass. The mules stood in their traces looking indifferent. Ida Mary let out a sob—a sudden burst as though a hand had slipped from her mouth.

One of the mules jumped.

Mrs. Kohl screamed from under her wagon, "You can't have my boy!"

The man turned to her and cocked an eyebrow. "We're gonna take your boy one way or another, ma'am."

"No!" Mrs. Kohl screamed again, her voice cracking. "You can't ... you can't ... !"

The man laughed. "Well, sure we can."

"Take me!" Wilomene yelled. "You can have me!"

"Don't want you."

Lang's chest tightened when he saw the woman crawl slowly out from under the wagon with the little girl clawing at her dress.

"Wilomene!" Imbert Kohl yelled. "Get back!"

"Take me," the woman said again, pushing the screaming Ida Mary away. "Leave my boy alone!"

The Norwegian girl crawled out behind Wilomene and grabbed Ida Mary. "Please, Aunt Wilomene ... don't do dis!" she begged.

"Take me," the older woman pleaded, walking toward the man, who sat his horse frowning.

Imbert Kohl was yelling and squeezing his rifle and moving around in front of the mules.

Angry, the rider said, "I want the boy and I want him now."

The woman kept coming, one slow step after another, hands laced beneath her chin, begging the renegades to take her in place of her son. She was crying; tears streamed down her pale cheeks. The folds of her skirt blew against her legs. "Take me. . . . He's just a boy. . . ."

The other pilgrims yelled at her to stop. Mad with sorrow, she ignored them.

"Take me. . . . *Pleeeeeease!*"

Feeling his control slipping away, J.L. grew more and more incensed. His horse was starting to booger, jerking its head and lifting its tail. J.L. had to pull on the reins to keep from bolting or getting thrown.

The woman was about ten feet from him when he slipped both reins into his left hand, drew his pistol, and clicked back the hammer. Imbert Kohl was on the other side of his mules now, still yelling. When he saw the rider draw his pistol, Kohl lifted his rifle.

"No!" he barked, and squeezed off a round. The rifle cracked. The rider's hat flew off his head.

His horse lurched and twisted around, and the man pulled back on the reins, too busy with the horse to react to the shot. His face was flushed and creased with anger, his jaw set. His teeth flashed in his dark face beneath the white band left by his hat.

Awkwardly, the man followed the woman with his pistol, reaching around behind him as his horse turned and bucked. He steadied the weapon at the woman's forehead.

No, Lang thought, taking heavy, involuntary steps forward. Oh, my god . . . *no!*

The gun barked. Flames and smoked geysered from the barrel. Wilomene's head snapped back. She stopped in her tracks and crumpled.

Lang stopped, feeling his knees buckle. *Oh, sweet Jesus.*

Behind Mrs. Kohl, Corinne screamed.

"Wilomene!" Kohl yelled.

It had all happened so fast, Lang couldn't get his bearings or figure out what to do. He stood frozen for what seemed minutes, his legs shaking. Then he heard more gunfire and turned to see the other riders bearing down on the wagons with their carbines puffing smoke.

He raised his revolver and fired at the first rider. The man didn't so much as flinch at the wayward shot. He bore down on Lang and squeezed off two rounds; they whined around Lang's head like hornets. Lang fired again and ran to the wagons for cover.

Holding onto his frightened horse's reins, the first rider dismounted and casually picked up his hat. Heart thumping and dizzy with adrenaline, Lang ducked under a wagon and fired another round from behind the wheel, but his hands were shaking too much to hit anything.

The man smiled at Lang and snugged his hat on his head as casually as if he were out for a Sunday stroll. "Why, you couldn't hit the broad side of a barn from inside the barn!"

Lang's fear succumbing slightly to anger and frustration, he scowled and fired again. The bullet creased the man's shoulder, instantly transforming his expression to rage. "You fuck!"

"Fuck you!" Lang retorted, voice cracking.

Before he could get another round off, the man lifted his pistol quickly and fired. The slug tore into the wheel two inches from Lang's face, the sound of the impact clanging like an anvil in Lang's ears. Shrapnel from the slug and the wheel cut his cheek and neck.

In pain, he lowered his head. Guns popped around him. Ida Mary wailed and the women screamed. Lang lifted his eyes, wincing, blood dripping down his face. The gunman was moving forward on his horse, grinning. "Say your prayers," he said, and raised his pistol.

Lang's moment of courage had left him as suddenly as it had arrived. His fight was gone. He dropped his eyes, pressed his head against the ground, and waited for the end.

19

Nordstrom slept fitfully, the pain in his side keeping him from a good night's rest. He wished he'd had more of the firewater that had sent his camping companions into long, luxurious snores once they'd settled down.

He rose when dawn was still only a pearl smudge in the east, pushing himself carefully and painfully up from the travois, knowing the bullet wound could tear open and start bleeding again. But he didn't have the luxury of spending the day in his bedroll.

He needed to stay ahead of the renegades and find the emigrant wagons.

When he'd managed to climb to his feet and had gotten his land legs, he glanced around the camp and saw that all the Indians were gone, which meant he must have slept after all, for he hadn't heard them stir.

He saddled the grulla and rode east all morning, following creeks and ravines toward the old stock road he figured the emigrants had picked up across the Deadman River. The pain in his side came and went, but he thought it was giving some ground. He stopped often to spell his horse and to change the bandage, for the riding had set the wound to bleeding again, turning the bandage into a wet mess.

It was just after noon when he heard the distant cracks of intermittent gunfire, and spurred the grulla up a ridge lined with ponderosa pines and boulders. Below, in a gentling valley, a creek meandered through a narrow, shallow cutbank lined with cattails, scrub box elders, and occasional cottonwoods. In a horseshoe of the creek, under a big cottonwood, sat the wagons.

Around the wagons were three horseback riders, weapons drawn.

Nordstrom fired his pistol in the air and took off at a gallop. He slid his Winchester from the saddleboot under his thigh, took his reins in his teeth, and jacked a shell into the chamber. When he was about a hundred yards from the creek, smoke puffed and fire licked from the barrel of a raised rifle pointed his way. He lowered the Winchester and took aim at the horseman this side of the creek.

As he squeezed the trigger and the gun popped and kicked, he heard what sounded like Indian war whoops. Swinging a look to his right, he saw four Crow warriors descend the ridge into the valley toward the wagons, hair flying out behind them, rifles popping, the hooves of their horses rumbling like distant thunder and kicking up dust and sod.

Nordstrom recognized Hawk and his three hunting companions, and felt the knot in his gut loosen a little. They, too, had heard the gunfire and had come to help.

After seeing the Indians, it didn't take the renegades long to light a shuck out of there. Suddenly they were outmanned, outgunned, and outflanked. The man nearest Nordstrom rode downstream at a gallop, keeping his head down and slapping his mount with a quirt. The other two bolted over the ridge behind the wagons, the Indians about sixty yards behind them.

Nordstrom touched the grulla with his spurs and galloped across the creek, slowing to a canter when he reached the camp. He knew instantly that someone had been shot, for the little girl was screaming and a strange hush had settled over the other pilgrims. Nordstrom's heart banged when he thought of Corinne.

Rounding the wagons, he saw her kneeling and Imbert

Kohl standing over the body of his prone wife. Corinne was hunched over the woman sobbing. The little girl, Ida Mary, pulled at her mother's hand and screamed.

"How bad's she hit?" Nordstrom asked automatically.

No one offered a reply and, moving closer, Nordstrom needed none. He dismounted and stepped up beside Kohl. At the farmer's feet his wife lay with a bullet-sized hole in her temple from which dark red blood gushed. The woman's chin was tipped back and to the side. Her eyes were half-open and glazed with death.

"For Christ's sake," Nordstrom muttered, feeling sick.

Kohl turned to him with wild, baffled eyes. Sweat beaded his face. "They *killed* her," he said, as though trying to absorb the fact himself.

Although Kohl watched him as if waiting for an explanation, Nordstrom knew from experience there was nothing he could say that would make any difference.

Finally, to fill the silence, he said, "God, I'm sorry, Kohl," knowing how wooden it sounded.

They stood there for several more minutes. The major and Douglas and Cynthia Townsend came out and stood behind them.

"Oh, my god," Cynthia said quietly, clutching a handkerchief to her mouth.

Nils appeared, walking slowly with his head down. He knelt beside Corinne, hands on his thighs, and observed the dead face of his mother, his eyes flat with mute emotion.

When Corinne pulled the little girl away and took her back to the wagon against her wailing protestations, Nordstrom said, "I'll bury her for you, Kohl."

"We both will," John Lang said, coming up beside the rancher.

Kohl just stood there, soundlessly moving his lips and looking down at his dead wife with that same white look of incomprehension.

"I'll bury my wife," he growled at length.

He knelt down and shoved his left hand under the woman's neck, his right under her knees. Grunting, he stood, stumbling a little with the weight. Blood strung in the bending grass. Kohl moved forward slowly, the woman's head and legs bobbing stiffly as he carried her off.

"That poor woman," Lang said. "She was just trying to save her son. . . . Who were the Indians, anyway? They saved my life. Saved all the rest of us for sure."

"Friends of mine. They'll give those savages a taste of their own medicine—you can be sure of that."

Turning to him, Nordstrom saw that the school-teacher's face and neck were matted with blood. "You need some attention there," Nordstrom said.

Lang dropped his eyes to Nordstrom's side. "So do you."

"Later," the rancher said, retrieving his dangling reins. "I'm gonna go give Hawk and his pals a hand."

He poked his boot in his left stirrup and felt his right knee buckle. Lang grabbed him.

"I don't think you're goin' anywhere for a while, Nordstrom."

Nordstrom pressed his face against the saddle and gave a sigh. "I think you're right, teacher."

Nordstrom rested for an hour, then walked down through the weeds to the creek. He struggled out of his buckskin tunic and tossed it aside. Kneeling, he cupped the murky water to the wound, cleaning it.

"You need stitches," said a female voice behind him.

He turned and saw Corinne. Her face was pale with the horror of what she had just seen, but there was a strength there, as well. A practical sense.

"Come. I will stitch it closed."

"It's not bad," Nordstrom said. "It'll heal on its own."

She shook her head and sucked her upper lip. "It will not stop bleeding until it is stitched."

She turned and walked back up the bank to where

Nordstrom had set up his camp. The grulla stood nearby, eating grass. The saddle lay beside him on the ground.

Nordstrom grabbed his shirt and threw it over his shoulder. He followed Corinne up the bank. "You know how to stitch?" he asked her.

"What woman does not know how to stitch?" she said. "Sit down."

He did as he was told, looking skeptical. Corinne produced needle and thread from a pocket in her skirt and knelt beside him. "You have a match?"

Nordstrom reached into his saddlebags and pulled out a box of lucifers.

"I'm sorry about Mrs. Kohl," he said. "I'm sorry about . . . everything," he added with a shrug, feeling stupid. How could he ever sympathize with this girl, so far from home? How he could ever imagine how she felt?

Corinne struck a match. Cupping it in her hand, she ran it up and down the needle, scorching it, then let the breeze snuff the flame. "Lay back," she said.

Nordstrom lay back on his elbows, watching the needle and bracing himself.

"This will hurt," she warned.

Nordstrom lifted his eyes from the needle to the girl's face, concentrating on the firm white flesh of her cheeks and neck, the blueness of her eyes, the milky valley between her breasts, which he could not help stealing a look at when she bent over him and her dress fell away from her neck.

He feasted on details—a freckle about two inches down from her left ear, a tiny mole at the base of her throat. She pinched the tattered flesh around the bullet hole, poked it with the needle, and pulled the thread through.

Nordstrom yelped.

"It hurts?"

"I'll say!"

"I told you it would hurt."

She worked slowly and deliberately, as though stitching a pillow cover, occasionally glancing at his face for signs of pain. There was no more soothing sight than hers, no lovelier visage, no feeling more comforting than her long tawny hair brushing his naked chest as she worked.

"It still hurts?"

"It's getting better," Nordstrom said, able to smile.

"It doesn't?"

He smiled and shook his head.

"Now turn over," she said, finishing with the entrance wound and cutting the thread with her teeth. He found the act arousing despite his pain.

He turned onto his left side so she could stitch the exit wound. He crooked his elbow and rested his head in his hand.

"Ouch!" he said, feeling the prick of the needle piercing the tender flesh.

"I thought you said it didn't hurt."

"I can't see you from this angle."

The needle poked him again, and as he felt the thread pulled taut, he squelched a yell.

"*They* shot you?" she asked.

"Yes," he replied, knowing who "they" were. "But I don't think they'll be causing any more trouble. Not after those Crow hunters get done with them, anyway. They may give the whiskey traders more business than they should, but they're still Crows. Only thing deadlier's a Flathead."

When she said nothing in reply, he turned to see her face. It was creased with concern.

"It's OK, Corinne. Those men are dead. You're safe—or as safe as you can be out here."

"I don't know," she said thoughtfully. "Evil is hard to kill. . . ."

Five minutes later she finished with the stitches. She cut the thread again with her teeth, wiped the blood from the needle with her fingers, and brushed her hand in the grass. She produced a roll of gauze from her pocket and wrapped it around his waist. He felt her warm breath on his back, the gentle caress of her hands, as she slipped the gauze under his side and pulled it through and tied it.

"Thanks," he said.

He turned and caught her staring at him. Her eyes were warm and wanting, her full lips slightly parted. "I am so frightened," she whispered.

He knew she felt as lonely and displaced as she did frightened, but he said, "There's nothing to be afraid of anymore, Corinne."

"I have been afraid for so long, I don't know what it is to not be afraid."

In his mind, he reached out, took her face in his hands, and kissed her . . . felt her full lips press against his.

In reality, he reached into his saddlebags, pulled out a spare buckskin tunic, and dropped it over his head. "You best get back to the Kohls," he said tersely. "They'll be wonderin' where you are."

A shadow swept her face. She frowned. "But . . ."

"Thanks for the doctorin'," he said, turning away and wincing. He would have given anything to have known her in a different time and a different place.

But here and now was hopeless.

He turned back to explain but she was already gone.

20

Before dark, Nordstrom climbed the ridge behind the wagons and looked around. The sun had fallen behind the western buttes, and long shadows stretched across the prairie. Sweeping his eyes across the sage-strewn hills gashed with black rock, he decided that he and the others were alone out here, and relatively safe.

Part of him regretted that safety. It meant he wouldn't get his chance to give the renegades their due, and that's what had driven him since he'd found Charlie's body. Now he felt wayward and hollow. Where would he go? What would he do?

The obvious answer was to go back to his ranch and build a new cabin before the snow flew, but the thought of returning to the graves, the charred cabin, and the rotting carcasses of his dead mustangs went down like camphor.

He sat down and smoked a cigarette, watching the shadows thicken and the moon become a polished silver coin in the east. After long thought, he decided to head for Milestown at first light. A friend of his owned a ranch that way. Nordstrom knew he could work there until he had enough cash to fill his larder.

He gave no thought to Corinne. No conscious thought, anyway. He could not deny that he felt a connection with

the girl, but there was no room for her in the life the
renegades had left him.

Returning to his camp, he moved the grulla to fresh
grass and turned in, resting his head against his saddle
and bringing his blanket up to his chin. He woke up
suddenly in the dark. Something rustled the grass
nearby.

He threw off the blanket, grabbed his revolver, and
crept into the weeds, crouching and waiting. A figure
appeared—the silhouette of a man holding a rifle.
Soundlessly, Nordstrom moved toward the figure and
snugged his pistol behind the man's ear.

"Evenin', Major. Out for a walk?"

The man stiffened. The rifle sagged. He turned his
head. "That's right . . . out for a walk."

"Nice night for it, but kinda dark for shootin', don't
you think?"

The major didn't say anything, but Nordstrom could
hear him breathing.

"I know what you're up to, Major, and to tell you the
truth, I don't blame you. I tell you what I'll do. I'll turn
around and you can finish me right here and now."

He gave the major his back. After a few seconds, he
heard the hammer of the major's old muzzle loader clatter back. He stealed himself for the bullet. The major
breathed heavily. After several seconds, he gave a grunt,
cursed, and depressed the hammer. Nordstrom heard him
walk away through the grass, and turned to watch him
go.

Beleaguered, he decided to light out before the others
rose. He drew on his boots, gathered his gear, and saddled his horse. Pointing the grulla south and letting the
horse choose his path in the dark, he rode up the ridge
and onto the flatland beyond.

It was full light when he smelled something foul on
the wind. It was a sickly sweet stench he couldn't place.
A quarter hour later he saw five stationary figures in the
distance, about six feet apart. White dust swirled near
the ground around them.

Nordstrom got a dark feeling. He put his horse into a gallop and rode over.

"Oh, my god," he whispered, reigning the grulla to a halt. Climbing slowly from his saddle, he cupped his bandanna over his mouth to muffle the overpowering stench of burned flesh and peered unbelievingly at the horrific image before him: five half-burned humans tied to posts.

The five heads sagged forward, wisps of long black hair—Indian hair—sliding around the blistered skulls over which the cooked skin had cracked and melted, oozing a thin red fluid. The bare torsos were similarly charred and cracked, the skin peeling away from the muscles and bones so that the affect was of half-revealed skeletons. What was left of their moccasins mingled with the ashes of the brush and branches that had been piled around and set aflame.

Nordstrom took short breaths through his mouth, fighting the vomit his stomach was trying to force into his throat.

The outstanding size of the man farthest left was all that told him it was Hawk. *Had been* Hawk. The man's lips had been burned away, revealing the roots of his teeth as if in a sneer.

Still cupping his bandanna to his mouth, Nordstrom stood frozen. His ears rang, and his tongue tasted coppery. Regaining his senses, he turned to look around him, drawing his pistol.

The renegades could be nearby, but Nordstrom saw only endless expanses of sage-bristled prairie dotted with buttes under big, white clouds aglow with autumn sunlight. The clouds swept shadows all around, adding to Nordstrom's muddlement.

There were no renegades in sight.

Which meant they were after the pilgrims! The thought hit Nordstrom like a hammer, and he swung into the saddle and galloped the grulla back in the direction from which he had come.

Varying his speed to keep the horse from playing out,

Nordstrom got back to the emigrants' camp in an hour. As he had suspected, the wagons had already left, leaving a smoldering breakfast fire and the freshly mounded grave of Mrs. Kohl on a small hill. A rough cross was the only marker. A brown blotch in the grass marked where the poor woman had fallen.

Nordstrom rode north for half an hour and came upon the Kohl and Lang wagons in a wide, grassy flat west of a rocky bench strewn with wind-stunted pines. The wagons were moving single file, following a deep-cut trail. The thick dust smelled like dried buffalo dung.

"Where are the Townsends?" Nordstrom demanded, reining his horse to a skidding stop beside Imbert Kohl's wagon, about fifty yards behind Lang's.

Kohl indicated north with a nod. "They vamoosed before sunup. The major was all agitated, said he needed to get movin'."

"What's the matter, Nordstrom?" Lang called from ahead, peering around his covered wagon box.

"The renegades are still on the prowl," Nordstrom said as he rode past. "Keep your weapons handy and your eyes peeled. I'm gonna ride ahead and warn the major."

Following the tracks of the major's party, he spurred the grulla ahead and into a narrow crease between benches that sloped into a canyon with eroded walls pocked with swallows' nests. A spring bubbled in a rocky hollow. He halted the grulla for a blow and a drink.

Antsy, he walked around the horse, peering up at the canyon walls, knowing he was a sitting duck down here. But the major had come this way. By the wheel marks gouged in the mud around the spring, Nordstrom knew the major and his son and Cynthia had stopped for water—about an hour ago, it appeared.

Continuing on, he kept his eyes on the ridges widening and narrowing around him. He galloped through a buffalo herd, scattering the cumbersome beasts in every direction. A prairie dog chortling or a porcupine

rustling the dry grass was enough to spook him. Even
the grulla jumped, his senses bristling at the nearly pal-
pable evil here.

Where the trail dipped to a dry creekbed, a horse appeared sniffing a dogwood. As he rode near, Nordstrom
recognized the major's gold stallion, Windjammer. The
horse was bridled but saddleless. The reins dangled as
he tentatively lowered his muzzle to forage the grass
around the shrub, a skittish cast in his eyes.

"What the hell's goin' on here, boy?" Nordstrom
asked the horse, the blood chilling in his veins.

He tied the major's horse to his saddle and continued
north. A quarter hour later, riding out of a grassy swale
that swung westward, he saw a wagon cover about a
mile ahead. It was not moving, and as Nordstrom rode
closer he saw the wagon lying on its side, its contents
strewn. The mules were gone. Apparently the frightened
beasts had ripped the wagon tongue from the undercar-
riage and fled.

Riding amid the wreckage, Nordstrom found the major by a boulder, his head and chest a mass of blood.
No telling how many times he'd been shot. A meaty red
swath covered with flies was all that remained of his
hair.

Nordstrom followed the tracks of the other wagon on
foot, his rifle held up close to his chest. He found the
other van in a shallow ravine about a hundred yards
ahead. It lay on its side, the cover torn away to expose
the broken hickory bows, both mules dead and hideously
twisted.

Running and sliding down the eroded bank, he
jumped onto the overturned wagon and found Douglas
Townsend crushed beneath, only his torso visible above
the box, arms flung out above his head, teeth bared in a
silent scream. Like the major, his hair had been lifted
with a hasty thrust of a bowie, leaving a ghastly wound,
black and abuzz with insects.

Nordstrom looked around and called for Cynthia. He

peered around both wagons and scoured the brush. Nothing.

When his adrenaline settled down and he could think, he looked for tracks and saw that she'd run up the ravine, three men walking behind her. She'd stumbled in a foxhole, and run on, plunging into a hawthorn thicket. Swatches of torn clothes clung to branches.

Pushing through the thicket, holding the spiky limbs away with his rifle barrel, Nordstrom stopped suddenly and stifled a yell. Like cats toying with a mouse until they'd had their fill of fun, the renegades had caught up to her here.

He swallowed to keep from vomiting and turned away from the blood-soaked clothes hanging in the branches. He'd taken two steps when he heard a low, almost inaudible gurgle behind him.

He turned back. His eyes widened. Blood banged in his head.

She was still alive.

Nordstrom brought his rifle up in one quick motion and fired, silencing the horrible sounds rising from the shrubs. Cursing, he turned and stumbled out of the brush. He fell to his knees, pressed his fists to the ground, and retched.

What he'd only surmised since his wife's slow, agonized death he knew now to be unequivocally true:

There was no God.

Nordstrom rode south with his eyes riveted on every shrub, tree, and boulder he passed. He knew from the hair standing on the back of his neck that he was being watched, and that an ambush was imminent.

The ominous feeling in his bones was validated when a shot rang out and a bullet buzzed past his face and spanked the butte on his other side with a twang. He hunched low in the leather and put the grulla into a gallop, weaving to make as hard a target as possible. Swinging a look up the low volcanic cone to his right, where the shot had come from, he saw nothing.

He galloped unharassed for a mile, then stopped to give the grulla a blow. He looked quickly around. Where were they? What were they doing? He was beginning to feel like the mouse in their game, and he didn't like it a bit.

He shucked his Winchester, jacked a shell, and fired into the air.

"Come on out here and fight like men!"

The only reply was the ringing of the mustang's shod hooves on stone as he moved out, and the rasp of the wind funneling between the buttes.

A few minutes later the emigrant party—what was left of it—appeared cresting a knoll. Nordstrom could see Lang in the driver's box, his white-bandaged face glowing against his sunburn.

"Where's the major?" the teacher said as he halted his mules, scrutinizing Townsend's horse with a frown.

"Didn't make it."

"What?"

"Neither did Douglas and Cynthia."

"Oh, my God," Lang said softly, expelling a slow sigh. "What happened?"

Nordstrom shook his head. He looked as grim and ragged as he felt. He slouched in the saddle, hands crossed on the saddle horn. "You don't want to know. Any sign of the renegades?"

Still whirling from the news, Lang's face was pale with shock. "No," he said absently. His eyes found Nordstrom. They blinked several times. "Maybe . . . maybe they don't know where we are."

Nordstrom gave a grunt. "They know exactly where we are," he said, wrinkling his nose in a savage grimace. "They ain't attacking 'cause they've had their fill for the day. But they will come after us soon enough—you can count on it." He hooked a thumb over his shoulder, to where a broad, blue mesa shelved into the valley, its base strewn with boulders. "Let's head for that high ground there and set up camp."

"Kind of out in the open, isn't it?"

"We need high ground, Mr. Lang. Out here in these buttes, we're just like ducks in a row. No sense makin' it any easier for 'em than it already is."

The teacher shrugged. "If you say so."

Nordstrom rode back and told Kohl the plan, then loped ahead, scouting a trail up the mesa's east side. It was rocky and pocked with gopher holes, but the mules threw their shoulders into the work as though they sensed the danger behind them.

Near dark, the party reached the flat, grassy cap of the mesa and set up camp. Nordstrom unsaddled his horse and hobbled it on the east side, knowing the horse would warn them if danger approached from that direction.

"Will there be a fire tonight?"

Nordstrom turned from the horse to see Corinne standing only a few feet away. Her big eyes regarded him coolly. He felt a flutter in his chest, a tightening in his stomach. The sun was a purpling flame behind her, the grass a silver rug buffeting shadows.

"Sure, why not?" he said with a shrug. No doubt the renegades had seen where they'd gone. There could be no harm in a fire.

She nodded, lingering. Then she dropped her gaze, turned, and walked away.

"Corinne," he called. But she did not turn back.

Repelled by his longing, Nordstrom watched the girl disappear among the wagons, then hefted his saddle with a curse and went looking for a place to spread his bedroll.

Later, he accepted the supper Mrs. Lang offered, and ate with her husband and Kohl beside the Kohl wagon. He was aware of Corinne and Mrs. Lang moving around him putting food away, washing dishes, and spreading blankets, but he did not regard the girl directly.

Nils sat in the shadows, quiet and thoughtful as always, cleaning a rifle. Ida Mary sat at his feet, staring and silent. In the distance a wolf howled. Nordstrom and the other two men ate without speaking.

Finally, Kohl said, "You can see a long ways from up here, but we're gonna have to go down sometime."

"Tomorrow," Nordstrom said. "And we're gonna be a hell of a lot lighter and a hell of a lot faster."

"What're you talkin' about?"

"At first light we abandon the wagons, ride out on mules."

Kohl nearly jumped out of his chair, spilling beans from his plate. "The hell you say! All I own's in the back o' them wagons!"

Lang chimed in, agreeing. "There's no way you're gonna get Grace on a mule, Nordstrom. And like Kohl says, everything we own is back there."

"Must be some mighty valuable stuff," Nordstrom said.

"It is," Kohl said.

"Worth your lives?"

Lang looked away, thoughtful. Kohl stared at Nordstrom darkly.

The rancher said, "Those renegades are going to attack us tomorrow, sure as shit in a stock barn. And if we stay with the wagons, we'll have no chance of escape."

"I'm not leavin' my wagons," Kohl said stiffly.

"Then you'll die with them." Nordstrom rose and threw the rest of his coffee on the fire. "I'm leavin' at dawn. Whoever's goin' with me better be on a mule at that time . . . and ready to ride for their lives."

21

J.L. heard something and came awake with a start, drawing his gun.

Pete Hill jumped back and raised his hands. "Jesus Christ, J.L.—I only threw some kindlin' on the fire!"

Blinking sleepily, J.L. depressed the hammer and smiled. "You just about bought it, Pete. I just about greased ya."

"What's goin' on?" Big Jim said, lifting his shaggy head from his saddle.

"Nothin'." J.L. hawked phlegm from his throat and reached for his tobacco pouch and papers. "I just about plugged Pete is all. Thought he was one of them Injuns come back from the dead. Pilgrims still up there, Pete?"

"I ain't took my eyes off that mesa since first light. They're still there. Must be sleepin' in this mornin'."

"They're feelin' pretty safe, I s'pose—sitting up nice and high so's they can see us when we come for 'em." J.L. gave a grunt, eyes on the quirley he was shaping with his fingers. "Or so they think."

He pushed himself up against a rock and smoked leisurely, a soft light coming into his eyes as he remembered the sounds of yesterday—the men yelling, the woman screaming, the Indians chanting their death songs as the flames licked their bare thighs. J.L. didn't know why, but killing Indians and lifting scalps always gave him a thrill. It made him feel like he was the biggest, meanest *hombre* in the whole world.

He almost wished that trash his mother had married back in Missouri when J.L. was five was still alive, so J.L. could kill him all over again, and take his scalp. Just like he'd done when he was fourteen, just like he'd read about the Injuns doing out West. Only now he'd burn him at the stake, to boot.

His thoughts turned to the girl they'd killed yesterday. . . . My god, the girl! A real Southern belle! He and the boys probably shouldn't have messed her up like they had. They could have sold her to some Indians for a pretty string of mustangs. Or they could have taken her up to Canada and sold her to that little Frenchman who ran the hogpen on the Milk. He paid cash money, J.L. knew. But then, Frenchy preferred chink women, said white women didn't take to the strap like the chinks did.

J.L. flicked away his quirley and stood. Stretching, he made a mental note to consider the Frenchman when they caught up to the Norski girl. Frenchy might prefer chinks, but he hadn't seen the girl riding with the pilgrims.

When J.L., Jim, and Pete had broken camp and saddled up, they followed a draw to the base of the mesa. It was mid-morning, and the sun was before them, but J.L. didn't think it mattered. The rancher was the only one who'd probably know to take advantage of the sun's position. The others would be standing around with their thumbs up their asses while J.L. and the boys filled them with lead.

He thought of the kid who'd crept into their camp the night they'd attacked the Norski girl, and slit Dew's throat. J.L.'s heart thumped as he imagined what he was going to do to that kid in just a few short minutes. A smile grew on his dark face.

When they'd ridden out of the draw and climbed a bench that gave them a good view of the mesa's top, the grin faded. There were only two wagons sitting, wagon tongues drooping, among the rocks and short grass. He

saw neither hide nor hair of the pilgrims or a single
mule. The breeze kicked up cold ashes from a long-
defunct breakfast fire.

"What the jesus, Pete? I thought you said you were
keeping an eye on 'em!"

"I . . . I was, J.L."

All horns and rattles, J.L. looked at him. "No, Pete,
you were lookin' at two wagons. Two fucking wagons!
The pilgrims slipped right out from under your nose."

"They musta piled in one wagon, and headed out
early," Jim put in.

Pete moved his lips and studied the mesa, but no
words came out.

"Save it, shit-for-brains," J.L. said, touching his
horse with his spurs and starting down the bench.

When they'd climbed the mesa to find the camp de-
serted, as expected, J.L. removed his hat and scratched
his scalp, smiling confoundedly. Pete watched him warily.

"Sorry, J.L."

J.L. sat his horse smiling at Pete. He shook his head
and snugged his hat back on, securing the strap under
his chin.

"Jesus Christ, J.L.," Jim yelled from behind the wagons. "They left their plunder!"

"They did, did they?"

"Come on!"

"You go ahead, Jim." J.L. turned his horse to look
over the valley. Far away in the breezy distance, the
white blotch of a covered wagon crept northwest.

"Yeah, you go ahead, Jim. You and shit-for-brains
help yourselves to all those jewels. Me, I got scores to
settle . . . and a little Norski girl to get re'quainted
with."

Driving his wagon through a valley where old volcanoes
stood sentinel, where a single hawk soared over his
head, and where rattlers thick as fence posts sunned

themselves on occasional rocks lining the trail, Imbert
Kohl felt like the last man on earth.

His son, niece, and daughter were riding muleback
with the others. They'd refused to join him in the wagons, and there wasn't a goddamn thing Kohl had been
able to do about it.

"Good riddance to all of ya, ya goddamn sheep!" he
yelled to the silent prairie. One of the mules turned its
head and rolled an eye at him.

Kohl's blood boiled as he thought of what Nils
had said when Kohl had told him to harness the mules
to his wagon: "Pa...I...I...wanna go with them,
Pa...!"

The boy nodded at Nordstrom and Lang, wrestling
hackamores over mules' ears in the light of the breakfast
fire.

Kohl had given the boy a savage scowl. "You'll do
as I tell ya!"

Nils swallowed. "I don't wanna die, Pa."

"You won't die as long as you do as I say. Now, get
your cousin and your sister into the wagons and help
me harness the mules."

Brainwashed by Mrs. Lang, Ida Mary gave a howl
and clung to the big woman's skirts. That's when Nordstrom intervened.

"Leave it up to the boy, Kohl. He's old enough to
make up his own mind about livin' and dyin'."

Kohl wheeled to face the rancher. "This ain't none
of your business. Stay out of it!"

"If you want to commit suicide, go ahead. But you
can't expect your family to go along."

"I told you, this ain't none of your business!"

Nordstrom gritted his teeth and kept his voice low.
"I'm making it my business."

"You're the one in charge, that it?"

Nordstrom made no reply. He said to Nils, "Why
don't you ready two mules for you and Corinne?"

"Those are my mules, and I'll say how they're used,"
Kohl barked, fisting his hands and taking a step toward

Nordstrom. "And I say they'll be harnessed to my wagons."

Nordstrom stared at Kohl. He moved forward until he stood only a foot away from the farmer, and spoke calmly. "We're taking two of your mules—one for Nils, one for Corinne. That means you'll have to leave one of your wagons, and that's too bad, but those are the cards you've drawn. Now you're welcome to join us. If not, stay out of our way."

Nordstrom turned back to his work. Kohl lunged at him. Nordstrom wheeled, deflected Kohl's fist with his forearm, turned, and wrapped his muscular arm around the man's neck, immobilizing him.

In a split second he had his knife at Kohl's throat. The farmer was panting and wheezing and cursing through gritted teeth, spittle stringing from his chin.

"We don't have time for this kind of foolishness," Nordstrom said into Kohl's ear, pressing the point of the knife into the gray stubble over his jugular. "You either join us or stay out of our way. I won't tell you again."

He released the farmer and shoved him aside. Kohl stumbled backward and fell against his wagon. Chest heaving, face flushed, he massaged his neck and glowered at the rancher. "This is stock theft. You'll hang, Nordstrom."

Then he brushed himself off and angrily began harnessing his mules.

"Go ahead, you pantywaists!" he yelled now at the hawk tipping its wings high over his head. He was still incensed by the indignity he'd suffered, still brooding over his family's rebellion. "I'll see ya all in hell!"

They were about three miles ahead of him now, he figured. They'd left the camp before he did, and they were traveling about three times faster. But the way Kohl saw it, abandoning the wagons was a shameful display of weakness. He'd be goddamned if he'd let those savages murder his wife *and* steal his plunder *and* see him run with his tail between his legs.

It was time to draw a line in the sand.

Approaching a rimrock, he stood in the wagon box to look for Nordstrom's trail. He'd lost it a half mile back in a hollow. Seeing something out of the corner of his eye, he turned his head to scan the prairie rolling south to a willow copse and beyond to several low hills and then more woods and a high, flat-topped ridge tracing a creek bed.

He brought his eyes back to the willows and, squinting, made out a small cluster of dark dots before them. Staring, he saw that the dots were three men on horseback. Kohl reached for the rifle beside him, brought it to his chest, and turned back to the dots.

They were gone.

"What the hell?" he growled, twisting around to look behind.

He scanned eastward. Nothing. Only a coyote slipping over a knoll and tossing a sheepish look behind. The riders had disappeared as quickly as they'd shown themselves.

But they could have been deer, Kohl thought. Or antelope or elk or even bear, for that matter. He hadn't gotten a good look, and his imagination could have been playing tricks. But as he set his rifle down and flicked the reins lightly against the mules' backs, he knew deep down that the dots had been the renegades.

All doubt faded when, an hour later, he heard the crack of a rifle and turned to look behind him. About a half mile away three dark-faced, buckskin-clad men sat their mounts about fifty yards apart, rifle barrels pointing at the sky. They were sitting still, watching him.

Kohl slapped the reins and yelled, putting the mules into a lope. He knew he couldn't outrun them, but this was no place for a fight. As the wagon bounced crazily over rocks, gopher holes, and prickly pear, nearly throwing him out, he scanned the distance for cover.

About five miles ahead was a range of purple hills. Swinging a look right, he saw a ravine, but the rocks between here and there would tear the wagon apart.

Nearby, there was nothing—no cover for a wagon, no high ground from which to make a stand.

Kohl's heart pounded, and he felt a stone grow in his throat. He tossed a look behind him, expecting to see the renegades closing. He was surprised to see that they were not there. He looked around, eyes sharp with fear. He rubbed his chin and pursed his lips, thoughtful.

Once again they had vanished.

Not taking any chances, he continued a breakneck pace for the hills. When he'd followed a twisting trail around the first rise, he halted the wagon in a dry wash, grabbed his rifle and ammo pouch, and ran back up to the ridge.

He fell to his chest three feet from the top, and brought up his rifle. Lifting his head above the hill's grassy crest, the smell of sage sharp in his nose, he surveyed his backtrail. The sere-brown prairie, relieved by swales, bowls, and hummocks, was empty. The wagon trail followed a pale course disappearing over the first knoll and reappearing on another a quarter mile away.

The renegades were not there. The only dust he saw was that which his own wagon had kicked up.

"They're comin', I know they're comin'," Kohl growled, hearing the blood wash in his ears. His lungs felt like sandpaper from his run up the ridge. He lifted his hat, ran a thick hand over his thinning, sweat-matted hair, and cursed. "Come on, come on, goddamnit! Let's get on with it!"

A rifle cracked. A bullet thudded the grass near his elbow. He gave a startled yell and turned. The three renegades stood on the acclivity behind, aiming their rifles. All three weapons puffed smoke. The reports were nearly simultaneous.

The slugs tore into the grass only inches from the farmer. He felt their impact with the ground, smelled the dust and hot lead.

Yelling, Kohl buried his head in his arms. Another rifle cracked. Kohl's hat flew off. As far as he could tell, he hadn't been hit. Another rifle exploded. The slug hit the wagon with a wooden thunk.

They were toying with him.

Kohl lifted his head, reached for his rifle, brought it to bear, and fired blindly at the ridge behind him. He scrambled to his feet and ran over the hilltop. He hit the ground on the other side, laid the old single-shot Springfield across his knees, and reached into his pouch for ammo.

Reloading, he poured powder down the barrel, pushed the bullet home with his thumb, drew the ramrod, and pushed the projectile down. Pulling back the hammer, he fit the percussion cap to the nib, then swung the barrel up over the hill's brow and snugged his cheek to the butt, aiming.

There was nothing on the ridge but windblown grass. Above the grass, sky. The renegades were gone.

"You sons o' bitches," Kohl said weakly.

He lay there for a long time, looking around and trying to work up the nerve to stand. Finally, he pushed himself to his feet, blinking his eyes and jerking his head around. He swallowed and licked his lips.

"Tryin' to drive me nuts, that it?"

He gave a plaintive sigh and walked back down to his wagon. He heard water puddling and saw that they'd shot a hole in his water barrel, which meant he would have to camp by a creek tonight.

Face pale with fear, he climbed weakly onto the wagon and headed out. He took several deep breaths to calm his nerves, but it was no use. His knees trembled, his hands were slick with sweat, and his stomach felt as though he'd chugged a gallon of bad milk.

The next several hours of travel were miserable. He knew the renegades could appear out of nowhere at any second, and he grew half-mad with dread and anticipation. The horror was no less pointed for his knowing it was all part of their plan. Like kids pulling legs off a spider, they were having fun.

At sunset he camped in an arroyo near a spring and

picketed his mules in a cottonwood grove. He built a small fire in a cleft, put coffee on to boil, and sliced bacon into a pan. Although he was not hungry, he knew he had to eat.

He jumped at every night sound lifting from the darkness. His chest felt tight and raw.

Finally, he curled two strips of bacon into a dry biscuit and poured a cup of coffee. Scuttling into the cleft and pressing his back against the rock wall, he finally felt his nerves ease. His stomach loosened a notch.

A minute later a rock rolled down the ledge above him and landed at his feet. He gave a start, put his hand on his rifle stock. A branch snapped in the tangled shrubs and stones across the fire. In the chill night air the sound carried like a gunshot.

Someone laughed tauntingly, close enough to rattle Kohl's eardrums. He grabbed his rifle, scrambled to his feet, and peered into the darkness. He dredged up his voice from deep in his chest.

"OK . . . I've had enough o' this! Come out and show yourselves!"

The laughter came again. They were moving around in the darkness, circling the fire. Kohl heard a boot kick a stone.

A scream lifted behind him. He turned and fired, the kick of the Springfield knocking him back a step.

Taking another step back from the fire, he reached into his ammo pouch and frantically reloaded, spilling as much powder as he poured down the barrel.

"Never shoulda let that boy kill my brother," a man said casually.

Kohl was pushing the bullet down the barrel with the ramrod and cursing with the effort. "I never . . . I never let him!" he cried. His knees shook visibly. "He done it his ownself!"

"You're his father, aint ya?"

"The man appeared at the edge of the fire, the light dancing on his dark, sharp-featured face.

Laughter sounded only four or five feet behind Kohl. He turned, swinging the rifle around, and fired. The boom echoed and died. No one was there.

From the corner of his eye, Kohl saw a shadow move toward him from behind. He turned slowly, eyes wide, heart tattooing his breastbone.

The man stood only a few feet before him. He held a pistol down at his thigh. His face was expressionless, eyes without light. The hollows of his cheeks were filled with darkness.

"Please . . . I never . . . I never woulda let him—"

Kohl watched the pistol rise to his face. It took a long time. He stared down the barrel, lowered his chin to his chest, squeezed his eyes closed. He sobbed.

The man spoke with measured calm. "The father should pay for the sins of the son, don't you think . . . you old stumpsucker?"

Kohl took a ragged breath. His last thought was that he should have listened to Nordstrom and run for his life.

22

Corinne awoke to crows cawing angrily in the cotton-woods down by the seep. She didn't think she'd ever really lost consciousness, but only dozed near dawn. How could one sleep on the hard, cold ground without even a pallet? There seemed to be rocks or roots or lumpy grass clumps everywhere you turned.

She heard the clinking of a saddle cinch, and turned her gaze to Nordstrom, saddling his horse beyond the breakfast fire. He spoke softly to the mustang as he worked. The wily, graceful animal slid his eyes to him, as though he understood what the man was saying.

Corinne had never known anyone like the rancher: a rough yet gentle man, bold but strangely humble. She felt drawn to him as though to a warm fire on a cold night. But his gruff manner told her the feeling was not mutual.

Asleep beside her, Nils stirred, cried out, and rested his head on her shoulder. She ran her hand through his hair affectionately, then slid out from beneath him, gently removing his head from her arm. She stood and smoothed her dress, swept her hair back from her face.

"Mornin'," Nordstrom said as she approached.

"Good morning. How did you sleep?"

Nordstrom shrugged. "Same as always."

"I do not sleep so well on the ground."

"You get used to it."

She watched him saddle the mules. He did not look at her. His jaw was set and his brow was furrowed. His round shoulders stretched his fringed buckskin shirt taut across his chest. His forearms bulged. She could not help imagining how it would be, wrapped in his arms. The pain would leave, the bad memories . . . the loneliness. . . .

"Where are we going, Mr. Nordstrom?"

"Glenn."

"What?"

"Might as well call me Glenn. We only have about two days left. The Melby Stage line runs just north of here, about sixty miles. We should hit it tomorrow." He reached under the mule he was saddling for the latigo, then tightened the cinch with a grunt. "It's on the other side of Blood Mountain, due west of here. If the gap's where I remember it to be, we should get there about six o'clock tomorrow night."

"Blood Mountain?"

"That's what the Indians named it—the Blackfeet. With the sun a certain way—this time o' year, as a matter of fact—it turns the color of blood."

Feeling a chill, Corinne crossed her arms over her breasts and frowned. "What will happen when we cross this Blood Mountain and reach the Melby station?"

Nordstrom eyed a stirrup, adjusting it. "Then I put you all on the stage for Fort McGuire." He turned and flashed a smile. "You'll be safe, then. Those boys' horses will be too tuckered to keep pace with a stage. Besides, they'll have me runnin' interference for you then, too." He gave her a wink and turned back to his work.

Corinne hesitated. "I . . . don't . . . understand."

"What's to understand? You're goin' home—or back where you came from, at least. The roundabout way, but it's the only way. At Fort McGuire, you can hook up with another stage line to Denver. From Denver you can get back to St. Louis relatively easy, then back east. . . .

Back where you came from. You folks sure as hell don't want to stay out here . . . not after all this!''

"I see," Corinne muttered after a moment, thoughtful. Even after all that had happened to her, she hadn't considered the possiblility of going home. Her true home was thousands of miles across the sea. Of course, she'd longed for it—the sights, the smells, the familiarity—but going back was impossible. For better or worse, her home was here . . . somewhere.

"Your mule's ready," Nordstrom said. "We'll pull out just as soon as everybody's had a bite to eat and a cup of coffee."

"Yes," she said, giving a weak smile and turning away.

"How you holdin' up?" Nordstrom called after her.

"I'm OK," she said over her shoulder.

"You're probably sore from ridin', but just remember, we've only two days left."

She nodded, her heart breaking at the formality of his tone. She gave her back to him, not wanting him to see the hurt in her eyes, and knelt down to awaken Nils.

John Lang was up and saddling Grace's mule. Grace sat with her big legs curled beneath her, staring vacantly into the fire, spiritless. Her blond hair had flattened out and hung in her eyes. Her round face was dust-streaked. Ida Mary, who had taken up with the woman after her mother's death, sat beside her with the same blank stare. The girl refused to ride with anyone but Mrs. Lang. Neither of them had said a word since Mrs. Kohl was killed.

Lang seemed to be holding up better than Nordstrom had expected. The man may have been green, but he listened, he learned fast, and he was dependable. Nordstrom was impressed by his sand.

He called to Nordstrom from the fire, where he stood warming a bridle bit, a trick the rancher had taught him, for a warm bit slipped through a mule's teeth easier than a cold one. "I was thinking about Kohl and wondering if one of us shouldn't hang back and watch for him."

Nordstrom led his saddled grulla to a tree. Tying the

reins to a branch, he shook his head. "I don't see the point in that, teacher."

"What do you mean?"

Nordstrom glanced around to see if the others were listening. "Kohl didn't make it."

Lang licked his upper lip and squinted his eyes. "How do you know?"

"Just take my word for it." Grimly, Nordstrom turned to the fire. Using a leather mitt, he lifted the blue enamel pot from a flat rock in the fire and filled a tin cup.

Blowing on the hot liquid, he sipped and glanced over the cup at Nils, who was rolling his blanket. Hoping to cheer the lad, he said, "You can ride point today, boy."

The young man shrugged. His eyes were flat, his shoulders slumped, his demeanor as withdrawn as always. "If you say so."

Nordstrom's gaze took in the others. "We move out in ten minutes," he said.

Mrs. Lang lifted her chin and gave a sob. "No, no, no," she cried, shaking her head. "No more!"

Ida Mary turned to the woman and broke down in tears.

"Come now, Grace, you're frightening the child," Lang said, moving toward his wife.

Corinne put her hands on Ida Mary's shoulder, and the girl turned sharply away. "No!" she grunted, and scuttled into the arms of the bawling Mrs. Lang.

"We've only two days left, Mrs. Lang," Nordstrom said consolingly. "Just two more days. Then we'll put you all on a stage for home."

"I don't want to go home! I don't want to go anywhere! I want to stay here! Oh, *John*!"

Lang knelt beside his wife and spoke to her softly. Nordstrom turned away, allowing them some privacy, and untethered Corinne's mule. When he'd led it into the camp, Mrs. Lang and Ida Mary were getting to their feet. The girl took the big woman's hand as Lang led them to their mount tethered behind the rocks.

As Nordstrom watched them, he knew that every mile

was going to get tougher and tougher. There was nothing harder than trying to save someone who no longer cared whether they were saved or not.

The morning was a rosy glow in the east when they mounted up and headed out. Nils took the lead. Behind him, in single file, were Grace Lang and Ida Mary on one mule, then Corinne and John Lang. Nordstrom flanked the group, leaving the trail occasionally to look around from a butte top.

He'd seen no sign of the riders since leaving the mesa. But they were out there. He sensed them the way an old Indian once told him he could sense when someone had cast a spell on him.

Mid-morning he rode down from a hillock. Lang was waiting for him on the trail. The others rode ahead—a dour, sullen group if Nordstrom had ever seen one.

"Any sign of 'em?"

Nordstrom shook his head.

"Maybe they've given up."

"Don't count on it."

"You'd think they'd have something better to do."

Nordstrom shrugged his shoulders and bunched his lips. "Nah . . . not them. They're havin' too much fun."

They turned their horses to follow the others along the trail switchbacking along an arroyo. The morning was clear, with serried ranks of high, thin clouds overhead. There was an autumn nip in the breeze. A storm front brewed on the horizon.

Nordstrom knew he'd have to keep an eye on it. This time of year was ripe for hail, and twisters were not out of the question.

He and Lang rode side-by-side, slowly, resting their horses. They'd pick up the pace again in a few minutes.

The teacher turned to Nordstrom. "What you said to Grace back there—about picking up the stage? I'm not going back East."

"Don't you think your wife has been through enough?"

"No," Lang said, shaking his head. "I don't think

either one of us has been through near enough."

Nordstrom shrugged. "Whatever you say, Teacher," he said with a sigh, and touched the grulla with his spurs, picking up his gait.

At noon they stopped for a quick lunch of jerked beef and coffee boiled over a smokeless fire. An hour later they drove along in half darkness, watching a thin blue line growing ahead of them, feeling the wind pick up and get colder. Finally, the front blocked out the sun and inundated them with pea-sized hail.

They were down in a hollow with no cover, so Nordstrom pushed them on. They rode, wincing, with their heads dipped to their saddle horns, hands holding their hats secure. Ida Mary wailed. Corinne buried her head in her arms and let her mule find his way. Grace Lang dipped her chin slightly and bunched her cheeks, as though this were only one more in an infinite series of indignities—no better, no worse.

As abruptly as it had dropped, the front lifted, and the party rode out into soft sunlight under a cloudless sky. Nordstrom rode up a bench for a look around, halting just below the ridge so he wasn't outlined against the sky. He dug around in his saddlebags for his spyglass, brought it to his eye, and twisted the lens until a distant ravine swam into focus.

Each a fuzzy outline from this distance, three riders traced a curving trail along a brushy creek, heading this way.

As Nordstrom turned to his party riding single-file through a crease in the hills below, Grace Lang brought her mount to a halt and crawled clumsily out of the saddle, catching her foot in a stirrup and landing in a pile beneath the horse. Alone on the mule, Ida Mary made a high, thin noise, watching the poor woman.

"Hey!" Nordstrom yelled.

Lang had been watching him, probably hoping for good news. He turned now to his wife about fifty feet ahead. "Grace!"

Lang jumped down from his horse and ran over to his

wife. "No, I don't want any help!" the woman screamed. "Leave me alone!"

Nordstrom galloped down the ridge. "What's going on?" he said sharply. Time was slipping away, and the riders were closing.

"I'm stopping," Grace said. "I'm not going one step farther!"

"Grace!" Lang said.

Nordstrom sighed. "Lady, you're holding us up."

"Go on without me. I'm staying . . . I-I'm staying here!"

Lang knelt down and took the woman by her shoulders. "Grace, you don't mean that."

"You're the one who brought me here! I didn't want to come! Now, look what's happened!"

Nordstrom stepped forward, ready to slap some sense into the woman. Behind him, Ida Mary sat the mule—face bunched with pain, tears rolling down her gaunt cheeks. Although her mouth was open, she didn't make a sound.

Thinking of the precious time they were losing to the renegades, Nordstrom knelt down and shouldered Lang out of the way. He stared into the howling woman's tear-washed eyes. "Lady, you either crawl back into that saddle, or I'll throw you in it and tie you there!"

She threw back her head and bawled like a bogged calf. "We're all dead. . . . We're all dead, anyway!"

"Grace!" Lang yelled.

Nordstrom cocked his arm to slap the woman, but someone touched him lightly on the shoulder. Corinne stepped between him and Lang, lifted her skirts, and knelt down.

"Let me talk to Mrs. Lang," she said.

Nordstrom and Lang stepped back while Corinne wrapped her arm around the big woman's wide waist and led her away. Nordstrom heard the Norwegian girl speaking to the woman in a soothing tone.

They walked about twenty feet away, then turned and faced each other. Corinne was obviously trying to bol-

ster the woman's spirit. After several minutes, she
hugged the woman. The size difference made it an awkward embrace, but it seemed to do the trick.

Mrs. Lang brought her eyes up to Corinne's, brushing
the tears away with the back of her hand. She nodded.
Then she and Corinne turned and walked back to the
others.

Wordlessly, Grace moved to the horse and allowed
her husband to help her into the saddle. Nordstrom held
Corinne's mule by the bridle as the girl mounted up.

"Thanks," he told her.

Corinne shook her head and reined the animal away.

"Sorry about that," Lang said.

"It's not your fault, but we have to keep movin'."
Nordstrom walked to his horse cropping bluestem, reins
dangling. He snugged his hat down and slapped traildust
from his chaps.

"What did you see up there?" Lang called after him.
"They comin'?"

"Yep," Nordstrom said gloomily, leather creaking as
he climbed into his saddle. "Let's break a leg while we
still have one to break."

Watching the rancher put his mustang into a three-
pointed gate up the trail, the teacher muttered, " 'Yea,
tho I walk through the valley of the shadow of death'
. . . please give me the balls not to make an ass out of
myself."

He swung his tender butt into the leather, tossed a
wary look behind him, and galloped off.

23

Nordstrom did not like running anymore than he cottoned to being chased. He'd always settled his disputes up front—mostly with words and a handshake, though a time or two he'd had to resort to the iron hogleg on his hip.

But he'd never run.

Most of the troublemakers he'd encountered had backed down to his impressive physical presence. One didn't easily draw or lift a fist against the resolute eyes under the heavy blond brow, the firm jaw, broad shoulders, and big, hard-callused hand hovering near the Colt holstered butt-forward on his hip.

The few who had—there was a sharp-tongued drover from Nebraska, for instance, and a freighter from Missouri who'd cheated him and three soldiers at cards in Julesburg—had long since gone to their respective boot hills. He was no gunslinger; he hated the breed. But he could be accurate when he needed to be, and he was willing, and that combination almost always counted for more than speed.

No, it was time to stop running and give the tables a little turn, he thought as his mustang rode into a wedge between two rimrocks. . . .

He pulled up lightly on the reins and the grulla came to a stop, lifted its head, and blew. Nordstrom peered

into the cleft. A small fieldstone hut nestled in sage and
boulders at the bottom of the rock-strewn slope.

It was a curious place for such a structure—out here
in the middle of nowhere. Nordstrom had seen such hov-
els before, left by the anonymous adventurers who'd
been coming west longer than most people realized. Dismounting and walking over for a look, he saw that the
roof had fallen in, and tough brown grass had grown up
around the fallen stones inside the cabin.

There were two rooms divided by half a crumbling
rock wall. At the top of the wall sat a salamander, its
sides heaving in and out, tongue out collecting flies.
Startled by the intruder, it turned and disappeared in a
silver-green flash.

Nordstrom left the grulla at the cabin and walked up
the cleft, finding a live spring amid sage and scoria. He
knelt, cleared the film of seeds and algae from the largest
of the two pools, and drank from his cupped hands until
his temples throbbed. The water tasted only vaguely of
minerals.

He dampened his bandanna and cleaned the dust and
sweat from his face, letting the icy water dribble under
his lathered tunic. Standing, he gave a tired sigh, tied
the bandanna around his neck, and walked back down
the cleft to the cabin. Mounting the grulla, he cantered
back to the other riders.

They were crossing a dry streambed where crows
cawed from twisted box elders.

"It's gettin' late," Nordstrom said. "We'll hole up
for the night in that cleft. There's a cabin."

He looked for any sign of relief on their faces, but
they were all stony-faced with fatigue.

Nordstrom reined the grulla around and lead them into
the cleft. When the mules were unsaddled and hobbled
near the spring, and buffalo chips were gathered for a
fire, he climbed the rocky slope behind the cabin. He sat
there for a long time, watched the sun go down, heard
the first bats whorling like spirits in the cooling air above
the rimrock.

Chewing a hunk of jerked beef and nibbling dried apple slices, he watched a distant pinprick of burnt-orange light gather life and substance as the violet sky darkened and the salmon streaks of cirrus receded farther and farther westward.

It could have been the light of an Indian camp, but Nordstrom knew better. He waited there until full dark, then made his way down the rimrock, choosing his steps carefully around the sharp-edged rocks and boulders.

Keeping watch, John Lang stood outside the hut where the others slept. He stood back from the fire and hefted his rifle when he heard Nordsrom's boots grinding stones.

"It's me," the rancher said. "Everything OK?"

"I keep hearing grunting sounds coming from up the trail to the spring," Lang said, not as much worried as curious.

"Grunting sounds?"

"You probably couldn't hear them up there, but every once in a while I hear—I don't know—something like a . . . There it is—listen."

Nordstrom heard the guttural sounds rising from up the wedge between the rimrocks. The mules thrashed, spooky.

"Bear," Nordstrom whispered, tipping an ear to listen. "Grizzly. Two of 'em, fixin' for a fight. That scratchin' you hear now is one rakin' his claws on a tree. One's probably a rogue trespassing on the other's private property. Nothin' makes 'em madder."

Now a worried expression etched itself on Lang's round Indiana face. The campfire's flames danced in his wide eyes. "Grizzlies?"

Nordstrom nodded and shrugged. "Nothin' to worry about. They'll make a hell of a racket before the night's over, but they're too pissed at each other to pay us any heed."

"Jeepers, Nordstrom. *Grizzlies?*"

Nordstrom smiled and clamped his hand on the teacher's shoulder. "It ain't like what you've heard. A grizzly won't bother you if you don't bother him. You just have to stay out of his territory, that's all.''

Lang inflated his chest with a deep breath. "If you say so.''

Nordstrom's smile faded. "Keep your eyes peeled, will you? I'm gonna take a ride. Be back to relieve you in a couple hours.''

"Where are you going?''

The rancher plucked the iron from the holster on his left leg, and gave the cylinder a spin. "I spied the renegades' fire from up on the rimrock. I'm gonna go over and say hello.''

Lang blinked, frowning. "Are you crazy?''

"Probably," Nordstrom said. "Just the same, keep your eyes peeled.''

He turned and walked away in the darkness.

There was no moon. That was good, but the trail was lit enough by starlight that Nordstrom was finding his way.

To muffle the hooves and cover the tracks, he'd wrapped the grulla's feet with deerskin. While the smoky mustang could move all day on a hatful of water, it had never been the best night horse in the rancher's remuda, and tonight it was living up to its reputation. Spooked by the slightest sound, it stopped suddenly to sniff the air. It gave a jerk and a short whinny at a distant wolf's howl, then at a horned owl lifting from a boulder.

Nordstrom tried to assure the horse with pats on the neck, and with gentle commands. Nordstrom could feel the horse's muscles expand and contract beneath him, see its ears twitch. Still, the grulla strode onward like the stout-hearted cavalry mount Nordstrom had trained it to be.

The air was chill and Nordstrom could see his breath. What day was it, anyway? What month? Hell, it must be September by now.

Gently, he turned the grulla from the Indian hunting trail, and headed southwest along an ancient riverbed.

Half-buried driftwood littered the rocky ground. Nord-strom's night vision picked out seashells and bone chips in cut banks webbed with roots.

Something scratched the sand, rustled a sage bush to Nordstrom's left. The horse stopped, tensing. Nordstrom raked the .44 from its holster and thumbed back the hammer. There was another, indistinguishable sound from farther away.

A retreating coyote, maybe a wolf.

"Don't worry, it wasn't a grizzly," he whispered in the grulla's ear, forcing a smile.

He rode as far as he dared, then dismounted and tied the grulla to a tree. Removing his spurs, he draped them over the saddle horn. He shucked his Winchester and looked around, memorizing as many details of the place as possible.

Jacking a shell into the breech and releasing the thong over the hammer of his pistol, he started out . . . quietly, one step at a time, sliding his gaze slowly from left to right.

From here the land looked very different than it had from the rimrock, and he had only a vague sense of where the renegades' camp might be. He knew he might never find it, but he had to try.

The renegades would never expect it.

He smelled the cedar smoke before he saw the burnt-orange glow about fifty yards ahead. As he hefted the rifle before him and stole along the rocks of the arroyo, the encampment grew in the darkness until he could see the light wavering on the stony bank behind it.

He moved off to the right and traced a wide circle around the camp, stepping behind a lightning-topped box elder. He slid his gaze around the trunk. The flames of the campfire danced about twenty-five yards ahead.

A man sat on a stone beside the fire, his elbows on his knees, his head in his arms. His shoulders jerked and his head rolled with what appeared to be laughter, but he was too far away for Nordstrom to be sure.

The man held a pistol in his right hand, and he appeared to be running it across his forehead.

Another man—the big bastard with the beard—materialized from the darkness behind the fire. He looked at the other man askance as he knelt and rummaged in a leather pouch beside a saddle, producing a thin-bladed skinning knife. He stood and regarded the other man, said something Nordstrom couldn't hear.

The other man lifted his head and jumped to his feet. He raised his arm, aiming the pistol at the big man with the beard.

"Get the fuck away from me, ya here!" The yell was loud and shrill. It resounded in the chill night.

The big man spread his hands placatingly and backed away, said something unintelligible. Then he turned and disappeared.

Nordstrom scrunched up his eyes. What in blazes . . . ?

The first man gave an agonized sob—there was no doubting the nature of the sound now—and shuffled around the fire to a pile of branches and buffalo chips. The gun hung low at his thigh. His shoulders slumped, and his head sagged. Clipped sobs escaped his parted lips. He cursed and shook his head.

Nordstrom thought he'd never seen a man so miserable. He smiled.

The man dropped a long branch on the fire and stepped back to watch the glowing cinders rise on smoke wheels. As the man was giving Nordstrom his chest, the rancher knew he could take him now with the Winchester. One quick shot through that repugnant heart . . .

He stepped around beside the tree and raised the rifle. He knew the man could not see into the darkness beyond the fire.

Nordstrom snugged the rifle to his cheek, closed one eye, fit the bead at the end of the barrel into the notch on the breech, and snugged them both on the man's hide-covered chest, over the heart.

He held the position for several seconds, willing back the first knuckle of his trigger finger, but it would not move. He whispered a curse, lowered the rifle.

It was just too easy. The man wouldn't even know what had hit him. He'd die without knowing who'd killed him and why. Nordstrom wanted his face to be the last face old Snake Eyes saw. Just like old Snake Eyes was the last face poor Charlie saw.

Nordstrom watched the man sit back down on the rock beside the fire, bury his head in his arms, run the pistol along his scalp as though it were a talisman. He sobbed like a child.

The rancher moved away from the tree, widening his circle around the camp, looking for the other two men. They had to be out here somewhere. He wanted to take them all out in one fell swoop, in one holy hail of lead, but they had to know who was turning them toe down. They had to know why. Nordstrom wanted to finish the ordeal tonight, but he could not resist turning the tables on these men. He could not resist stalking them, so they knew what it was to be hunted.

He'd crept twenty feet when he saw another fire. Moving closer, one step at a time, planting his feet carefully so he wouldn't snap twigs or kick stones, he saw that the light originated from a torch hanging upside down from a branch.

The two men stood in the sphere of light, near a deer carcass hung from the same branch as the torch. The hind legs of the deer were splayed, and the big man was hunkered in the cavity, dressing it out. His raised elbows bobbed as he worked. The head of the big, horned buck brushed the ground and turned this way and that as the knife assaulted its loins. Shadows swirled.

The men were not positioned well for a clean shot. The deer and several low branches were in the way. Nordstrom considered continuing forward until a clean shot presented itself, but looking that way, he saw several bushes and old deadfall bearing dry, spindly branches that would make a hell of a racket if stepped on.

Then the joke would be on him.

He hunkered down behind a shrub and licked his lips, taking a deep breath to calm his nerves. He smelled the smoke from the quirlies the men were smoking, heard their muffled voices.

He tensed his finger inside the trigger guard, breathing quietly through his mouth. He was trying to figure a way of getting the drop on both men without getting shot by Snake Eyes, when the big man piped up: "I said get me some water, goddamnit!"

"Get your own goddamn water!" retorted the other man, who stood several inches shorter. He took a number of steps back, limping, cigarette smoldering between his lips. "I near broke my foot when we was chasin' that girl—you know that," he whined. "I cain't walk all the way down to the creek over them rocks!"

"Oh . . . you *goddamn* pantywaist!" the big man said. He stood glowering at the smallish man, then turned, gave a sigh, and stuck the knife in the carcass. He retrieved a canteen from a log, then walked off, ducking his head under branches and cursing.

"I near broke my foot, Jim!" the short man barked after him.

Limping exaggeratedly, he turned, sweeping his eyes over the ground as though looking for something. Pain twisting his face, he backed up to the tree from which the deer hung, and sat awkwardly down. He cursed. He took the cigarette from his mouth and peered at the ember, gave it a blow.

Nordstrom breathed his own quiet curse. His heart drummed in his temples and fingertips. His hands were sweating. The situation was getting away from him. Now the uglies were scattered, and his chance to bear down on them all was evaporating before his eyes. He should have taken out Snake Eyes when he'd had the chance.

He knew the thing to do now was to sit tight and wait until they were all asleep, then wander into camp with his Winchester cocked. But like killing Snake Eyes, he couldn't do it. He was out of control and he knew it, but there was nothing he could do about it. He had to do *something*—something just as evil as what these men had done to him and Charlie and the pilgrims.

Keeping to the shadows, he crept a few feet ahead, until he was directly behind the tree the man was using as a backrest. Here, there were only a few branches to avoid. Moving his gaze from the ground to the tree and back again, he stole silently up to the trunk and knelt down.

The man was only a foot away, on the other side of the tree.

Biting his lower lip and holding his breath, Nordstrom holstered his pistol and unsheathed his knife, gripping the big bowie firmly in his right hand. He was hot and tense; at the same time, he felt strangely agile. His heart drummed a slow but persistent rhythm. His senses were as alive as they had ever been.

He watched the man's shadow. It sprawled on the ground to his right. The flickering torch bounced it to and fro. A breeze brought the smoke from the man's cigarette to Nordstrom's nostrils.

He breathed deeply, sprang from his haunches, and lurched around the tree. He fell to his knees, facing the man.

The man gave a start. "Hey—!"

Nordstrom stifled the yell by smashing his cupped left hand over the man's mouth and holding the knife to his throat. He held the man's head firmly against the tree. He could see by the man's eyes that it hurt. Bark flecks fell to his shoulders. Beneath Nordstrom's hand, the face felt coarse and leathery and wet.

He looked deeply into the man's befuddled eyes. Then the man recognized him. Horror replaced the surprise in his eyes, which widened with the recognition of what was about to happen.

He bucked and kicked against the rancher's weight pressing him down.

Nordstrom drew the knife across the throat as suddenly as if he were slapping the man's face. He held the

mouth for several seconds, and watched the fear fade
from the man's eyes as the life drained from his body.
Blood bubbled down his chest and onto his lap. It pud-
dled on the ground between his thighs.

Nordstrom tensed as he saw the shadow of the deer
move when a breeze scuttled. He wiped the blade of the
bowie on the dying man's shirt, stood, and crept through
the woods, in Snake Eyes' direction. It was time to in-
troduce himself. One man was dead and the other had
gone for water. Snake Eyes would be alone.

When he came to the boulder silhouetted against the
fire where Snake Eyes had been crying, he put his left
hand on it, steadying himself, breathing steadily through
his mouth. For several seconds he listened but could hear
nothing but the snapping fire, see nothing but shadows
bouncing from the orange glow the flames cast on the
surrounding trees.

Pressing his tongue against the inside of his lower lip,
he brought the Winchester up to his waist and bolted
around the rock. He gazed around the fire.

No one was there. The dry pine Snake Eyes had been
using for fuel crackled in the circle of rocks. Boot prints
marked the finely ground dirt and pine needles. The
darkness beyond the fire was like a wall. He could see
nothing.

Feeling suddenly claustrophobic, knowing Snake
Eyes could be crouched in the shadows, Nordstrom
jumped quickly back behind the rock and waited for the
bark of a gun.

Nothing. Only the sigh and mutter of the fire, the quiet
ringing of the night, the rush of the pulse in his head.
He'd blown his chance. Snake Eyes was gone, and
Nordstrom knew he couldn't wait for him. There were
two men out there with guns.

The tables had turned again, and Nordstrom had no
one to blame but himself.

Creeping quietly back the way he'd come, still
pumped with adrenaline, he saw the deer the big man
and the man he'd killed had been dressing. Upside

down, it turned a slow half-circle as the breeze caught it, lifting the bristly fur. It shone in the velvety light of the dying torch.

An idea occured to him, and he recognized its madness. "Gonna get yourself killed," he warned himself.

But it was no madder than anything else he'd done tonight.

Big Jim dipped the canteen in the thin stream of water trickling over the stones. The creek was nearly dry, and it took a long time to fill the canteen. As he did so, he watched the stars and perused the horizon for the moon, but it was nowhere in sight.

He frowned and wrinkled his big, wide-nostriled nose. There went his theory that the moon was the instigator of J.L.'s sour moods.

"Sour," Jim said to himself with a mirthless grunt. "I'll say it's sour. Sour like green rhubarb!"

Jim had never known anyone who got as dark as J.L. Wood. He'd seen grim people with long faces aplenty—you didn't come from where he came from and see a whole lot of grins!—but he'd never seen a grown man get so down for no reason. J.L. was the only man he knew who could go from a wild night of drink buying and poker playing and skirt chasing to a morning of weeping like a baby and stroking his pistol like a dead pet rabbit.

Jim had never seen a man who could take your head in his hands and give your beard a friendly rub one minute, and turn his dark eyes on you the next and threaten to tear your lungs out if you didn't stop lacing his whiskey with beaver piss.

No—J.L. was a new one on Jim, and if Jim knew one thing, he knew to cut J.L. a wide swath the first night of a waxing moon. Listening now to water bubbling into the canteen and staring up at the velvet sky sprinkled with crisp, white stars, he decided to revise that vow to every goddamn night of his life.

Because there was no sign of a moon tonight—wax-

ing, waning, or anything else—and J.L. was as looney
as a rat trapped in a nest of diamondbacks.

For that reason, when Jim had capped the canteen and
headed up the slope, around the stunted ponderosas and
loose talus, he gave the camp a wide berth. He wasn't
going anywhere near J.L. again tonight, not after he'd
been threatened once already. In fact, tonight he was
going to take his saddle and bedroll and spread out under
a tree far, far away from that looney son of a bitch, and
hope the mood passed by morning.

If it didn't, Jim would just go ahead and shoot the
bastard—put him out of all their miseries. J.L. might be
the brains of the outfit, but Big Jim didn't have to put
up with that kind of shit.

"Well, here's the water, no thanks to you, you worth-
less sack o' shit," he told Pete as he ambled under the
tree from which the deer hung. "You better heal that
ankle o' yours real soon, or I'm gonna take an ax and
lop it off, really give ya somethin' to holler about. How
'bout that?"

Big Jim stopped beside the tree, fished in his shirt
pocket for a cigarette he'd rolled earlier, and brought the
quirley to his lips. He scrutinized it to make sure the
ends were still tightly twisted, then scratched a lucifer
on his thumbnail.

Touching the flame to the end of his cigarette, he
lifted his head. Before him, buckskin leggings soaked in
blood hung where the deer should have been. Blood
dripped like red molasses from the tips of the worn
boots.

"What the fu—?" he cried, raising his eyes from the
blood-matted buckskin shirt to the head of Pete Hill.

There was a rope around the neck. Jim couldn't see
much of the rope because of all the blood, but he saw
the end tied to the branch.

Pete's head rested on his shoulder, and his eyes were
lightly closed, lips pooched out.

Jim turned his head sharply. The gutted deer carcass

rested against the tree, its hollow cavity opening like a big, laughing mouth.

Big Jim dropped the canteen and took one lumbering step backward, nearly falling.

"J.L.!" he muttered, eyes fixed on the blood-soaked corpse casting its shadow over his face. "*J.L.!*"

24

Outside the stone hut, Lang sat by the fire, staring into the flames and listening to the skirmishing grizzlies. The raspy, high-pitched roars were intermittent, at times piercing the night and echoing off the buttes, then dying to low growls, snorts, thrashing brush, and snapping branches. They gave an ethereal quality to the night, like a waking nightmare.

He cradled the rifle to his chest, ready to drop the barrel and pull the trigger. He hoped Nordstrom returned soon. If the rancher got himself killed . . . A sharp chill ran from his feet to the top of his head. He not only had human marauders to worry about now, but grizzlies, to boot.

Maybe Grace was right. Maybe they shouldn't have come west. Maybe the dull schoolkids of Oakville were not quite as dull as they'd seemed.

He pressed his back against the rock and considered his favorite literary hero, Odysseus. The old Greek warrior had gone through worse than this and survived. It was a comforting thought. It took the edge from Lang's worry, and he grew sleepy. After a quarter hour of head bobbing, his chin came to rest on his chest and the rifle dropped to his lap.

At the same time, inside the hut, his wife opened her eyes and stiffened. The inhuman sounds had penetrated her sleep, and she lay listening unconsciously for several minutes, giving agitated grunts and murmurs, arms and legs jerking, until somehow the sounds became a summons.

A celestial call.

Suspended between consciousness and slumber, she tossed away the blanket and climbed heavily to her feet. Without stopping to put on her shoes, she stepped around the fallen stones, over Nils and Corinne, through the low doorway, and into the night.

Her half-seeing eyes did not register her husband sleeping by the fire. They sought only a path toward God and home.

Finding it, she moved up the trail past the mules toward the spring—barefoot, ignoring the sharp stones beneath her feet, eyes wide and expectant, almost smiling. Her breath puffed in the chill air.

"Wait," came a voice from behind her.

Grace stopped, turned stiffly. A short, thin, long-haired figure stood on the trail behind her. Ida Mary.

"Where . . . where you goin'?" The voice was small and muffled with sleep and confusion. She rubbed an eye with a fist.

Grace smiled and held out her arm. "Come, child. Come with Grace."

"What's that noise?"

"That's God, child."

"What's he want?"

Grace said nothing. She smiled and beckoned with the fingers of her outstretched hand.

The girl stepped forward and took the woman's hand. "Where we goin'?"

"You come with Grace, Ida Mary. We're going home."

Holding hands, the woman and child disappeared up the trail.

Behind Nordstrom, pistols cracked and men yelled.

He walked quickly back the way he had come, glancing behind him to see if the men were anywhere near. The only sign of them was the flickers of their barking pistols far off in the darkness. They receded farther as Nordstrom moved toward his horse.

"We know you're out there, rancher," one of them yelled.

Voice shrill with rage, the other screamed, "Get your ass back here!"

They knew he was near but couldn't see him in the dark. Their wild shots and shouts bespoke their frustration. Nordstrom knew they wouldn't pursue him and risk getting bushwacked. All they could do was hold their positions and hope he came to them, which he had no intention of doing.

Reducing the renegades to two, and frustrating them— frustrated men often made mistakes—was enough work for tonight, he thought. Tomorrow was another day.

Spying the black figure of the grulla under a tree, its head up and nose working, Nordstrom untied the skittish mustang, speaking softly to ease its jangled nerves, and mounted up. He gave the horse a slack rein and allowed its keen nose to guide him back to the hut.

He hailed Lang as he neared the guttering fire outside the cabin, reined the horse to a halt beyond the sphere of light, and looked around. Lang was nowhere in sight. Movement attracted his eyes to the cabin's doorway. It was Corinne. Holding a blanket around her shoulders, she gazed across the fire, brows furrowed, blinking.

"What is it?" Nordstrom asked sharply, sensing that something was wrong.

"Where is Mrs. Lang and Ida Mary?"

"They're not inside?"

Corinne shook her head.

"Lang's not here, either." Nordstrom reined the grulla around and peered into the darkness. He cleared his throat. "Lang?"

There was no reply.

He turned back to the girl. "Get back in the cabin. I'm gonna look around."

"Oh, my god," the girl said in a thin, quavering voice, lifting a hand to her mouth.

Remembering the pistol and her vow to use it, Nordstrom jumped down from the horse and took her in his arms.

"No," he said forcefully. "It's not the renegades. I know where they are, and we don't have to worry about them tonight." He pushed her away to look into her eyes. Sharp with fear, they gazed back at him unseeing. He shook her gently. "Do you hear?"

Her eyes softened a little, blinked. Before he knew what he was doing, her face was in his hands, and he was kissing her. Her body softened against him; her lips opened. Flushed and befuddled, he stumbled backward, turned, and mounted the grulla.

Not looking at her, he said, "Get back inside," as he rode away.

Her face creased with confusion and longing, Corinne stood there, watching the place in the darkness where he had disappeared atop the mustang. She was not aware that, behind her, Nils had awakened at the sound of Nordstrom's voice, and had seen the kiss.

Sick to his stomach, the boy lay back on the ground, his head on his saddle, and saw the embrace again in his mind—the rancher's arms enfolding his beloved Corinne, and Corinne doing nothing to stop it. Distracted, he did not notice that Mrs. Lang and his sister were gone, or wonder what all the commotion had been about.

He turned on his side, folded his arms across his chest, squeezed his eyes closed, and stifled an angry sob.

Following three sets of tracks beyond the glowing coals of the fire, Nordstrom rode up the path to the spring. The mules were nickering and stomping around on their hobbled feet.

Nordstrom called for Lang, letting his voice rise only a few decibels above normal, for he did not know how far it would carry in the still night. He did not want to take even the minimal risk of betraying their position to the renegades.

He stopped the horse and listened for a reply, but heard only a nightbird chattering in the distance and a vagrant breeze rustling grass. Cursing, deciding Lang's wife and the girl had run off, and Lang had gone after them, Nordstrom moved up a rocky bench and stopped suddenly as a knee-numbing roar lifted from the wide, dark valley opening on the other side.

The grulla stiffened and jerked its head, took two steps sideways. "Easy," Nordstrom said, holding the reins taut.

Another, louder complaint split the night, and the grulla turned full around and bucked. Nordstrom said nothing, just held tight to the reins and set his jaw, letting his free hand stray to the rifle butt poking up beneath the horn.

A gunshot sounded, muffled with distance. Two more followed close on its heels. Nordstrom wrestled the grulla around, pointing it down the valley, and gave it the spurs.

Jerking its head from side to side, the horse complied, but Nordstrom felt the reluctance in its tight-muscled gallop and the wary arch in its neck. The rancher shucked his Winchester and jacked a shell as the screams and roars lifted the hair on his neck and sent a chill like a knifepoint deep in his loins.

He'd gone maybe a hundred yards when a figure broke away from the velvet darkness and gathered human shape before him. The object moved erratically, as though stumbling, half-running. Then Nordstrom heard the labored breath and clipped groans.

"Lang!"

The rancher brought the horse to a sliding halt and jumped down. Seeing Nordstrom, the teacher dropped his rifle and fell to his knees. He pushed his head to the ground and gave a horrible yell.

"Lang, what is it? Where's your wife?"

The teacher cried and ground his head against the

grass and gravel as though trying to bury it. Nordstrom squatted on his heels beside him. "Come on, goddamnit! What happened?"

The teacher sat up on his knees and lifted his head, chest rising and falling, eyes squeezed shut. His shirt was torn. Long, curved gashes shone bright with blood down his arms and chest. "Grace . . . she . . . !"

"What?"

"Grizzly . . ."

Nordstrom froze, blinked once. He stared at the teacher, who groaned as though in unbearable pain then lowered his head to vomit.

At length, the rancher licked his lips and said, "Ida Mary?"

The teacher was too busy retching to reply. It was answer enough. Nordstrom rose slowly, stiffly, trying to gather his wits. Then he pulled Lang to his feet and led him back to the encampment with the skittish horse in tow.

"Sit down by the fire," Nordstrom told the teacher, retrieving a log to add to the dying coals.

"If you think there's any chance they might still be alive . . ."

Lang wiped his mouth with a handkerchief and gave a rueful laugh. "There's no reason to go down there."

Nordstrom heard a foot grind gravel. He turned to see Nils standing behind them. In the light from the dancing flames, his face was expressionless.

"Boy . . . your sister . . . ," Nordstrom began, tentatively choosing his words.

"I heard—the bears got her," Nils said crisply, and walked away.

Nordstrom watched him, frowning, not knowing what to make of the odd lad.

Then he saw Corinne sitting several feet away on a fallen log, clutching a blanket around her shoulders. Her eyes met his and held his gaze knowingly. Then she slid her look to Lang. Rising, she moved to the teacher and knelt down beside him, touched his arm.

Softly, thinly, she said, "Your wounds need tending."

Lang shook his head. "I fell asleep."

"No, Mr. Lang," Corinne said, her bright, sympathetic eyes filling with tears.

"If I wouldn't have fallen asleep—"

"No, Mr. Lang," Corinne cooed, shaking her head. She bit her lower lip to cease its trembling. "I will clean your wounds."

As she poured water from a canteen, Nordstrom stepped away from the fire to locate the boy. He didn't need anyone else wandering off and getting mauled.

He found Nils sitting a ways up the grade behind the hut. "You all right?" Nordstrom said.

The boy said nothing for several seconds. Nordstrom could see only his silhouette. "I ain't gonna run off, if that's what you're thinkin'."

"OK," Nordstrom said with a shrug. "If you need anything, you let me know."

As he turned to rejoin the others, the boy said gruffly, "Keep your hands off her."

Nordstrom turned to him sharply, frowning. "What?"

There was no reply.

Realizing the boy must have seen the kiss, he flushed and turned away, unable to make sense out of his own confused emotions, much less the boy's.

What the hell kind of trouble would he land next? he wondered.

25

They saddled the mules and doused the breakfast fire before dawn. Nordstrom unhobbled the mount Mrs. Lang and Ida Mary had ridden, and turned it loose with a spank. They had no use for it; Indians would probably pick it up, or white buffalo hunters.

Seeing the riderless mule trot off gave Nordstrom a sick feeling. He knew what had happened to Grace and Ida Mary was as much his fault as Lang's. If he hadn't gone stalking the renegades like some gun-for-hire, he could have stopped them from leaving the camp.

He shook his head. What had possessed those two? Their own worst fears come to life, he figured. He'd seen it before. In fact, he'd felt the surrendering urge himself, but Charlie had been there . . . and his land and his cabin and his remuda of wild mustangs.

He, Corinne, Nils, and John Lang mounted up and headed out as the sun shouldered an opal smudge onto the western horizon. He wanted to get a jump on old Snakes Eyes and the big shaggy bastard. After Nordstrom's visit to their camp, they'd no doubt be scouring the country for him at first light, and seething with as much primal hate as those grizzlies.

Mid-morning, Nordstrom rode up a tabletop mesa and scanned their backtrail with his spyglass. Several dust tails lifted on a grassy flat. Squinting, he counted seven riders. They were mere dots from this distance, but the vigor with which they rode told Nordstrom they were Indians. Probably hunters, he told himself, and returned the glass to his saddlebag.

He rejoined the others cantering their mules on the sage flats north of the mesa, but said nothing about the Indians. There was no point in worrying them if there was nothing to worry about. He kept an eye on their backtrail throughout the morning.

There was no sign of old Snake Eyes and his shaggy sidekick, but the seven riders were still there, kicking up dust in earnest, sticking to Nordstrom's trail.

"What the hell do *you guys* want?" he said with a groan as he lowered the glass. He raised it again with the irrational hope they'd be gone. They weren't, and they were Indians, sure enough. What's more, they were Sioux—probably of Sitting Bull's band, all lathered up after their victory on the Little Bighorn. They were near enough now that Nordstrom could make out war paint through the spyglass. His stomach gave a little turn. He cursed and rode down to the others.

Lang lagged behind Nils and Corinne. By the way he hunched his shoulders, Nordstrom could see that his wounds were smarting, and they probably smarted worse the faster his mount moved.

"How you holdin' up?" he asked the teacher.

Lang pursed his lips and shook his head. His face was pale and drawn. Nordstrom hoped it was due to pain and heartbreak and not infection.

Lang said tightly, "They're behind us, aren't they? I can tell by all the times you've scouted our backtrail this morning."

"There's seven mounted Sioux sticking to our trail like orphan foals."

Lang closed his eyes. "No," he said tiredly.

"We need to get through the Gap and to the Melby Stage station pronto. No lunch break today, I'm afraid."

"Where is this Gap, anyway? We anywhere near it?"

Nordstrom aimed his arm northwest, to a long, dark

blotch lifting above the prairie. In the middle of the blotch, to the left of the blotch's highest point, there was a V-shaped cleft.

"That's it—about twenty, twenty-five miles away. Blood Mountain Gap. Just beyond it, through some badlands, is the Melby station."

"What are we waiting for, then?" Lang said, lifting his head with a determined air and putting his mule into a wound-jarring gallop.

It took them the better part of three hours to make the hogbacks and badlands near the gradual, rocky upthrust of Blood Mountain—a dead volcano spurred with shaley dikes, cut with slides, and covered with short, tough grass and occasional pines.

The land around was rough and gouged by shallow canyons and ravines. Several times, Nordstrom had halted the group to spell the mules. He wanted the animals fresh when they shot the Gap, off the southern slope of Blood Mountain.

He'd been through the cleft only once or twice before, but he remembered the going was tough, for only a narrow game trail meandered between the rocky slopes. There were several muddy springs, and much of the ride was uphill, to an unprotected saddle.

Now he lay on a knoll's brow, three hundred yards from the Gap. Corinne, Nils, and Lang hunkered below, sullen, while the mules cropped behind them. Nordstrom scanned the mountain and the Gap with the spyglass, then trained the lens on the low, round-topped mountain humping up on the Gap's other side, opposite Blood Mountain.

He felt a ratlike gnawing in his stomach. It was a bad sign. He hadn't seen the renegades all day, and he wondered if they'd skunked him, taken a shortcut he didn't know about. If they had, they were ahead of him, waiting in ambush either in the Gap or on the butte above it.

He lowered the glass and fingered his chin, thinking. Then he turned, walked down the knoll, squatted on his

heels beside John Lang, and cut his look between all
three as he voiced his doubts.

"What are you saying?" Lang said when he finished.

Nordstrom turned his eyes to Corinne, then Nils. "I
want you three to head straight through the Gap, as fast
as the mules will take you. I'm going to climb to the
top of that low ridge and cover you. I have a feeling
they're either in the Gap or on the ridge, and I'm betting
they're on the ridge."

"What if they're in the Gap?" Lang said.

"First sign of 'em, you take cover and return fire. I'll
get to you as fast as I can."

Lang lowered his head and gave it a slow, resolute
wag. "No."

"No, what?"

"You're better with a gun than I am. You go with
Corinne and the boy. I'll be more use to you up there."
He nodded at the ridge, upon which a slate gray sky had
lowered; two golden eagles spread their huge wings
against it.

"Not a chance, Teacher."

"You don't have a choice." Lang looked at him directly. "You don't want them going through alone, do
you?" A wry, cunning smile tugged at his lips.

Nordstrom considered it. Corinne and the boy *would*
be safer with him, and all Lang had to do was trigger
some lead to distract the renegades until Nordstrom was
out of rifle range. It was dangerous, but then either op-
tion was liable to get them all killed.

Nordstrom sighed, looked at Lang with reluctant ad-
miration, and said heavily, "All right. I'll cover you
from here until you're on the mountain. Then you'll be
on your own. Find a spot that'll give you a good view
of the whole Gap—it's only about a half mile long, as
I recall. You got twenty minutes, then we're heading out.
I'll lead your mule and leave it in the Gap, about midway through. Remember, you've got seven Sioux braves
making fast tracks behind you."

"Don't linger, is what you're saying," Lang said.

"You got it."

"Sounds like a plan," the teacher said jovially—maybe a little too jovially, Nordstrom thought.

Lang moved out with his rifle, jogging around the knoll and across the open plain toward the base of the mountain.

"What about me?" It was Nils. He looked at Nordstrom with furrowed brows and incredulous eyes. He slid his gaze to Corinne and back again.

"What about you?" Nordstrom said, puzzled.

"I ain't no snot-nosed kid."

"I didn't say you were."

"What can I do?"

"Oh, Nils . . . ," Corinne said, as if reading the boy's mind.

He jumped to his feet and turned his anger on Corinne. "He ain't so goddang holy. That Mrs. Townsend, she visited his bed. I seen 'em!"

Nordstrom looked at the boy, astonished. His face warmed like a cast-iron skillet. To Nils, he said tightly, "Get on your mule."

"I ain't doin' nothin' you say."

"Get on your mule!" Nordstrom barked, clenching his fists. "This isn't the time or the—"

"Nils—please," Corinne pleaded, cutting him off. "Get on the *mule*!"

Abashed, Nils's face softened. He turned and untethered his mules' reins from a scrub cedar. "I will for *you*, Corinne."

Nordstrom turned to the girl. Cutting her eyes away from him, she walked to her own mule, put a foot in the stirrup, and swung into the saddle. Sitting there, awaiting Nordstrom's call to head out, she brushed her hair back from her face and stared at her saddle horn with a troubled crease in her brow.

Nordstrom watched her, then turned to watch Lang moving toward the base of the mountain. He gave a mirthless chuff. So what if Corinne knew he'd slept with Cynthia Townsend? he asked himself. There was noth-

ing between him and Corinne. There was nothing between him and anybody.

He ushered the whole silly issue from his mind, and
watched Lang start up the mountain, following a switchbacking game trail, rifle held at his chest. When the
teacher appeared to be in position to cover them, Nordstrom stood and walked down the knoll to his horse.

Regarding neither Corinne nor Nils, but keeping his
hat tipped low, he said, "Let's go," and mounted up.

Lang lifted his collar against the breeze and made his
way along the game trail toward the edge of the mountain, where he'd have a clear view of the Gap. He made
sure the slope was always behind him, so he was not
outlined against the sky.

Looking around, he saw no one. He'd seen no foot-
prints, either, which meant the renegades were probably
still behind them or in the Gap.

If they were in the Gap, he needed to spot them and
warn Nordstrom. Looking for good cover, he decided on
a black-rock shelf fifty yards below the summit. A wind-
twisted ponderosa jutted from a crack in the rock, and
there were several boulders that would hide him from
below.

He took position behind the tree and craned his neck
to peer around the rocks. Nordstrom had been right. The
Gap was roughly a half mile long. Each end narrowed
in the distance, but he had as good a view of the Gap
as he was going to get, he decided.

He sat down and lay the rifle across his knees, scanning the hillside around him and the Gap below. A thin
smile creased his face as he thought of his father- and
brother-in-law back home in Indiana. If they could only
see him now, on a grade over Blood Mountain Gap
scouting for bandits! The throb of life hammered in his
chest and made him almost giddy.

The reverie was snuffed when he saw Nordstrom,
Corinne, and Nils enter the Gap on his right, the mules
moving awkwardly on the narrow, uneven trail. Lang

could not hear the footfalls, but he saw stones roll away from the lumbering hooves.

The three rode single file, with Nordstrom in the lead. The rancher's hat brim hid his face as he eyed the trail before him; it snapped back as he combed the topography. From this distance, his face was featureless, but Lang could tell his jaw was set like iron. He held his rifle in one hand, reins in the other.

Lang sucked in his breath. The beat of his heart was strong and irregular. If something was going to happen, it would happen within the next three or four minutes. He scuttled forward and hunkered down with his rifle up at his chest, ready to fire the moment he saw something.

The thought was still reverberating when a dark form separated from a boulder about seventy yards below and to his left. It slid around the left of the boulder, until the boulder concealed all but a sliver of the gunman.

Lang gave a start, felt a grunt catch in his throat. He brought the rifle to his shoulder and aimed, but the man had flattened against the boulder, giving Lang only about six inches of his back. If the teacher fired now, he'd probably miss and betray his position. If he didn't fire, the gunman would surely draw a bead on Nordstrom's group moving toward him on the trail below.

In about thirty seconds, Lang figured, Nordstrom would be directly below the gunman.

Lang knew he had no choice. He moved out from behind his cover, and ran, crouching, to his left. He stopped when he was directly above the gunman, who stood with his back pressed against the boulder and staring downhill, waiting. Lang knew if the man happened to look up the hill, he'd be discovered, for he was right out in the open with nothing but the mountain rising behind him.

Lang lifted the rifle to his chest and snugged his cheek against the stock. The man gave him only a profile view, with his head turned, looking downhill. Lang's hands shook, fouling his aim, as his mind raced through his options.

He knew he couldn't hit the man from this angle. He either had to continue forward until he had more of the man in view, and risk being discovered, or call to the man and get him to turn his way, allowing him a full-body shot.

Before he could make up his mind, a boom broke the silence and echoed. Lang nearly jumped out of his boots. A horse gave a hair-raising whinnie, a girl screamed, and a man yelled, "Go . . . *go*."

It was Nordstrom.

Lang turned his head back to the man before him, who was facing him now and raising his rifle. Smoke puffed and fire poked from the barrel, and Lang felt the wind rush of the slug above his head, heard the thunk of the lead into the ground behind him. Feeling a strength and a strange inner calm steel him against panic, he raised his rifle again to his cheek, took a deep breath, held it, and squeezed the trigger.

Cracking, the rifle leapt in his arms.

The man's arms spread, and he sprang backward off his feet, flinging his rifle above his head. Then he was on the ground, and all Lang could see was the soles of his boots, the toes pointing skyward.

Lang couldn't help staring, amazed, at his fallen quarry. After several seconds had passed, he whispered, "I got him. I killed the bastard."

The last sounds he heard were his own words of self-congratulation, because a moment later a large-caliber slug tore through the volume of Shakespeare's sonnets tucked in his vest and proceeded through his left lung and spine.

He jerked around with the force of the blow, positioning himself just right for the next bullet, which took him through the heart. He fell as the man he'd killed had fallen, on his back, the soles of his boots facing uphill.

He was still alive as, below, Nordstrom shouted "Go!" over and over again. But he didn't hear a thing, saw nothing but a growing darkness which quickly turned black.

26

Nordstrom's right leg was pinned beneath the fallen grulla. Hit through the lungs, the mustang was taking a long time to die, and it wasn't doing it quietly, either. Frothy blood sprayed from its nostrils; it jerked its head from side to side, and gave great, ear-piercing cries, threatening to roll even farther up Nordstrom's leg as it struggled to gain its feet.

Wincing at the pain of the brute in his lap, and trying with all his strength to pull himself free, he dashed a look ahead and saw Corinne and Nils reining their mules back to help.

"No!" Nordstrom shouted at them. "*Go—keep going!*"

Two rifle shots boomed above the nightmare din of the dying horse. Helpless with the horse on top of him, Nordstrom yelled again at Corinne and Nils. "Keep moving, goddamnit!"

Ignoring the order, Corinne had nearly turned her mule full around to return to him when Nils grabbed her mule's bridle to head the animal up the trail.

"No!" she screamed, craning her neck to regard Nordstrom with frantic eyes.

But Nils held tight to the bridle, put his own mule into a hard canter, and led Corinne, screaming and throwing desperate looks behind her, through the Gap.

Nils coaxed their mules with hoarse yells in which Nordstrom read the boy's fear, and Nordstrom was grateful
the lad had been able to conquer panic and take control.

In a few seconds, he and Corinne had diminished to
specks and a thin dust cloud, and Nordstrom was left
alone with the struggling horse. He swept the mountainside with his gaze, hoping to spot Lang, wondering why
in hell the teacher wasn't laying down some fire. He got
his answer when he saw two men sprawled beside a
rocky shelf. One was the big shaggy hombre—Snake
Eyes' sidekick.

The other, arms stretched above his head, hat tumbling over the grass away from him, was John Lang. He
wasn't moving, and by the way he was lying, Nordstrom
could tell he'd never move again.

The rancher reached over the horse for his rifle, but
in the grulla's death throes, the boot had slipped down
the mustang's side, and was wedged beneath the belly.
Nordstrom cursed.

The rifleman on the hillside took another shot, the
boom lifting and the lead thunking into the fender of
Nordstrom's saddle, setting the horse into even more
paroxysms, threatening to grind the rancher's leg into
pulp and powder.

Nordstrom unsheathed his pistol, set the barrel behind
the animal's ear, said, "Sorry, old boy—you've been
more horse than a man could ask for, but it's either you
or me," and silenced the beast with one shot. The head
bobbed once, then fell sideways to the ground. The legs
kicked spasmodically for several seconds.

Nordstrom brought his left foot up against the saddle
and pushed, but it was no use. The right leg wasn't going
anywhere.

Trapped beneath the horse, all he could do was wait
for the gunman's bullet. Not wanting to make it easy for
old Snake Eyes, he flattened his body against the ground
and slid as close to the grulla as he could. To get a clear
shot, the gunman would either have to move farther up
the slope, or come down. If he came down far enough,

Nordstrom would have a chance at the bastard with his pistol.

But he knew that Snake Eyes hadn't lived this long making stupid mistakes.

A voice drifted down the hill. "Hey, rancher—that horse has *got* to be heavy." Snake Eyes laughed.

Following the voice with his eyes, Nordstrom picked the man out of the mountainside. He stood about half-way up, rifle butt snugged on his hip. Nordstrom saw that it was a big-caliber gun—probably a Sharps—the buffalo gun he'd seen in the man's saddle boot.

"Come on down here, and let's talk about it," Nordstrom said, feeling his leg going numb.

"Throw out your pistol; then I'll come down."

"What fun would that be?"

The man gave a slow chuckle, then walked down the mountain, moving several yards to Nordstrom's left, where he'd have a better shot at the rancher. The man stopped, sat on his butt, brought up his knees, and used the right one as a rest for the barrel of the long rifle. The man tipped his head to the butt and poked his finger through the trigger guard.

Nordstrom cursed and lay his head flat, hunkering as close to the horse as he could. He didn't know why. If the gunman didn't get him, the Indians would, and he'd have preferred a buffalo slug between the eyes over a long afternoon with the Sioux.

Still, he pressed his head sideways in the dirt and felt a ball slap the ground beside him and, just above, heard the cannon pop, the rasp of the lever ejecting a shell.

"How close did I get there, rancher?"

"Why don't you come down and I'll show you."

Nordstrom lifted his pistol awkwardly and snapped off two rounds toward the gunman, but the shots fell short. The man was not only too far away for anything but a lucky shot, but at the wrong angle for Nordstrom's awkward position. He couldn't lift his head enough to get a decent bead on the man.

"That hogleg ain't gonna do you any good," the gun-man said, as if reading his mind.

The next shot spanked the ground an inch from Nord-strom's side. He felt the wind brush his shirt. He shot an angry look uphill. He'd never felt so helpless. Fear, anger, and frustration burned within him.

Another boom, and another shot tearing grass and spitting sand in Nordstrom's face. He spit and shook his head, rubbing the dirt from his eyes.

The voice floated down the hill, irritatingly conver-sational: "Well—now I'm too far right. What the hell?" There was a short pause. "That's what I get for lettin' Pete sight the thing in for me. But you took care of him, didn't you, rancher? You gave us a hell of a little romp last night—had us worried there for a while."

Nordstrom cursed himself for not taking out old Snake Eyes last night, when he'd had his sights on him. "Fool," he grated. "You get what ya pay for, and you're payin' now, aren't you?"

"What's that?" the man yelled.

"I said go diddle yourself!"

The gun flashed and a split second before the report carried to Nordstrom's ears he felt a bullet tear the flesh of his upper right arm. It burned, sent needles of razor-sharp pain down his elbow and wrist. He clutched the wound with his left hand and grunted against the pain, half wishing the son of a bitch would just get it over with.

Then he heard something to his right. It sounded like hooves, a galloping horse. Nordstrom thought it was the Indians, but then realized the sound came from up the Gap, not down. He jerked a look that way and saw Nils riding hell-for-leather atop his mule, hat brim pasted against his forehead, approaching Nordstrom at full speed. Corinne was nowhere in sight.

"No—get back!" Nordstrom yelled.

Nils approached in a cloud of dust and a din of pound-ing heels, and jumped from his mount while the mule was still in stride. Yanking on the reins, he halted the mule, and dropped them next to Nordstrom.

"Hold these," he ordered.

Nordstrom was too bewildered to do anything but grab the reins and hold them while the mule gave agitated jerks and lunges and Nils grabbed his rifle from the boot. The boy took three quick steps toward the mountainside, knelt to one knee, and fired the single-shot muzzle-loader at the gunman, who stood on the slope frozen, staring curiously at the unexpected development below.

Nordstrom watched the bullet strike about two feet above the man's head, puffing dust from the dun sod. The man gave a curse and ducked. Nils set down the old muzzle-loader, stepped over the head of the dead grulla, bent down, and pulled Nordstrom's Winchester from the boot with some effort. Nordstrom heard his raspy, frightened breathing.

Snake Eyes took an errant shot from the slope. Fearful but determined, Nils turned with the Winchester, knelt, and sent a hail of lead up the mountain, shaking and jacking the lever awkwardly, but getting it done.

Lead split the air, thunking and spanging around the gunman, sending up dust puffs at his feet and around his head. Nordstrom smelled gunpowder, saw the smoke rising around the kid's head, and heard the chinking of the empty cartridges spitting from his rifle.

The man jerked to his right, stumbled, fell, rose to a knee, and tried to get a shot off, but Nils's cracking rifle gave him no reprieve. The man lurched to his feet and gave an angry curse. He bolted up the side of the mountain, dodging between isolated trees and rocks and cutting baffled, angry looks behind him at the young gunman working the rifle.

"I'll be goddamned," Nordstrom said.

When Snake Eyes was out of sight, Nils turned and dropped the smoking Winchester to his side. Setting the rifle down, he knelt and wrapped his hands around Nordstrom's saddle horn, giving the dead horse a tug.

"It's no use," the rancher spat. "Grab my lariat and

tie one end around the neck and dally the other to your horn.''

Nils quickly did as he was told, mounted the mule, and spurred it forward, tugging at the dead horse. The mule lowered its head against the weight and ground its hooves in the dirt and sod. The grulla rolled up a few inches, and Nordstrom pulled his leg out with a painful sigh through gritted teeth.

"Is it broke?" Nils asked.

Nordstrom shook his head. His face reddened as he struggled to his feet. "I don't think so, but it's twisted good." Gaining his one good leg, he balanced himself with the other and his rifle.

He held out his hand to the boy. "Give me a hand, will ya?"

When he was on the mule's back, behind the boy, and they were cantering up toward the saddle, he asked about Corinne.

"I left her on the other side of the saddle," Nils said. "She's waitin' for us there."

"You shouldn't've come back for me, son," Nordstrom said.

But he had to admit, it had been a relief to see Nils bounding toward him, and to watch the boy open fire on old Snake Eyes. Still, it left the boy and Corinne in a prickly situation, and Nordstrom hoped with all his soul they didn't die because of him.

They found Corinne in a hollow below the saddle, in a small grove of cottonwoods and willows through which a dry creek meandered. She stood holding the reins of her mule, watching them approach, an anxious look in her keen blue eyes.

"Where is Mr. Lang?" she said as Nils reined his mule in and Nordstrom climbed tenderly down from the saddle.

"In a better place," Nordstrom said gruffly. He grabbed the reins of Corinne's mule away from her. "You ride with Nils. I'll take your mount."

"Mr. Lang . . . he—"

"Didn't make it, goddamnit!" Nordstrom yelled at her. He was tired and in pain and feeling helpless. What's more, he loved the girl. There was no use in denying it, and it made him feel all the more vulnerable, all the more helpless.

"How is your leg?" she asked, probing with her eyes.

"Forget it—mount up." Nordstrom turned his attention to the mule Corinne had been riding.

The stirrups had to be lengthened or he'd have a hell of a rough ride with a sore leg and a wounded arm. The bullet had only creased his arm, but he'd bruised his leg pretty good. He felt a painful drumming in his knee.

Nils helped Corinne onto the mule while Nordstrom adjusted his stirrups quickly, balancing on his good leg. He cast anxious looks behind them, at the backside of Blood Mountain and the Gap, expecting to see either old Snakes Eyes or seven mounted Indians heading their way.

When he was through, he loaded his Winchester from his cartridge belt, mounted awkwardly, and led Nils and Corinne westward out of the hollow. As he rode, casting cautious looks behind, he saw why Blood Mountain had got its name.

The west-falling sun turned it from burnt-orange to blood red. It seemed to hover, suspended above the broken prairie—a giant, flame-shaped, blood-splattered rock straight from an Indian legend.

A chill leapfrogged the rancher's spine, and he turned his eyes and thoughts ahead, to the Melby Stage station and safety.

He just hoped the red mountain over his shoulder wasn't the bad omen it appeared to be. . . .

27

Melby Station was originally an army outpost, abandoned for typically obscure governmental reasons. Story had it the place was so remote that supply wagons couldn't find it, and garrisoned soldiers went apeshit from boredom.

Observing it from a knoll, Nordstrom saw why the soldiers had come unhinged. The long, gray cabin, corrals, and two unchinked barns sat alone on the flat, featureless prairie. The unceasing wind had the whole place leaning slightly to the southeast, and tumbleweeds had collected at the base of the cabin walls and corral posts. They looked like they'd been collecting there for a long time.

For miles in three directions, there was nothing but rough prairie with tough brown grass, and occasional rocky shelves and rimrocks. Blood Mountain rose austerely in the east.

Dog tired, Nordstrom clucked to his mule and lead Nils and Corinne to a barn. It was dusk. The air was cool and the sun was a salmon disk in the west. He hailed the cabin, but the wind slapping the outhouse door was the sole response. He climbed gingerly down from his saddle and swung the barn doors wide.

A thick-waisted, gray-bearded man in a ragged derby hat stood before him in the shadows, the butt of a

double-barreled shotgun snugged against his cheek. The
gray beard brushed the man's chest like a bib. Nordstrom stared down both bores and stiffened.

"Steady, fella," he said evenly.

The man's voice was as shrill as an old woman's.
"Who the hell are ya and what the hell ya want? Speak
now or forever hold your peace!"

"Glenn Nordstrom."

"That's a start," the man prodded. For all his horns
and rattles, there was a lack of resolution in his bearing.

Nordstrom jerked his head. "This is Nils and this is
Corinne. We were hopin' we could hop the stage."

"Why?"

"We're being tailed."

"Law?"

Nordstrom licked his lips and hoped the greener
aimed at his face didn't boast a touchy set of triggers.
"Seven Sioux and a white man."

A pained expression creased the man's rugged face,
and his eyes turned even darker. "Lovely." He rolled
his eyes and tilted his head away from the shotgun stalk,
letting the barrel drop a few degrees. Looking beyond
Nordstrom, the man said, "Did you hear that, Anna?
He's got Sioux on his tail."

Nordstrom swung a look behind him. A stout, dark
woman with an oval face stood before the cabin door.
There was a buckskin shawl about her shoulders. She
held a rifle with a shoulder strap, up high and trained
on the visitors. Nordstrom watched her for several seconds, and she didn't blink once. Her face was expressionless.

Turning to the man, Nordstrom said, "I'm sorry for
the trouble, but we have nowhere else to go. Our mules
are exhausted."

The man scowled and swept his gray eyes across the
visitors, sizing them up. He lowered the shotgun and
spat a stream of tobacco juice in the dust and straw at
his feet.

"Well, get your animals in here," he said gruffly,

stepping aside. "As if I don't have enough to worry about . . ." He lifted a hurricane lamp from the wall, trimmed the wick, and lit it. The dull yellow light chased shadows to the back of the barn. Somewhere in the rafters pigeons cooed.

"Much obliged," Nordstrom said, leading his mule into the barn. Behind him, Nils followed suit. Corinne remained in the doorway. The man stood a few feet away from her.

"Don't linger now," the man ordered, unable to keep his eyes from Corinne. "If I'm gonna be attacked by Sioux, I wanna be in the cabin with Hank."

"Who's Hank?" Nordstrom said.

"Expert Injun fighter." The man's eyes were still on the girl. It irritated Nordstrom.

"So it's not just you and the woman here?" he asked.

The man gave a snort and a snicker, finally turning his eyes to the rancher. "I'll say it's not!"

Removing his tack, Nordstrom eyed the man warily. Long wisps of thin gray hair poked from his sweat-stained derby, which sat at a sly angle. The long, gray beard swept his chest. His face was pale and round as a coin, and his translucent gray eyes were bright with folly.

"When's the next stage?" Nordstrom asked him.

The man was holding the lantern high. "Two, three days. Depends on how many passengers board in the Black Hills."

"Telegraph?"

The man shook his head and pursed his lips. "Been out all summer."

Nordstrom draped his bridle over a stall partition and sighed. "That's lady luck, for you."

"Fickle bitch, ain't she?"

When the tack was hanging from posts, and the mules had been given a cursory rubdown, the man led his visitors to the cabin.

Inside it was smoky and dark. Two rough wood tables sat parallel with the door, one behind the other. A potbelly stove squatted between them, a battered black flue poking through the ceiling, its seams leaking tongues of blue smoke.

The woman brought a stew pot and bowls out from the kitchen. "Food," she said tersely, and walked back to the kitchen, returning a moment later with a chipped enamel pot.

The air was thick with the musky smell of burning buffalo chips and boiled meat—antelope, Nordstrom thought. His mouth watered. How long since he'd enjoyed a hot meal?

"Coffee," the woman said with a nod, setting the pot on the table before slinking back to the kitchen.

Nordstrom watched her.

Chuckling, the man said, "Don't mind her. That's more than she's said to me in the past twelve years."

"Your wife?" Nordstrom asked, helping himself to the stew.

"Could say that. Shoshone. Won her in a card game in Wyoming, at a rendezvous on the Sweetwater. She don't look like much now, but back then she was worth a whole passel o' beaver pelts."

Nordstrom limped to the window, glanced out, then sat in a straight-back chair before it. He poked his fork in the stew, hungrily eating. "I gave you my handle—what's yours?"

The man stood peering out the half-open door, shotgun in his arms. "Avery Taggart." Nodding at the kitchen, he added, "That's Anna."

Taggart slid his eyes to Corinne, picking at a bowl of stew on the rough pine table. Nils sat next to her, at the end of the table, watching Taggart defensively.

"She yours?" Taggart asked Nordstrom with a cool, lascivious smirk.

Lifting her head, Corinne looked at the man, then at Nordstrom. Nordstrom considered the question a moment, then shook his head. Meeting Nils's gaze, he said, "No."

Corinne looked down at her food. Nordstrom felt his

own supper turn against him. He stood and set his bowl on the table. "You said there was an expert Indian fighter here," he reminded Taggart, changing the subject.

"So I did," Taggart said, shifting his gaze to Nils. "Boy, watch the door, will ya?"

When Nils had moved around the table and taken position by the door, Taggart looked at Nordstrom's swollen knee. "Can you climb?"

"Climb?"

"Into the loft."

Nordstrom's eyebrows knit skeptically. "Hank's in the *loft*?"

Taggart guffawed, tipping his head back and showing his small, V-shaped teeth. "Ol' Hank's a might antisocial, he is. His laughter boomed, then settled to a chuckle. "Follow me."

The man waved at Nordstrom and walked to the ladder at the back of the room poking through a six-by-four-foot hole in the ceiling. The man gripped both sides and climbed, his breath labored, the ladder creaking and bending with more give than Nordstrom considered safe.

When Taggart was wheezing at the top, Nordstrom climbed, taking his time with the sore knee. In the loft he cursed his throbbing leg and said, "This Hank better be one hell of an Injun fighter."

"Oh, he is . . . he is," Taggart sang, heading for the front wall.

He lit a lantern, dimly illuminating several worn cots and trunks, cobwebs, and swallows' nests. A mouse scuttled under a shredded newspaper. Nordstrom figured the loft had been the soldiers' sleeping quarters, unused since the army had pulled out.

Except by Hank.

Taggart stopped by a dark hulk at the back of the room. He turned to Nordstrom.

"Mr. Nordstrom—meet the incomparable . . . Hank."

With a flourish, Taggart swept a canvas cover off the hulking dark figure, and lowered the lantern to reveal a

Gatling gun standing about four feet above the floor. All set up and ready to go, its tripod spread, it resembled a giant steel grasshopper on wooden legs. The smooth-polished bronze breech housing glistened in the gold light.

The smell of gun oil filled Nordstrom's nostrils, and the rancher blinked, lifting his gaze to Taggart. A devilish smile tugged at the station manager's cheeks.

"You steal this?" Nordstrom asked.

"Army left it," Taggart said with a conspiratorial grin. "I found it in one of the sheds. Brand-spanking-new. The crate hadn't even been opened." Taggart gave a naughty-boy chuckle, produced a handkerchief from his pocket, and caressed the barrel lovingly.

"You have ammo?"

"Hee-hee," Taggart hooted. "Five cases worth!"

He stepped back, swinging the lantern, to reveal a stack of pine shipping crates. He pulled the lid from one, revealing a bed of .45–70-calibre shells with brass casings and snub-nosed slugs.

He whistled.

"My guess is those soldiers were so antsy to get out of here they didn't care what they left behind." Taggart moved to a dust-covered foot locker, tripped the hasp, and lifted a sooty brown bottle up for Nordstrom's inspection. "They made their own spirits, too." He pulled the cork with his teeth, spat it out, and tipped back the bottle. His throat worked noisily and the liquor gurgled.

After about five seconds, Taggart brought the bottle back down, withdrew his lips reluctantly, blinked his eyes widely, and smacked his lips. Beads of sweat popped on his forehead and glistened in the lantern light. His face paled.

"Not bad," he said hoarsely. "Snort?"

Nordstrom took the bottle and sipped. The snakewater took a long time going down, and tongue to gut, he thought it must have peeled off three layers of skin. The rancher coughed and returned the bottle to Taggart. His voice was about five octaves higher than normal.

"Obliged."

"My pleasure," Taggart said, giving the bottle another pull.

"Easy there, Taggart," Nordstrom warned, still swallowing to keep the firewater down. "If those Sioux show tonight, even with your old buddy Hank here, we're gonna want to be clear."

Taggart corked the bottle with a sigh. He looked at Nordstrom with rheumy eyes. "Friend . . . if those Sioux show tonight, with or without ol' Hank . . . it ain't gonna matter whether we're clear or not."

Nordstrom scowled, knowing the man was probably right. Then he turned and headed for the ladder.

Downstairs, he limped across the room and sat heavily down in the chair before the window. Nils watched him curiously. Corinne was not in the room, but from the sound of pans clattering in the kitchen he knew she was in there, helping Anna with the dishes.

"Who's up there?" Nils said.

Nordstrom told him. "It ain't gonna do us any good in the dark, though. But chances are the Injuns'll wait for morning to attack. They need to see us as well as we need to see them."

"What'll we do till then?"

Nordstrom shrugged his shoulders. "Keep watch, be ready." He thought for a moment, trying to come up with a strategy. He turned to Nils. "Son, I'd like you to keep watch in the barn loft the first two hours. Me and Taggart'll keep watch from here and spell you."

Nils nodded, eyes wide and eager.

"Take a cup of coffee with you," Nordstrom said. "Try to stay alert. See anything, give a yell."

Nils filled his tin cup from the pot at the table, hefted his rifle, and headed out the door. Nordstrom watched him go, confident he could depend on the lad. After all, the kid had saved his life earlier. There must be a hard layer of bedrock beneath that calm, brooding surface.

Tonight and tomorrow, he'd need it.

• • •

Several hours later, Nordstrom sat in the chair by the
window, his legs propped on a bench, rifle across his
knees. His eyes were closed. He was in a controlled
doze, half-awake, half-asleep, listening.

Taggart and Anna slept in their tiny bedroom off the
kitchen. Nordstrom had heard the station manager's
snores for the past two hours. Corinne was asleep on
one of the cots set up for stage passengers on Nordstrom's right, blankets strung between them for privacy.

A floorboard creaked. Nordstrom came full awake but
resisted the urge to lift his head. He opened his eyes and
saw a dark figure standing before one of the blanket
partitions.

Nordstrom lifted his head. It was Taggart, clad in ragged long johns, the butt hole parted to reveal his hairy
ass. He was holding a quilt away from Corinne's cot,
and peering down at her. Nordstrom heard the man's
heavy, raspy breaths.

Nordstrom came soundlessly to his feet and snugged
his rifle to the man's ear.

"When I said she wasn't mine earlier," Nordstrom
whispered harshly, "I didn't mean she was yours."

Taggart stiffened, turned away without even glancing
at Nordstrom, and tiptoed across the room. He entered
his bedroom and quietly latched the door behind him.

Nordstrom turned to the blanket. Unable to help himself, he pulled it back, and looked behind it. Corinne lay
curled on her side, blond hair fanned across her pillow.
The wool blankets rose and fell with her deep, even
breaths.

Nordstrom watched her for several seconds. Then he
realized her eyes were open, watching him. Hot with
shame, he released the blanket, turned on his sore knee,
and returned to the chair.

28

At dawn, Nordstrom was in the barn loft keeping watch through the open double doors. It had been a long, quiet, nerve-wracking night. Every wind gust was a storming Sioux, every creaking timber a rifle shot. The rancher hoped he'd never have to endure another like it.

Now the dawn grew from a thin line to a broad smudge silhouetting Blood Mountain. A chill breeze swept through the doors and funneled down Nordstrom's collar, lifting the hair on the back of his neck.

Boots scuffed on the floor below. The ladder creaked. "It's Nils," came the boy's voice.

The smell of coffee sharpened as the lad came across the hay-mounded floor and offered a steaming cup to Nordstrom, who took it eagerly.

"Thanks."

"See anything?"

Nordstrom shrugged. "A few raccoon. A few deer. Where's Taggart?"

"In the loft with his gun."

"Figures."

There was a pause. The breeze whistled in the un-chinked wall. Nils squatted down next to Nordstrom and looked out the doors. "I wish I coulda hit the man on the mountain," he said softly. "He was the one that shot Ma."

"I had a chance at him, too," Nordstrom confessed.

Nils laced his hands together and looked at them. "It ain't how I thought it would be," he said with a sigh.

"Killin'? How did you think it would be?"

Nils shrugged. "Easy. Like in the magazine stories."

Nordstrom cut a serious look at the boy. "When it gets easy, that's when you worry."

Nils turned his head to Nordstrom, giving the rancher an inquisitive gaze. "Pa's dead, I reckon."

"I'm afraid so. There's no way he could have outrun the renegades in that wagon. I don't know what he was thinkin'. I'm sorry."

"You tried to stop him."

Nordstrom sipped the coffee. It was good and strong and warmed his insides. He wanted to roll a cigarette to go with it but his fingers were too cold. "I guess your trip west wasn't exactly what you had in mind."

"It sure wasn't, Mr. Nordstrom."

"You got folks back home?"

Nils shook his head. "I'll stay out here, I reckon. There's nothin' back home."

"You can grow up fast out here. Sometimes too fast, sometimes not fast enough."

"I can handle a gun pretty good. I'll make it," Nils said.

"It ain't always a gun that decides if you make it," Nordstrom warned. "Tryin' to make it by a gun will only get you shot."

Nils got up slowly, thoughtfully, and walked to the ladder. He turned back to Nordstrom. His voice was so low that Nordstrom could barely hear him. "You . . . you love her? Corinne?"

Startled by the question, Nordstrom turned to him sharply. He thought for a second, then said, "She's all yours, kid," trying to sound flip. It didn't come off.

"She don't want me. She wants you. I see that now. I seen how she looks at you."

Nordstrom sighed, rested his elbows on his knees,

laced his hands together, and studied the lightening sky.
"She's all yours."

He heard the ladder creak and groan as Nils descended to the main floor. Boots scuffed the hard-packed
dirt. Trying to keep his mind off the girl, Nordstrom
fished in his shirt pocket for his makings, then slowly
shaped a quirley with his cold-stiffened fingers.

Before he had a chance to light it, a lone rider took
shape against the murky dawn, moving toward the station. Nordstrom could tell by the casual way the man
rode, head cocked to one side, that it was Snake Eyes.
Something white hovered over him. It looked like a flag.
A white flag.

What the hell?

Nordstrom stood, working his jaw, and tightened his
grip on his Winchester. "Nils! Taggart!"

"I see him."

Nordstrom looked left and down and saw the station
manager standing in the yard below, holding a coffee
cup and watching the rider, about a hundred yards away
and closing. "That your man?" Taggart asked.

"That's him."

"How's he armed?"

"To the teeth."

Taggart nodded. "OK," he said ominously, turning
and heading for the cabin.

Nordstrom brought his rifle to his shoulder and steadied the sites on the renegade. The man rode into the
compound as though to a Saturday night fandango, a
complacent smile curling his lipless mouth and lifting
his gaunt, bearded cheeks. But his eyes were dark and
deep-sunk.

A vein in Nordstrom's temple throbbed when he
realized the feathered felt Plainsman on the man's head
was the major's, and the horse cantering beneath him
was the major's mount, Windjammer.

The horse appeared exhausted and wild-eyed. At the
man's rough grip on the reins it jerked its head and
twitched its ears.

"Wouldn't shoot a man under a white flag, would ya?" the man said, halting the horse by the water trough and cocking a defiant eye at the rancher standing between the two open loft doors.

He was about twelve feet below Nordstrom, and thirty feet away. An easy shot.

"You sure must be betting I won't."

"You need me."

"How's that?"

"And I need you."

Nordstrom raised an eyebrow. "Come again?"

"There's seven war-whoopin' Sioux out there," Snake Eyes said, hooking a thumb over his shoulder. "They're gettin' all heated up for a raid on your little oasis here."

"And you want to help."

"You need my help as bad as I need yours."

Nordstrom gave a wry laugh, the rifle snugged against his cheek. "Why you—!" he growled, jacking a shell.

The man raised his left hand placatingly. "Don't be hasty now, rancher. Think about it. What have you got to lose?"

Nordstrom remained silent, shifting the unlit quirley from tooth to tooth and studying Snake Eyes bluntly.

"There're seven o' them," the man said. "How many of you?"

Nordstrom didn't say anything. The man tilted his head to the other side, waiting. Nordstrom wanted to blow the man out of the major's hand-tooled saddle, but his conscience wouldn't allow it. Even after all the man had done, Nordstrom could not kill him while he sat there under a white flag, even as he mocked him.

And Snake Eyes knew it.

"OK," Nordstrom said. "But you'll be unarmed till we need you."

The man dipped his head in agreement. "Sounds fair."

"Get down and lose the rifle and the gunbelt."

The man dismounted and dropped the rifle and the gunbelt in the dust at his feet.

"Now take your boots off and hold them upside down."

When, grinning as though he'd never had so much fun, Snake Eyes had done what he was told and had pulled the boots back on, Nordstrom said, "Now drop your pants and turn all the way around."

The smile faded from Snake Eyes' face. He gazed at Nordstrom, incredulous. Nordstrom squeezed off a round, blowing dust at the man's feet, and jacked another shell, waiting.

Scowling, the renegade undid his belt buckle and pushed his buckskin breeches down to his ankles. Awkwardly, nearly falling over the pants, he hopped in a circle in his ragged, faded long johns, until his scowling eyes once again faced Nordstrom.

"Clean as a whistle—see?"

"Nils, you there?" Nordstrom called.

"Here." The sound came from around the corner of the barn.

"Get his guns."

The boy ran out holding his rifle at the renegade. He crouched down and picked up the man's rifle and gunbelt. Standing, Nils faced him, his face taut with anger.

"Shoot him," he urged Nordstrom.

"Back up, kid," the rancher called. "He'll get his due once he's helped us deal with the Injuns."

Nils jerked an exasperated look at Nordstrom. "Soon as he gets a gun, he's gonna shoot us all!"

The renegade laughed spitefully. "Why—you stupid kid. If I did that, I'd be facin' those Sioux all by my lonesome!"

"Nils, get back," Nordstrom ordered.

Reluctantly, Nils backed off with the renegade's weapons. Blinking, the man gazed up at Nordstrom. "Can I pull my pants up now, rancher? I'm like to catch a chill."

Nordstrom said, "What hand's your shootin' hand?"

"What?"

"You deaf?"

The man gave a puzzled frown, blinking darkly. He hesitated. "Why . . . my right. Why?"

Nordstrom's rifle barked. Snake Eyes jerked around with the force of the bullet tearing into his left arm. Blood bubbled from a hole just above his bicep. He grabbed it with his right hand and squeezed, howling, then tripped and fell over his pants.

"You shot me, you son of a bitch!"

Nordstrom lowered the rifle and smiled. "Yes, but I didn't kill you. . . . Not yet, anyway."

When Nordstrom had climbed out of the loft and stepped into the yard, he called for Nils to set a chair about ten feet before the cabin door. Nils looked at him, curious, then turned and ran into the cabin.

Nordstrom walked over to the renegade squirming around on the ground and spewing epithets. The man's face was red with anger, eyes half-closed with rage. The major's hat was in the dust beneath him. His long, greasy brown hair was speckled with yard dust and seeds and dried horseshit. Nordstrom stood over him and puckered his eyebrows.

"That was for Charlie Decker," he said evenly, then bent down and hauled the man to his feet.

He dragged Snake Eyes to the chair Nils had set before the cabin door, and threw him into it; the chair and Snake Eyes went over backward.

"Ohhh—goddamn you son of a bitch!" he bellowed.

Nordstrom picked up the chair and wrestled Snake Eyes back into it, calling for rope. When Avery Taggart returned from the barn with a coil of sound hemp, Nordstrom tied the renegade's hands together behind the chair back, and his ankles to the chair's legs.

"Might as well shoot me now as leave me out here in the open for those savages to pink with their carbines," the renegade said, furious.

Blood soaked his left arm, but it was only a flesh

wound, Nordstrom could tell. As planned, he hadn't hit bone. If he had, the man would no doubt be in shock, and useless.

Nordstrom had opened his mouth to respond when he saw Corinne standing in the doorway behind the renegade, brown wool poncho hanging about her knees, round black hat tipped back from her forehead to reveal eyes bright with horror.

"Go back inside," Nordstrom said softly.

She shook her head, staring at the back of the renegade's hatless head. Her eyes filled with tears.

"Go back inside," Nordstrom said again.

Craning his neck to look behind him, the renegade saw Corinne. His face lit up and his eyebrows rose. "Well, hello, honey—ya back for more?"

Corinne pressed her white, even teeth to her bottom lip and regarded the man coldly.

Nils stepped forward, placed his hands on the girl's shoulders, turned her gently around, and led her back into the cabin. He closed the door behind them.

Nordstrom regarded Snake Eyes darkly. The man had just swung his smiling eyes from the door when the rancher brought his arm back slowly and jerked it forward, clubbing the renegade on the jaw with a gloved fist.

The renegade yelled and toppled into the hard-packed yard. Blood spurted from his lip. Nordstrom let him lie there, cursing, while he strode around the yard's perimeter, gazing over the dawn-purple sage for sign of the Indians.

Taggart had taken position in the barn loft. Nordstrom could see him up there, a woeful, gray-bearded visage in a dark derby, shotgun in his arms. He smoked and gazed across the prairie with an air of doom, talking to himself and shaking his head.

Returning to the cabin, Nordstrom lifted the renegade to a sitting position.

"It'll be full light in a half hour. They'll be attackin'

soon," the man said. "Better untie me and give me a gun."

"I'll untie you and give you a gun when I'm sure they're comin'."

"Oh, they're comin'," Snake Eyes promised, face bunched in a malicious grin.

"He's right," Taggart said, walking quickly across the yard, giving his head a slow wag. "They're comin'!"

29

When Nils saw the door burst wide and Avery Taggart stumble into the cabin, his heart jumped and he staggered several steps backward, clutching at his rifle. Taggart didn't seem to notice his fear, for which he was grateful. Taggart turned his red face to Nils, then to Anna shoving chips through the stove door.

"Ready your arms now—I seen two o' the red devils out in the sage!" He stomped across the floor, thrust his shotgun into Anna's arms, and headed for the ladder.

Gripping the ladder with both hands, the station manager faced them again, chest heaving. "Woman, you watch the back. Boy, you take the east winda. Shoot anything with long hair and war paint. I'll cover the front with ol' Hank." His voice was shrill and filled with adrenaline; spittle flew from his lips. Nils wasn't sure if the man was horrified or thrilled at the prospect of an Indian attack. He decided it was a little of each.

When the man had heaved himself wheezing up the creaking ladder, Nils moved between the cots to the window. He heard Corinne stir from the table, and he turned to watch the girl walk over to the rifle standing against the wall beside the door. She picked up the Spencer carbine, hefted it in her arms, and approached Nils.

Nils frowned. "You don't know how—"

"Yes, I do," Corinne interrupted, looking out the

window. "You might have to reload for me, but I can shoot."

He nodded slowly, almost smiling.

The dull pop of a rifle made them both jump and turn to the window. The report echoed. Nils's throat went dry and his pulse throbbed in the fingers squeezing his rifle. East of the cabin there was nothing but sage rolling to a distant, gray bench.

Another rifle popped, then another. They came from about a hundred yards away, Nils speculated. Corinne turned to him, her eyes fearful and inquisitive.

"Give me my fucking gun!" the renegade out the cabin door yelled. "Rancher—ya here? Before you get yourself killed, goddamnit!"

"It's OK," Nils told Corinne, reading her mind. "Nordstrom will be all right."

Then the window between between them exploded. Shattered glass blew in. Corinne screamed and ducked her head so quickly her hat fell off. Nils fell back against the wall yelling, "Look out, look out!"

He turned and poked his rifle out the window, but there was nothing to shoot at. He fired a round to let them know he was here, then jerked back against the wall and tried to quell his fear. But his knees kept knocking of their own accord. He could hear them.

Several rounds exploded into the cabin walls. Rifles popped in the distance. The renegade was yelling for a gun. The Indian woman gave a hideous yell and tripped both barrels of her shotgun. The boom rattled the timbers and sent dust streaming from the rafters.

Avery Taggart's voice came from the loft. "Anna, can you see them? I can't see them!"

"Seen one," the woman said calmly. It was the first full sentence Nils had heard her utter. "He dead now."

There were several more rifle reports. Then Nordstrom's voice lifted outside. "Nils?"

Nils ran to the door and cracked it. "Here."

"Cut the man loose and give him his rifle. I'll cover you."

Nils opened the door another foot, looked cautiously around, then stepped forward. Taking the Green River from his knife scabbard, he drew it between the man's wrists, cutting the rope.

"My feet, kid—my feet!" the man yelled.

Nils bent down and cut the rope binding the man's ankles. He held the killer's carbine in his left hand. He couldn't bring himself to give it to the man. Once free of the ropes, the man lurched forward and grabbed it out of Nils' halfhearted grip.

He jacked open the breech to make sure the weapon was loaded and turned his dark eyes to Nils, who watched him cautiously, rifle held across his chest.

"Don't worry, kid—I'm not gonna shoot ya," the man wheezed, grinning. His stringy hair hung in his face. He pushed his face close to Nils, until the boy could smell his rancid breath.

"I'm gonna cut your fuckin' throat!"

Then he turned and ran across the yard to the barn.

Nils turned and leapt back into the cabin, slamming the door behind him. He hurried between the tables and cots to the east window. Corinne stood with the rifle, her back flat against the wall. Her eyes were bright with fear, but there was a coolness there as well.

"See anything yet?" Nils asked her.

"No," she said, shaking her head. "Where are they, Nils? Why don't they show themselves?"

" 'Cause they're Injuns, I reckon," Nils said, as puzzled as Corinne. From the stories he'd read in *Wild and Wooly Tales of the West,* he had figured the savages would come all at once on horseback, whooping and hollering and flinging arrows every which way. Not this one or two at a time business—slinking up out of the sage like snakes, taking a potshot here and a potshot there. It was enough to drive you nuts!

Nils stood on one side of the cabin's east window, Corinne on the other. They heard several shots from out beyond the barn, heard two slugs thump into the cabin's log walls.

Otherwise, a maddening silence yawned. Daylight
grew and angled through the windows and between the
logs where the chinking had disappeared. The fire guttered breathily in the stove. The wind caught in the
eaves. A flock of Canada geese honked up high, winging
westward.

Nils smelled cigarette smoke and turned to see the
Indian woman smoking on the other side of the cabin,
facing him with her black eyes. Nils said nothing. Neither did the woman. Neither did Corinne. The wind scuttled and a single rifle cracked out amid the sage.

Nils was hunkered down by the window, staring out,
when Taggart's voice boomed in the loft. Nils's heart
leapt. Corinne jumped and lifted her head.

"Get ready, now! Get ready!"

Then the Gatling gun started booming and spitting out
shells so loudly that Nils thought the cabin was coming
down around his shoulders.

Ahead there was a shallow gully littered with metal tub-
ing—no doubt the remains of a still. Something scurried
across the gully's lip and disappeared. Nordstrom stared,
feeling vulnerable.

He knew the Indians were better at this game than he
was, and the knowledge was reinforced when a rifle
belched smoke above the gully, about seven feet left of
where he'd been looking, and a can bounced near his
face.

Not wasting a second, Nordstrom scrambled to a half-
sitting position, laid his sights on the thinning smoke,
and pulled the trigger. He jacked another shell and let it
go, but the Indian's dying wail rose and fell with the
echo of the first shot.

Ejecting the shell, Nordstrom heard the tinny clatter
of cans on the other side of the trash mound. Cans rolled
down around his knees. At the top of the pile, a man-
shaped figure rose with a rifle trained on the rancher.
Nordstrom rolled right, trying to bring his rifle up.

The Indian's gun exploded and Nordstrom felt the

burn of a bullet creasing his neck. He raised his rifle, snugging the butt against his belt, and fired. He was jacking another shell when the brave dropped his carbine and suddenly took flight, arms spread, and pounced on the rancher, punching and thrashing and screaming in Nordstrom's ear.

Nordstrom dropped the rifle and fumbled for the man's hands and a possible knife. As the two men struggled on the bed of debris, the Indian dug his teeth into Nordstrom's chin, grunting and snorting like a crazed bear. Nordstrom groined the brave with a knee and flung him aside.

His hands found the knife on his belt scabbard. He lifted the point to the man's chin and was about to thrust it deep when he realized the man's body had relaxed. Looking up, he saw the man's eyes glaze and roll back in their sockets.

The Indian gave a watery sigh, and blood bubbled on his lips. Nordstrom felt a wetness at his chest and looked down. The brave's buckskin tunic was covered with thick red blood. There was a long, slow sigh. Then the brave tipped his head back and died.

Nordstrom reached for his rifle and was turning his gaze forward, ready for another attack, when he heard the tinny clatter of the Gatling gun. Someone was yelling. Beneath the din of old Hank, Nordstrom heard shotgun and rifle fire. There was a scream.

Corinne . . . !

By the time he reached the barn corner and had the cabin in view, the yard was littered with dead and dying Indians and horses. The air was filled with blue smoke so thick that Nordstrom could not see Avery Taggart in the cabin loft, but he could hear Hank going at it without pause and could hear Taggart screaming insanely with every revolution of the revolving breech.

The heavy, 50-caliber slugs thunked into the ground and into Indians and horses. They splintered the barn and corral, splashed in the water trough, and spanged off rocks and the steel handle of the water pump.

Dimly through the smoke, Nordstrom saw an Indian on the cabin roof, creeping up the low peek to the chimney. Nordstrom lifted the rifle, took aim, and fired. The Indian fell sideways, grabbing his thigh. When he turned to look where the shot had come from, Nordstrom squeezed off another round. The man fell backward and lay still, his rifle sliding down the roof to disappear in the smoke below.

Nordstrom ducked back behind the barn corner to reload, then dropped to a knee and lifted his rifle to study the open ground between him and the cabin. Barely visible through the smoke, three dead riders sprawled on the ground near two dying horses. One warrior was hunkered under a buckboard wagon near the main corral, clumsily feeding shells to the carbine stretched across his knees.

Taggart had let up with old Hank. Without the din of the heavy gun, the wails of the dying horses rose.

Nordstrom took aim and shot the Indian beneath the buckboard, then crouched down behind the barn corner and waited for the smoke to clear. Slowly, Avery Taggart took shape across the yard, crouched over the huge smoking gun between the loft doors. His eyes were wide and his lips were parted in a crazed grin.

The shotgun sounded, a horse whinnied, and a woman's voice rose from the cabin in a witchlike cackle. The wounded Indian rider galloped his terrified mount out from the cabin's rear, crouching over what remained of his bloody right arm.

He rode screaming toward Nordstrom, trying to raise his rifle with his remaining arm. Seeing Taggart start cranking the Gatling gun, Nordstrom dropped below the line of fire. Lifting his head he watched the 50-calibers fairly shred the man, his head exploding and his chest blooming red.

Screaming, the horse fell on its side, the man beneath it, and if there was any life left in either horse or rider, the Gatling quickly stifled it.

Again Nordstrom waited for the smoke to clear and

for Avery Taggart's crazed, gray-bearded visage to take
shape across the yard.

"That it?" Taggart yelled.

"Not quite," Nordstrom replied. "You seen my
friend?"

A rifle cracked and a black spot shone on Taggart's
forehead. The man stiffened and fell over his gun.

"Right behind ya, rancher." It was Snake Eyes.
"Drop the rifle and turn around."

Nordstrom froze, cursed aloud, and considered his options.

"Don't even think about it, rancher. I got the drop on
ya."

Reluctantly, Nordstrom lowered his rifle butt to the
dirt and let the barrel fall. He turned around. Snake Eyes
stood before him, head tipped to the side, smiling and
working his mouth.

"You know," he said, "I had fun killin' that hired
man o' yours—fillin' him full o' holes, then stringing
him up high over your gate. Why, he squealed like a
nanny goat, he did! But I'm gonna be just tickled pink
puttin' a bullet between your eyes and cuttin' that boy's
throat."

He stared at Nordstrom, grinning darkly. "Then me
an' that pretty Norski bitch are gonna have us another
go-round . . . just so ya know."

He raised his rifle to his shoulder and squeezed his
left eye closed. The gun barked, and Nordstrom flinched,
stared at the barrel. There was no smoke, no fire. Snake
Eyes lowered the rifle and looked at Nordstrom dully,
blinking.

Nordstrom was too puzzled to do anything but frown,
his heart beating wildly. A misfire?

Snake Eyes staggered forward several steps, trying to
catch his balance. A curious smile pulled at his lips. His
hands opened and the rifle dropped. He turned and fell
on his back.

Corinne stood behind him, her pistol steady in her
outstretched hand. Smoke curled from the barrel. Her

eyes were dark beneath the brim of her black felt hat, and her lips formed a taut line.

The renegade lifted his head, looking at her, then lowered it. He grunted a laugh. "Why . . . that bitch . . . shot me. . . ."

"She did at that," Nordstrom said.

Snake Eyes looked at him incomprehensively, coughed, and died.

Nordstrom looked at Corinne. She was still holding the pistol. Her hand had fallen several inches, and a look of shock and surprise widened her eyes and paled her cheeks. Her lips were parted as though to speak, but she didn't say anything.

Nordstrom shook his head and grunted an incredulous laugh. "Crazy girl—coulda got yourself killed." His expression did not betray his immense relief at seeing the girl alive and unharmed.

Corinne stepped around him quickly and walked to the cabin.

Nordstrom watched her, his jaw tight, then walked over to where Avery Taggart lay on the ground under the smoking Gatling gun. Nils was there, standing beside Taggart and watching Nordstrom glumly.

Anna turned away from her husband's body and walked toward the rancher. Her dark eyes and round face betrayed no emotion. She carried the shotgun in her arms like a baby.

"Dat da one dat kilt my man?" she asked Nordstrom flatly, looking at the body behind him. Wisps of coal-black hair blew about her lips.

Nordstrom nodded.

The woman walked over to Snake Eyes. Nordstrom turned to watch her. The events of the past few hours had left him numb, befuddled, and more exhausted than he'd ever been.

Anna stood over the renegade's body for several seconds, looking down, her back to Nordstrom. Then she

lowered the barrel of her shotgun and tripped both triggers with a boom that punctuated the morning's vio-
lence. The breezey silence washed in behind it, more
dense than before.

30

Nordstrom had winced at the shotgun's double blast, imagining what the two exploding shells had done to Snake Eyes' head. He knew some tribes believed that disfiguring their enemies would keep them from the next world; apparently Anna was making sure Snake Eyes stayed right here on earth.

Nordstrom had never considered himself a religious man, but he'd always believed that twisted souls were doomed—here and hereafter. With or without Anna's help, Snake Eyes would stay in the crude hole they'd dig for him in the sandy dirt behind the barn.

He was thinking such thoughts as he knelt down beside Taggart, whose hands lay palm up on either side of his head. One knee was twisted so that the right leg was beneath him. Feeling an inexplicable urge—the man was dead, after all, and felt nothing—Nordstrom straightened it. Then he folded Taggart's hands over his chest and ran his thumb and index finger over the man's half-open eyes, closing them.

Whatever he may or may not have thought of the station manager, the man had died helping him and the others. Without him—and old Hank—Nordstrom was sure they'd all be dead.

"Rest in peace," Nordstrom whispered, then turned to see Anna stride to the cabin. Nordstrom wanted to ask her where he should bury her husband, but the set of her jaw and her dark eyes told him to wait.

Beside him, Nils cleared his throat and licked his chapped lips. His fearful eyes scanned the horizon. "What's to keep 'em from comin' back?"

Nordstrom inhaled sharply and shook his head. "There's bad medicine here. They'll warn the others."

An hour later, he and Nils were hauling off bodies in a buckboard wagon, dumping the dead Indians in a shallow communal grave a mile and a half south of the outpost, when a rider appeared in the outpost's direction. A packhorse trailed the rider on a lead rope.

Nordstrom grimaced, wary of strangers after all that had happened. Nils pushed one of the bodies over the side of the wagon and did a double-take, following Nordstrom's gaze. He reached for his rifle. Nordstrom grabbed his arm, gazing northward.

"It's Anna," he said.

Nils squinted his eyes, delineating the squat figure in buckskins, braids, and knee-length moccasins as the horses came within a quarter mile. He said nothing until the woman pulled the horses off the trail, giving Nordstrom and Nils a wide berth as she passed.

"Where do you think she's goin'?" Nils asked, squinting his eyes against the westering sun.

Nordstrom said nothing for several seconds. "Home, I reckon," he said, liking the sound of the word on his tongue. "Where she belongs."

He watched as the woman rode out of sight, never looking their way. When they had finished unloading the bodies and filling in the grave, he climbed onto the buckboard's seat, flicked the reins against the mules' backs, and pointed the wagon back toward the outpost. Nils sat and dangled his legs off the back end.

"I reckon I'll be leavin' now, too," the lad said, turning his head so Nordstrom could hear above the squeaking wheel hubs and clomping hoofs.

"What are you talkin' about?"

"Well, I gotta go somewhere sometime. May as well head there now."

Frowning, Nordstrom turned on the seat to take in the boy's clean-shaven face and youthful eyes, the wisps of sandy hair curling from under his floppy-brimmed hat and over his sun-peeling ears. Had he ever been that young? he wondered. He almost got a chill imagining all that lay ahead of the lad. But then, Nils had a lot behind him, too.

"No use rushin' things, son. I've been thinkin' . . . I'm gonna need me some help rebuilding my cabin. And next spring, I'm gonna string me some wire and run me a herd up from Oklahoma. The railroad's gonna be through any day now, and I'm gonna be ready for it."

He stared straight ahead as he spoke, his eyes bright and clear. He did not know what he was going to say until he'd said it. Having said it, he knew there was no other way, no other life for him. He was going home.

"I'm gonna need help, you see, is what I'm sayin'," he continued. "I won't be able to pay you much for a while . . . just a roof over your head and three square meals, but—"

The boy cleared his throat, politely interrupting. "Thanks just the same, Mr. Nordstrom, but I think it's time I go my own way."

Nordstrom turned to him again, his eyes derisive. "How old are you boy—fourteen, fifteen?"

"Fifteen."

"That's too young."

"Sir?"

"You better come back with me and let me rub some of that green off you before you try going it alone."

Nils turned and looked back at the brown, sunlit prairie. Eastward, antelope grazed around a rocky knoll, and several bucks eyed the wagon warily, lifting their black-and-white heads and curled horns, noses measuring the breeze. Closer by, tiny brown birds darted here and there above the tawny grass turning to autumn brown and stiffening from the recent frost.

"Thanks just the same, Mr. Nordstrom. But I'm old for my age. I can fend."

Nordstrom rolled his eyes and shook his head. There was no use arguing with the boy. Nordstrom remembered those very words rolling from his very own very young lips, and there'd been nothing anyone could have said to weaken his resolve.

Reading and hearing stories of the Great West, he'd needed to make his own way. Fortunately, a little industry and a lot of luck had seen him through—this far, anyway. He hoped the same for Nils.

Behind him the boy said hesitatingly, "I 'spose . . . Corinne will go with you?"

Nordstrom didn't say anything, just stared thoughtfully off. He hadn't wanted to admit it, but in the new vision of his life he'd acquired while talking to the boy, Corinne was there—in his cabin . . . by his side. . . .

"I reckon that's up to her," he said gruffly, and steered the mules into the outpost's yard.

He pulled up to the barn and set the break, crawled gingerly down, felt the exhaustion in every bone. His leg was feeling better, having loosened up from all the exercise. It would be good and stiff in the morning, though.

He swept his hat from his head and ran the sleeve of his shirt across his sweaty brow. Turning to the cabin, he saw Corinne standing by the door, back against the wall. Her hat was tipped back, and her arms were folded across her chest. The baggy poncho accented the slenderness of her figure.

She was looking at him, Nordstrom saw, and he felt his knees weaken like a boy's at a barn dance. He knew he could not let her go. Not a man given to expressing himself, he wasn't sure how to keep her. After what she'd learned of his trysts with Cynthia Townsend, maybe she had no intention of being kept.

Nils broke the reverie. "I believe I'll saddle one of the mules and take off now. I have several hours of daylight left."

Nordstrom turned to the boy, astonished. "Hold on, hold on! What's wrong with waiting till morning?"

"I figure I better go before I lose my spunk," Nils said with a nervous laugh. "I'll ride over to the gold fields at Cutter Creek. I read—"

"You read, you read," Nordstrom chided. "That's all you've done is read, boy—you have no idea what you're gonna run into at Cutter Creek. The kind of *men* you're gonna run into at Cutter Creek. You know those men been chasin' you for the past week and a half? Well, they're a dime a dozen in the gold fields."

He paused, watching the boy, hoping to frighten him. It didn't seem to be working. "You got any money?" he shot at the lad.

He shrugged. "I'll work in a livery. Swamp out a saloon until I have enough money for mining supplies. Then hell, maybe I'll hit the mother lode."

Nordstrom shook his head. "The mother lode! Jesus Christ, boy!"

"Nils, what are you talking about?"

It was Corinne. She'd walked up to them without either Nordstrom or Nils noticing.

"Maybe you can talk some sense into him," Nordstrom told the girl. He looked again at Nils. Seeing no give in the boy's chinking, he turned and walked to the cabin, leaving them alone.

A coffeepot gurgled on the stove. Nordstrom found a cup and filled it, then sat at the table listening to the pot sigh and the stove crack. He tossed his hat aside, scrubbed his face with his hand, yawning, and sipped his coffee.

After about fifteen minutes, Corinne called from the yard. Nordstrom got up and walked to the door. Nils sat his mule looking adventurous. Corinne stood at his stirrup, arms folded across her chest. Her brow had an aprehensive ridge.

"Good-bye, Mr. Nordstrom," Nils said. "Thanks for pulling us through."

"You're not through yet, boy." Nordstrom walked to

him and shook his outstretched hand. He glanced at Corinne.

"He would not listen to his older and wiser cousin," she said ironically. "He is a very bad boy, but I know he will fair well." Her voice cracked and her eyes filled with tears. Smiling, she looked up at Nils.

Nils gave Nordstrom a poignant look. "Take care of my cousin."

Nordstrom nodded and pursed his lips, glancing at Corinne. She looked down, flushing. "I will," he said laconically. "You behave yourself, kid. Stick to the stage road. You should make it to Cutter Creek in about three days."

Nils nodded and reined his horse around. "I'll write when I'm rich!" he said, giving his mule the spurs and trotting off, waving his hat in the air.

Nordstrom had to laugh at the kid's spunk and surprising lack of fatigue after all they'd been through. He wouldn't have been that young again for anything in the world.

When Nils had galloped into the distance, disappearing over the earth's curve, Nordstrom turned a bashful look at Corinne, not quite knowing what to say. She was still looking off across the prairie.

"Well, I reckon I'll bury Taggart now," he said with an uncomfortable sigh, and walked off.

Corinne watched him for several minutes, then turned into the cabin and closed the door.

Nordstrom laid the station manager's blanket-covered body in the back of the buckboard and hauled it to a slight rise east of the cabin. The soil was not as rocky here as elsewhere, and the digging was relatively easy, although the rancher's knee was beginning to bark with every swing of the spade.

His concern for Nils kept his mind off the ache, however, and before he realized it, he was standing in a hole deep enough to cover himself standing. He tossed out the spade and heaved his own weary bones from the hole. Using ropes wrapped around his shoulders, he lowered the station manager's body into the dark earth.

He stood staring at the blanket-covered body for several minutes, feeling a wave of melancholia so severe it buckled his knees. He fell to his good knee and reclined on his left arm, moaning almost inaudibly. Embarrassed, he looked around to make sure no one was watching, then gave a feeble grunt and stared into the cloudless sky where a rough-legged hawk traced lazy circles above him, curious about the carrion it spied below.

He laughed with amused contempt and studied the hole. After several minutes he got tiredly to his feet and covered the body against scavengers, his face expressionless, his eyes grave.

"Ashes to ashes . . ."

Late afternoon found him sitting on the other side of the rise, smoking a cigarette and watching Blood Mountain shoulder higher and higher above the prairie as the sun fell before it. It was turning a rosy golden on its way toward blood.

Nordstrom thought of John Lang lying above the Gap. If anyone deserved a decent burial, it was the teacher, but Nordstrom knew his bones had long since been stripped and scattered by wolves and lions and everything else.

The girl's voice sounded behind him like one of the angels he didn't believe in. He hadn't heard her approach. "I thought you'd like some coffee."

"Thanks," he said, accepting the cup.

He watched her studying the grave thoughtfully. "Will it ever end?" she murmured.

He said nothing, just sipped his coffee and studied her, his heart warming, the throb of life seeping into him again.

After a few minutes she turned from Taggart's grave and regarded the rancher cooly. "I just want you to know, Mr. Nordstrom, that I plan to be as little trouble for you as possible. As soon as we find a suitable settlement, you can take leave of me and go your own way.

I would have gone with Nils, but he assured me that the gold fields were not a place for a woman.''

She looked at her hands for several seconds, then stood stiffly, and walked away down the rise. Unable to find the words to stop her, Nordstrom tried to stand and follow her, but the ominous pounding of his heart and his throbbing knee compelled him to stay seated.

He watched her diminish in the gathering shadows, heard the cabin door latch, then watched the long, low hovel until it had purpled against the orange sun behind it. He stood and walked to it stiffly, jaw tight, eyes those of a man possessed.

Throwing the door wide, he said, ''Corinne?''

The cabin was dark and steamy. Peering into the shadows, he saw a quilt stretched before the stove. From behind it came the sound of splashing water. Below the quilt he saw the base of a large oak tub.

Suddenly, Corinne's face appeared above the quilt, blond hair piled on her head. ''I'm bathing,'' she said matter-of-factly. Then she disappeared again below the quilt. Water lapped against the sides of the tub. The fire in the stove roared. He felt its heat.

Nordstrom kicked the door shut, strode around the first table, and flung the quilt aside. The girl gave a start and slapped her hands to her shoulders, covering her breasts. Wet ringlets of tawny hair hung in her face.

She gazed up at him. In a second, the fear was gone from her eyes. Her chest rose. She swallowed, parting her lips and inhaling deeply.

When he bent down and lifted her to her feet, she did not resist. Standing, she dropped her arms to her sides, let him appraise her with his eyes, let him lift her gently in his large, powerful arms, and carry her across the room to a cot.

He laid her down and stared into her eyes. They were soft now, and bright with wanting. She smiled. He kissed her deeply. She wrapped her arms around his neck and opened her lips for him.

He pulled away and undressed slowly, watching her—

the rise and fall of her breasts, the flat belly, the long
and shapely legs. She turned on her side and brought a
knee up. She returned his gaze, caressing his chest and
shoulders with her eyes—his hard, knotted stomach,
muscular legs covered with fine blond hair . . .

He moved to her.

"Marry me?" he said, kneeling down before her and
taking her face in his hands. It wasn't so much a request
as a plea.

Her breasts rose and fell with each full breath. "I
think that is all I have ever wanted," she whispered.